PITY DATE

WHITNEY DINEEN

Made in the United States. May, 2023

Print ISBN: 979-8-391681-16-8
E-book ISBN: 978-1-988891-76-7

https://whitneydineen.com/newsletter/

33 Partners Publishing

ALSO BY WHITNEY DINEEN

Children's Books

<u>The Friendship Bench</u>

GRATITUDE

Being an author is my dream job. Seriously, it's right up there with french fry tester—and being that no one has approached me for that one, I'm pretty content where I'm at.

However, authoring is not a solo endeavor. A book is only as good as its editor, proofreaders, and team of people who believe in it. An author is only successful if they have a posse of loving and dedicated friends.

I raise my champagne flute to the following people:

Kristina Walker, who left her fancy Hollywood life behind to move to my town so we could take over the free world together. An added bonus is getting to sit with me and spend lovely afternoons trying to figure out what my books are going to be about. *Pity Date* was our first.

My daughters Faith and Anna, for whom my dynamic duo characters are named. Faith helped me plot and Anna read early pages and offered encouraging words of support. Also, thank you to my niece Esmé for letting me borrow her name.

Cheers to my loving husband, Jimmy. You are my rock!

Paula Bothwell is the first pair of professional eyes to see my books. She not only tackles grammar and spelling errors, but she calls me on all kinds of cray cray that I no longer can see after reading the book so many times. Paula, my friend, I would truly be lost without you.

Scott Schwimer is not only my literary attorney and link to Hollywood, he's my dear friend of many years. He makes me laugh and cry. He never questions me when I call him and say, "Scottie, this book is going to make the best movie!" He merely says, "I'm on it."

Special thanks to my fabulous assistant Melissa Martin, who takes care of all the nitty gritty that I don't have the head space to do. There's so much of it!

I have many lovely author friends who listen to me moan and complain when I feel overwhelmed. They help me back on the horse when I fall off. They are my pack. Diana Orgain, Melanie Summers, Becky Monson, Kate O'Keeffe, Kathryn Biel, and the rest of you, thank you for being my people.

And early thanks to whichever one of you reads this and gets me a side hustle as a gourmet french fry tester. Free books for life!

Pity Date is dedicated to everyone who brought my all-time favorite romcoms to life. A special nod to Julia Roberts and Hugh Grant who starred in most of them.

PROLOGUE

FAITH

I've had an invisible target painted on me that only members of the opposite sex can see. And boy are they determined to shoot me through the heart.

It started with Bobby McEntire in the first grade. My best friend, Anna, used to help me chase him around the playground as a way of declaring my undying devotion. He missed the point entirely and tripped me so that I fell face first into a mud puddle. That single act of war ended any love I'd once felt for him.

In the fourth grade, Kenny Franks caught my eye. He wasn't the typical boy girls pined for, which made me think he could possibly share my feelings. He had moderately bucked teeth, a nose that turned up just enough to appear porcine, and he wore glasses. Surely, *I* was enough to catch the heart of one such as him.

Alas, when I asked him to be my boyfriend on Sadie Hawkins Day that same year, he laughed in my face. *Laughed.* At me. The disdain I felt lasted through our senior year in high school. When he approached me at a friend's graduation party and asked why I hated him so much, I reverted to childish ways and threw my drink on him before walking away. *How dare he forget his trans-gression?*

Then there was that tourist I kissed—my first!—at a beach party the summer before my freshman year. I never got his name, nor did I see him any summers after that. I can't really say what I felt for him was love, but a definite hormonal reaction took place. Also, I may have pretended that he was my long-distance boyfriend at Katie Ramsey's big back to school sleepover the week before we entered the hallowed halls of Elk Creek High School. Go, Crappies!—as in the fish, not the poop emoji.

In high school, I was all about Adam Sanchez. Adam was so far out of my league, I knew nothing could ever come of us, but that didn't stop my fantasies. I spent the whole four years imagining scenarios where he would claim me for his own. My favorite was the one where he strode into the lunchroom like a rock star taking center stage. He stopped right in front of me before loudly declaring my perfection to one and all. Then he got down on one knee and asked me to homecoming/prom/the spring formal—basically, whichever dance was on the horizon. None of that ever happened.

Obviously.

Junior year in college, I thought I'd found my life partner in Trevor Blake. Trevor was your typical tall, dark, and handsome specimen. He was sporty *and* studious. But more important than both of those things, he had a sense of humor that kept me laughing. The only problem was that after a year of dating, Trevor still hadn't put any serious moves on me. When confronted with why, he claimed it was because he wanted us to save ourselves until we were married.

He saw us getting married, so, yay! But also, we did not live in Victorian times, so it was kind of hard to trust that was the real reason. In retrospect, I'm hugely grateful I didn't believe him. A happenstance that was firmly cemented when I caught him making out with his roommate at a kegger their fraternity was throwing. As far as gaydar goes, I didn't have any.

I dated a few different guys in my twenties, but none of them sent my heart into atrial fibrillation. I simply enjoyed going out with them while I was waiting for "the one."

Enter Astor Hill. I knew he was it for me the night we met. One look at his sandy-haired Leonardo de Caprio (from *Titanic*) savoir faire, and my heart rate took off like a particularly vigorous Fourth of July fireworks display. Boom, boom, boom! Everything about him shouted he was destined to be Mr. Faith Reynolds. Although, I'm sure I would have taken his last name instead. I mean, Faith Hill worked so well for, you know ... Faith Hill, that I was sure to have equal success. Even though I was no singer ...

But then Astor showed his true colors and once again I was left behind. That's when I should have probably converted to Catholicism and committed my life to God, a la the convent life.

I might have actually done that too, had it not been for the pity date ...

CHAPTER ONE

FAITH

Anna and I have been planning our weddings since we were in Pull-Ups at the Little Sunshine Preschool on Maple Street. Of course, we're going to be each other's maid of honors. To be precise, I'll be Anna's maid of honor when she gets married next month, and she'll be my matron of honor, seeing as how she's getting hitched first. Not that I'm officially planning my wedding. Not yet. I have an inkling of who my groom might be, but nothing's set in stone.

My prospective fiancé is none other than Astor Hill. Not only is he Anna's fiancé's best friend from law school and office mate, but we're walking up the aisle together for the ceremony. We haven't been a couple that long, but as you near your thirties— and I'm twenty-nine and three quarters— most of us have dated enough toads to know when we're being courted by a real prince. Astor is a real prince if there ever was one. *His name alone, am I right?*

"Faith, are you coming out or not?" Anna yells through the curtain of my changing cubicle. That's when I realize I haven't even taken off my street clothes yet, let alone put on the brides-maid dress.

I start to fumble with the button on my jeans. "I'm almost ready."

"Are you daydreaming about Astor again?" she teases. "Girl, you've been nonstop mooning over that man since your first date. I'm starting to think you might be the next one to the altar."

I subconsciously put my hand to my heart in a gesture of pure, unadulterated, "Who, me?" Astor hasn't mentioned taking our relationship to the next level, but that doesn't mean he's not thinking about it. He lives in Chicago, and I live in Elk Lake, Wisconsin, which means we only see each other on the weekends. But as absence makes the heart grow fonder, it's been a very workable arrangement. Especially since it's only temporary.

Astor and I met on a blind date nearly ten months ago while I was visiting Anna. We hit it off so spectacularly that I've taken the train down to Chicago most weekends since. It's just over two hours from my door to his.

Ripping off my t-shirt, I gingerly step into the pool of silver *poult-de-soie* at my feet. As I pull the sheath dress up, it gets stuck on my hips. "Crap," I grumble under my breath. One of the bene-fits of falling in love is that my appetite for food has decreased considerably, which is obviously the reason I made such a rookie mistake as to think I could get into this dress the same way a supermodel might. While my hips have shrunk a size since Astor and I have been together, they have a ways to go before making the pull-up maneuver possible.

"How's the house hunt?" I ask. Anna met Christopher when she was a realtor in Chicago. She sold him his condo. Once they got engaged, they decided he would hang his shingle in Elk Lake and the two of them would get busy starting a family. When she's not planning the wedding, she's looking for their first home as a married couple, as well as office space that will suit Chris's lawyering needs. Astor is planning to join the mass migration to

Elk Lake and set up shop with him. For this reason alone, it would appear he sees a future with me.

"I've found a couple places that I like but neither one of them is perfect. The one on Elk Lake is slightly preferable. Three bed, two bath, its own dock."

"You've always wanted to live on the lake," I remind her. *I've* always lived on the lake. Actually, I'm still in the house I grew up in. My parents bought a condo in Boca several years ago, so I've got the place all to myself. Which, honestly, is the only reason I'm still there. My mom is too much of a control freak to cohabitate with on an ongoing basis.

"It's the old Turner house down the road from you."

"I love that place! All it needs is a good coat of paint and maybe a new porch."

"And a new roof, and potentially a new septic ..." she groans.

"Oh boy, that sounds like a lot." As I put the dress over my head and scooch the silk material down my hips, I decide that two more pounds ought to be enough for this confection to be a perfect fit. I could manage it now, but I wouldn't be able to eat supper and I'm really looking forward to the meal I helped Anna pick out—prime rib or wide-mouth bass served with prosciutto wrapped asparagus, balsamic glazed new potatoes, and the triple layer Black Forest cake I'm making for their wedding cake. *Seriously yummy.*

"Yeah, but it's a steal," she says. "I'm going to show it to Chris over the weekend and see what he thinks."

"Has Chris said anything about Astor popping the question?" I ask, trying my best not to sound as hopeful as I've started to feel.

"No, but that doesn't mean anything. You know men, they don't talk like we do." *Life would be so much easier if they did.*

My heart races like I just hurdled over the twenty-yard buffet at the Rib Barn. "I don't suppose there's any way you could ask?"

"Chris?"

"Of course, Chris. I don't want you asking Astor," I practically hiss. The disaster potential of approaching an unsuspecting man with such a question is seriously staggering.

The next thing I know I hear what I suspect is Chris's phone ringing. "I didn't mean now!" I holler.

Instead of hanging up, Anna pushes her way into my dressing room and sits down on the chair wedged in the corner. "Hey, babe, what's up?" Chris's deep voice is a near baritone which is odd as he's rather slightly built. It's kind of a Rick Astley situation. You know, that singer from the eighties. How *that* ginger isn't a giant Black man is anyone's guess. Chris is a moderately statured Japanese-American with a flat Midwestern accent that belies his genetics.

"Faith and I are at the bridal boutique for a fitting. I just got done and I thought I'd call you and tell you how much I love you."

"I love you too, babe." He sounds distracted which is par for the course. Lawyers aren't known for having vast amounts of free time to chit chat during business hours. "Is there anything else? I have an important meeting in ten minutes. I need to jet."

Anna jumps right in. "Has Astor said anything about Faith? You know, about asking her a big question?"

My face heats up to the point where a glance in the mirror confirms I've taken on the color of a steamed beet. My complexion matches the auburn highlights in my hair.

"I'm not on speaker phone, am I?" Chris's question prompts a flock of butterflies to take flight in my lower abdomen.

My friend shakes her hands in the air like she's wielding a pair of imaginary pompoms. *Oh. My. God. This is it. I'm about to find out what my future holds and I'm not sure I'm ready.* No, I'm ready. I'm so very ready. How much fun will it be to have a practice run up the altar at Anna and Chris's wedding knowing we'll be next? I make a mental note to catalogue every detail of this moment so I can accurately write about it in my journal tonight. *"Dear Diary, this afternoon my whole life changed …"*

"Nope, not on speaker," Anna lies with a twinkle of anticipation in her eyes. Her body practically vibrates with excitement. Meanwhile, I lean against the mirror to keep my knees from buckling.

"It's like this, A," he says after exhaling what feels like the longest breath in history. I'm suddenly not sure good news is forthcoming. "Astor's been waiting until after the wedding, so he doesn't make things uncomfortable for us."

Anna barely lets him finish his sentence before announcing, "I wouldn't be uncomfortable if they got engaged before our wedding. Would you?"

"Um, no." Chris clears his throat loudly. "But Astor's not going to ask Faith to marry him."

"But you just said ..." She looks at me with panic in her eyes and makes a motion to take him off speaker. I shake my head fiercely. I want to hear what Chris has to say. I *need* to hear it.

"Astor isn't going to ask Faith to marry him because he's going to break up with her."

"Excuse me?" Anna shouts. *Shouts.* "Break up with her? Why? They're perfect together!"

"He's met someone else." That one sentence obliterates all my emotional reserve, and the wall is no longer strong enough to hold me up. I fall to the floor like a discarded corn husk. The seams of my dress strain against themselves as though my body has become allergic to it and is swelling in an attempt to burst free.

"No!"

"Tiffany started working in our office last month. She and Astor have been practically inseparable ever since," he informs her.

"While he's been with Faith? That bastard! That no-account son of a bitch!" Even my friend's staunch support and anger isn't enough to pop the strange balloon of suspended reality that's formed around me like a protective shield.

A feminine voice interrupts her tirade. "Is there something I can help you with in there?" Missy Corner asks. Missy went through grade school and high school with me and Anna. She opened a bridal boutique with her mother the minute she graduated from college in hopes the karma of the whole thing would find her standing at the altar in record time. So far, she's as single as I apparently still am.

"No, Missy. We're fine," Anna tells her.

Suddenly, my skin feels like an army of fire ants are on the march to do battle with my nervous system. I'm hot and prickly and most decidedly *not* fine.

"Look, A, I've got to go. Let's talk about this tonight, okay?" Chris signs off, leaving me and Anna to stare at each other like we've just been told the nuclear button in the Oval Office has been pushed and we only have minutes before the end of the world.

The end of *my* world, anyway.

CHAPTER TWO

TEDDY

A string of curse words erupts out of me as I swerve to avoid hitting a giant pothole on the 101 Freeway. I'm so sick of LA traffic I could spit. The reason I moved to the Sherman Oaks hills was to avoid the congestion of Pacific Coast Highway in Santa Monica. I'd previously rented a tiny guesthouse only a block from the water. But once my last movie came out, I needed to buy something to protect the sudden influx of money that hit my bank account. Not to mention, I really needed a place behind gates, so every Tom, Dick, and Mary didn't have access to me.

I settled on the Contour property the minute I saw it. Half an acre with a house that probably would've been razed by anyone else who bought it. It was love at first sight for me. It's the perfect project to keep my hands busy. My grandpa was a master craftsman and he passed down to me his love of turning something ordinary—or disastrous, even—into something extraordinary.

When my phone rings, I hit the button on my steering wheel to connect it to my Bluetooth. I hear the voice of my agent and best friend, Theresa Ramirez, through the speakers. "Teddy Bearrrr!" She rolls her R's like a pro. "I have the best news for you."

"You found a mold remediation guy who won't charge a fortune?" I dare to hope.

"Don't be ridiculous. Mold is going to cost you an arm and a leg and probably six toes. You should tear that place down and build something modern and chic."

"No, thank you," I tell her firmly. "Part of the reason I love my house is that I can turn it into anything I want. It's a blank slate for my creativity."

"You know what else is a blank slate?" she asks derisively. Before I can answer, she tells me, "A vacant lot."

I click my turn signal on as I near the Woodman exit. "Yes, but this house has good bones, Terri. It's got something special."

"It's got mold," she says. "But I don't really care where you live as long as you keep showing up to work so I get paid."

"So that's all I am to you, a paycheck?"

"Don't you dare try to make me feel bad about you finally increasing my net worth. I've repped you for ten years and before your last film, you hadn't made me enough money to buy a decent car."

"That's because I've been making quality films that have turned the indie world upside down," I remind her. "It's not my fault they don't pay well."

"A werewolf anthropologist who discovers a love of taxidermy ..." Her tone is pure disgust. "Is that what we're calling quality filmmaking these days?"

"*Movie Maker* magazine said it was the best freak film of the year," I remind her. "*Nut and Crunch* said that because I didn't just eat the bodies once I killed them, but recycled them into works of art, it made it a socially conscious and highly watchable film."

"Yeah, well, freak films aren't going to put food on our table as we so well know."

"*Wolf Feast* is the reason the guys at Wonder contacted me to be Alpha Dog," I remind her.

"That's why I'm calling," she says. "It looks like the big boys are planning to introduce Alpha Dog to the Galaxy Platoon, and they want to make sure you'll sign on for another picture. I told them that of course you would, but then I thought I'd better call and make sure. You know, that you aren't too busy Bob the Buildering it out there in the boonies to actually do your job."

Ignoring her blatant sarcasm, I ask, "When does filming start?" It's not that I wouldn't move heaven and earth to do another Wonder flick, 'cause I would, but I've made plans for the next year of my life, and I'd like to know how this new project might alter them.

"Eighteen months. They have to write the script first, and that's the earliest they can get the whole crew together to shoot."

"I'm in," I say enthusiastically before reminding her, "I'm heading to Wisconsin to spend time with my grandpa tomorrow. I'll fly to Canada to film *Oxblood House* from there."

"Yup, I got the memo. I won't be putting you up for any leads before you shoot for Wonder because of timing issues, but I'll still submit you for some juicy side characters that won't interfere with your new leading man branding."

"I wouldn't be too bummed if you didn't," I tell her.

"Things going that badly for Theo?" she asks with a note of real concern. One of the many things I love about Terri is that her priorities are in line. Family first, everything else second.

"Gram has been dead for over a year, and he barely leaves their cottage."

"Poor guy. To have waited all that time to retire to the place where he and your grandma first met, only for her to have a heart attack. It breaks *my* heart."

"Mine, too," I tell her. "He started to build her a gazebo to paint in and when she died, he just scrapped the project. I'm hoping while I'm there I can encourage him to finish it with me."

"You're a good egg, Teddy," she says. "I've only met your grandpa a couple of times, but I'm guessing that if you ask him to finish it, he will. He thinks the world of you."

"Maybe you and Kay can come out to visit while I'm there. You know, get away from all the busy of LA for a week or so."

When the light on Ventura Boulevard turns green, I put my foot on the gas and almost get t-boned by some idiot running the light in the other direction. As I slam on the brakes, Terri says, "No, sir. My career is taking off with yours and I'm not about to miss any of the fun by leaving. Plus, contrary to stereotypes, Kay is not the outdoorsy type.".

My heart is beating so loudly in my ears from the near miss, I barely hear her. "Think of all the traffic you won't have to sit in," I say.

"Think of all the stars I'll sign while you're gone."

"Have it your way," I tell her. "But you don't know what you're missing. Elk Lake is straight up the best place on earth."

"Just because you learned to swim and caught your first fish there in no way suggests it's my idea of nirvana. I share my wife's love of luxury suites and meals I don't have to kill myself."

"My best memories were sitting on my grandparents' back porch and shucking corn for supper. They talked about everything with me. They made me feel like the most important person in the world," I recall fondly.

"Half of Hollywood currently thinks the same thing."

"Yeah, but they don't mean it and you know that. I'm just the flavor of the month."

"Speaking of flavor of the month, have you heard from Lindsey again?"

My stomach plummets into a sour pit of dread. Lindsey Flint was my girlfriend for three years, and my fiancée for four months. We met when we were both struggling actors waiting tables at an Italian restaurant on the West Side. She was so sure we were both destined for stardom that she pushed and cheered and finagled introductions for us like it was the only thing that kept her alive.

Then, once we were engaged and had started to actively plan our wedding, she got cast in a supporting role in an up-and-coming TV series. That's when everything started to change. She stayed out late, claiming it was work related. I had no reason not to believe her, but with my schedule, I felt like we barely saw each other.

I've replayed our final scene in my head a thousand times like I'm watching it on the big screen. It's a movie I would give two giant thumbs down and zero tomatoes on the Rotten Tomatoes website. The headline would read: **Worst Film of All Time**

I was sitting in our tiny living room trying to come up with some side hustles that would help us pay for the wedding when Lindsey walked through the front door. She said, "Teddy, we need to talk."

I stood up, walked toward her, and kissed her before replying, "I'm all ears. But if this is about adding fish or chicken to the reception dinner, I don't think we can afford it if you're still committed to having a cupcake wall in addition to a cake. We can't do it all."

She hemmed and hawed while taking off her jacket. Then she sat on the sofa and crossed her ankles like she was visiting royalty (I only know this because Lindsey is a dedicated royal watcher). That's when she dropped her bomb. "I don't think we should get married."

"Come again?" Lindsey and I had talked about our wedding for years. We'd planned both extravagant events and small ones depending on what our means might be. We discussed our future children's names for heaven's sake. "What do you mean we shouldn't get married?"

Staring me right in the eyes, she answered, "I just don't feel that you're committed enough."

"*Excuse me?* I'm the one sitting here wondering if I can hire myself out as a cage dancer at nightclubs to bring in more cash. If that isn't commitment, I don't know what is."

She clarified, "I don't think you're committed to your career."

I scratched my head like a trained chimp. Seriously, if this had been a movie, the director would have called me out on such a blatant use of an "idiot man" typecast. "I just finished another indie film," I told her. "It was my seventh."

This is where she stood up in a huff and started to pace back and forth, from wall to wall. "No, Teddy! You're not committed to getting *bigger* roles, to really making it as an actor."

Still reeling from her declaration that we should break up, I told her, "I'm lucky I'm getting cast in anything. You know how hard it is to make it in this town."

That's when she spun around and came at me with her pointer finger. She jabbed it at my chest like it was a dagger. "Not only is Tom starring in *Finding Dr. Hawks*, but he's also auditioning for major films every week. Every. Week. Teddy."

"Well, good for Tom." The way to my heart was not, nor ever will be, comparing me to someone else. "Tom has been at it longer than both of us, so it's no wonder he's farther along in his career."

"I don't think you're ever going to make it." Slapping me in the face would have hurt less. "And I want the big time, Teddy. I want red carpets and movie premieres. I want trips to Sundance and Cannes. I want everything."

At this point I was fuming mad. "Then make it happen for yourself, if you want those things so badly. It'll mean more than riding someone else's coattails."

With her hands on her hips, she told me, "I deserve to be with someone who is as big of a success as I'm going to be, Teddy. I want to hitch my wagon to a star, not to an old pickup that can't go from zero to thirty in two minutes."

The pressure in my head felt like it was building to a dangerous level, and it was going to explode Looney-Tunes style. "So you're leaving me to find someone you think is going to become a star?" I was beyond incredulous—I was incredulous to the tenth power. I was completely blown away.

"I'm leaving you for Tom." Before I could respond, she added, "I'll be back on Saturday to get my things. Please don't be here." Then she turned and walked out of my life. Almost three and a half years, gone like it never happened.

Terri pulls me back into the present by saying, "Earth to Teddy. Answer my question. Have you heard from Lindsey?"

Turning left onto Contour, I tell her, "Not since that night last year when she came by trying to get back together. Why?" I should have been strong enough to withstand Lindsey's seduction, but three scotches and a still-broken heart had made me weak. Luckily, in the morning I felt more myself. Her betrayal was simply not something I could ever overlook.

"She's been calling, trying to get me to take her on," my agent says. "I keep telling her it would be a conflict of interest." If I ever doubted Terri was as much of a friend as my agent, this proves her loyalty.

Even though I'm secretly glad Terri's not going to rep Lindsey, I ask, "How so?"

"It's a conflict because I love you and think she's Satan's spawn, that's how."

I'd almost feel sorry for her if it weren't so true. "She's hard to have any sympathy for, isn't she?"

"She's like ninety-nine percent of hopefuls who come to Hollywood with visions of stardom. The truth is, I'm actually surprised she stayed with you as long as she did before turning ho."

"Turning ho ..." I start to laugh.

"What else would you call leaving you for someone who was a bigger deal in the industry? And while Tom Callaway's career is doing well enough, he's no you."

When I get to my driveway, I open my window and punch in my security code. "If fame is all she was after, then she made a bad investment in her future. Had she only stuck it out with me, she could have had everything she ever wanted."

"Yeah, but then you would have been stuck with *her*," Terri says. "You dodged quite a bullet, my friend."

"I guess. But I really thought Lindsey was the love of my life. Had I become famous sooner, I might have never found out what a vicious she-devil she is."

"My poor, sweet, Teddy Bear," Terri croons. "You would have

found out. Lindsey's not the kind of leopard who changes her spots." —

"I guess." Opening the door to get out of my truck, I remind her, "Don't forget the mold guys are going to call you when they're done so you can set up the final inspection."

"I'll take care of *everything*," she says.

There's something in her tone that makes me nervous, but I don't have time to worry about that now. I've got to get myself packed for Elk Lake and help my grandpa rediscover his zest for life.

While I can't wait to see Theo, what I'm really looking forward to is anonymity that I can never have in Hollywood. Who knew I'd miss the days when I was nobody?

CHAPTER THREE

FAITH

In the two days since Chris spilled the beans about Astor's plan, I've spent all my time vacillating between crying my guts out and convincing myself it's not true. I woke up this morning to the following text:

> *Astor: Hey babe, I hate to bail on you, but I have to work all weekend. There's no point in you coming down just to sit alone in my apartment all day.*

I have no intention of going to Chicago, but I feel the need to toy with Astor. I'm not going to make this easy on him.

> *Me: Don't worry about entertaining me. I have a ton of shopping I can do while I'm there. Plus, at least we'll have our nights …*

> *Astor: Seriously, I'll probably spend my nights at the office.*

That slutty pig … Of course, I don't say that.

Me: Yay! I'll get the whole bed to myself!

Astor: Really, Faith, don't come. It's not a good time.

Me: But I already have my ticket. I'm not going to waste fifty bucks.

Astor: I'll pay for your ticket. Don't come.

At this point I've had enough. He'll pay for my ticket, will he? I do some quick math and am about to tell him he owes me a cool two grand for all my train and Uber fares in the last year, but I don't want to tip my hand that I know anything. Yet.

Me: Don't be silly. I'll see you later this afternoon. I might even stop by your office on my way to your place. I've gotta go pack now. See you soon!

I shut my phone off, hoping he's in a panic that I'm going to make a scene at his office in front of his new girlfriend. *What kind of name is Tiffany for a lawyer anyway?* Is she in charge of all the cosmetic lawsuits? Does she rep fashion models who fall off their high heels on the runway?

Logically I know her name has nothing to do with her intellect and more with the fact that her parents probably grew up on *Saved by the Bell*, but I feel the need to hate this woman on every level possible.

I throw my covers off in a fury. Look out, I seem to be rounding the corner on the second stage of grief at an alarming rate. How dare Astor string me along until after the wedding?

It would appear his plan is to avoid seeing me. And then what? Treat me like a maiden aunt the whole weekend? That lousy, good-for-nothing butt nugget. Only a slithering turd of a human being cheats. But to keep doing it on the pretense of not making things uncomfortable for his friend on his wedding day?

Sorry, asshat, you're only trying not to make *yourself* uncomfortable and you know it.

The sudden tidal wave of anger leaves nearly as soon as it hits, and I'm thrown right into a bargaining frame of mind. Maybe it's not Astor's fault. I should have moved to Chicago like he suggested a few months after we started seeing each other. What if he really loves me, and this *Tiffany* threw herself at him?

Maybe I *should* go to Chicago today and see if there's any way we can patch this up. After all, I've spent the better part of a year with the man, and I'm not getting any younger. If Anna and I are going to have our babies together, I really need to keep this train on the tracks.

Thankfully, common sense makes an appearance at the party in my head. *This isn't the 1800s, Faith. A girl doesn't have to get married to have a family. You don't need a man to validate your existence. You are enough on your own.*

While I appreciate the truth of these words, I still can't get over feeling sorry for myself. I may not need a man, but I want one. Why aren't I good enough for Astor? What does this Tiffany person have that I don't? I may not be a lawyer, but I am the best damn baker in all of Wisconsin.

I don't have any awards to support that claim, but no one makes sour cream coffee cake like me. Once, a guy on death row even asked for one of my scones as a part of his last meal.

If that's not something to hang your hat on, I don't know what is. And while it was a little nerve-wracking, there's certainly a worthy endorsement in there somewhere.

After showering and blow drying my hair, I'm practically hit over the head by the fourth stage of grief—actual grief. I feel like I've gained a hundred pounds in the last five minutes as depression fills every corner of my being. I want nothing more than to go back to bed, and I would do just that if I didn't have a huge coffee cake order to fill this morning for the Lutheran ladies' annual white elephant sale.

I told Esmé I'd bake them so she could stay out late last night.

She's only twenty-four and needs time for her own social life. Especially since she's been working extra-long hours with my grandmother so I could be down in Chicago falling in love with a cheater. What a waste of time.

Then the tears come. They start out gently enough, only needing to be wiped away every few minutes. But by the time I unlock the back door of Rosemary's Bakery—named after my grandmother when she opened it forty years ago—I've practically dehydrated myself.

I hang my jacket on a peg and then get to work. First, I pull twenty pounds of butter out of the refrigerator to soften. I wipe my eyes and blow my nose before getting busy grinding fresh cinnamon and nutmeg. When that's done, I start on the macaroon dough. By the time I look up at the clock, it's already six thirty. Nick, my counter guy, should have been here a half-hour ago.

Wiping my hands, I pull my phone out of my purse only to discover that it's still off. After turning it on, the notifications ping like a video game in overdrive. I open the text from Nick to discover that he threw up this morning, and there's no way he can come into work. *Great.*

Then, one-by-one I open the texts from Astor.

Astor: Faith, we need to talk. Call me as soon as you get this.

Astor: Seriously, Faith, quit playing games and call me.

Astor: Faith, do not come to Chicago today. I'm not kidding.

And finally:

Astor: I didn't want to do this before Chris and Anna's wedding, but I don't think we should keep seeing each other. Call me if you want to talk about it.

Call him? Never. I vow not to waste one more second of my life on that man. He's not worthy of me. I'm a strong, independent woman who knows how to laminate the crap out of croissant dough. Paul Hollywood would not only shake my hand in the Bake-Off tent, he would be hard pressed not to drop to one knee and propose! I make a mental note to consider the possibility of moving across the pond, but then I remember the rumors about Paul. Apparently, he also has a hard time keeping it in his pants. Grrr, men.

Even as I try to envision a brighter future for myself, tears of defeat flow out of me at an alarming rate. How in the world am I ever going to walk up the aisle with Astor by my side and maintain even a shred of dignity?

CHAPTER FOUR

TEDDY

As a kid, I went by Theo instead of Teddy. When I was twelve, I started teasing my grandfather by calling him by his first name. He teased me back by calling me Teddy. Both names stuck.

The last time I saw Theo was when he came out to LA to be my date for the opening of *Alpha Dog*. Even though we haven't seen each other in person for a while, we FaceTime a couple times a week. I've watched him deteriorate to the point where I knew I had to take real time off to spend with him.

I was swarmed by paparazzi the minute I stepped out of the Uber at the airport, which I can only assume had something to do with my driver's need to send several text messages before we left my house.

The flight to Milwaukee would have been bearable if not for the woman sitting next to me on the plane. She insisted on talking nonstop, and I now know way more about pickling beets and cucumbers than most farmers' wives. Somewhere over the Rockies, I finally told her I needed to sleep. Instead, I put on my sunglasses so she wouldn't know I was lying, and then inserted a pair of earbuds and listened to a Marvel podcast the rest of the way. I was left with so many questions. Like, why haven't Galactus, Lord of Latveria, Quake, and the Sleazoids shown up in the movies yet?

The rest of the flight passes quickly, and I'm currently standing at the rental car kiosk. "Next!" The counter lady knocks me out of my daydream about swimming in Elk Lake. The lanyard around her neck says her name is Twilla.

Putting a smile on my face, I step forward. "Hi there, Twilla, I have a car reserved." I hand over my driver's license.

She picks it up and looks at it. "Teddy Helms … why do I know that name?" She cocks her head to the side and narrows her eyes at me like I'm a bug under a microscope.

I shrug my shoulders innocently, hoping this doesn't turn into a scene.

She suddenly starts typing away on her computer while saying, "I've got you down for a premium SUV. Is that right?"

"Yes, ma'am," I tell her.

"Teddy Helms … Teddy Helms …" She repeats my name like it's become her own personal mantra. "Hey, Chantelle, why do I know the name Teddy Helms?" she calls out to a co-worker.

"Alpha Dog!" the woman I'm guessing is Chantelle answers.

Twilla's eyes pop open so wide I'm tempted to hold my hands out to catch her eyeballs in case they eject out of her head. "NO, WAY!!! You're Alpha Dog?" Heads swivel my way from all directions. "I'm not supposed to do this, but can I get your autograph?"

"Sure," I say quietly. "But would you mind keeping it down a little?"

She doesn't seem to hear me, because she yells, "And we *have* to do a selfie!" Pulling out her phone, she holds it out in front of her and instructs, "Turn around and smile!"

I do just that only to find that Twilla has launched herself across the counter, puckered up and is kissing my cheek. Snap.Snap.Snap.Snap.Snap.Snap.Snap. The burst shutter fires off with lightning speed.

By the time she's handed me the rental car keys, and her phone number, a small line has formed with other hopeful fans looking for interaction. I haven't been famous for long enough not to be flattered by the attention, but it does have a way of adding extra time to what should have been a simple endeavor.

It takes the whole drive to Elk Lake for me to finally start to decompress. By the time I reach the city limits, I'm so hungry I decide to make a stop on the way to my grandfather's house. My grandma used to take me to Rosemary's Bakery when I'd visit during the summer. I remember them having the best gingersnaps I've ever eaten. Gram used to think they put white pepper in them for the extra kick, but Rosemary would never confirm her suspicion. She told Gram it was such a closely guarded secret that if she ever disclosed it, she'd have to kill the person immediately after.

As I drive down Main Street, I realize that Elk Lake looks a lot like Stars Hollow from that old TV show *Gilmore Girls*. I was nine when it came out, and my mom used to make me watch it with her. It wasn't the hardship you might think as I had a mad crush on Alexis Bledel. I mean Rory Gilmore, am I right? Few girls possessed that unassuming combo of beauty and brains. Rory had that in spades.

Like Stars Hollow, Elk Lake has a small-town charm that makes you want to move here and never leave. It hosts old buildings with the kind of character that mattered in decades past, a park in the center of town where children run wild, and people strolling happily through town smiling and holding doors for each other. It's everything I've ever wanted in the place I chose to live. LA is *nothing* like it.

I park in front of Rosemary's Bakery and get out. The first thing I do is look up at the sky and feel the early summer warmth on my face. I inhale the faint scent of Japanese lilac trees that line both sides of Main Street, which causes that strange combination of pure joy and otherworldly optimism that is usually reserved for characters in Broadway shows right before they break out into song.

My dream has always been to make it big and buy my own house here so I can bring my kids during the summer. But now that my grandpa is all alone, I'd never not stay with him. Also, what kids? I'm nearly thirty-two and, thanks to Lindsey, am nowhere near having the family I thought I'd be starting by now. Ever since my dad died when I was sixteen, I've felt like I needed to become a father relatively young, in case like him, I wasn't destined to live a long life.

As I enter the bakery, the bell over the door announces me. Looking around, I notice the style has changed considerably since my childhood. It no longer has that eighties vibe of mauve, black, and chrome. The tables are light oak surrounded by mismatched chairs of all colors. It's eclectic and welcoming at the same time. It's also practically empty. I look at the clock on the wall and realize that four in the afternoon must be their downtime.

"Hi there," I call out to the woman standing behind the counter. She appears to be around my age with wavy auburn hair pinned up on top of her head. She's eating a cookie.

Her brow furrows as her gaze narrows behind her glasses. She looks like she might be about to recognize me. *Please don't let her recognize me.* I briefly consider shaving my head or dying my hair for the summer so no one will know who I am.

"Can I help you?" she finally asks.

As I step toward the counter, I notice her skin is blotchy and her eyes are rimmed in red like she's been crying. She must be allergic to lilacs. "I've been dreaming about one of your gingersnaps," I tell her.

She looks at the cookie in her hand before saying, "This is the last one."

"Oh." I'm disappointed, but as I'm here for another couple of months, it's no real hardship. "How about one of your chocolate chip cookies? From what I remember, those are spectacular as well."

"I ate the last one an hour ago," she says with no emotion whatsoever.

I force a smile, wondering if she took this job so she could eat cookies all day. While nicely curvy, she doesn't look any the worse for it. "What would you suggest then?" I ask.

"Coffee cake. I have a lot of coffee cake."

"Sounds good," I tell her. "I'll have a cup of peppermint tea and whatever cake you suggest."

Turning to find a table to sit at, I see a couple of old ladies chatting away near the window. I decide to sit in the corner where no one can see me from the street. They likely won't even notice me if they come inside.

Minutes pass and I start to wonder where my tea and cake are when the old ladies get up to leave. As they walk by me, one of them turns and says, "You look familiar."

"I have one of those faces," I tell her. I can't imagine this woman is a superhero movie fan.

"That's not it," the other woman says. "You look like Abigail Fischer's husband Theo when he was younger." She turns to her friend. "Doesn't he, Marge?"

Marge snaps her fingers. "That's it! You're not by any chance their grandson, little Theo, are you?"

I smile at them. This is the kind of recognition I like. "I am, but I go by Teddy now. Teddy Fischer," I lie easily. I may have just found a way to keep my anonymity while maintaining a shred of truth.

"I was so sorry to hear about Abigail," Marge says. "We used to have a lot of fun when she and Theo spent their summers here. They were away for so many years though that we kind of lost touch. I only saw her a handful of times after they finally moved here."

I nod my head sadly. "My grandpa's still here. I don't suppose you see him around much?"

They shake their heads in unison as Marge declares, "Abigail was always the outgoing one between them. Wasn't he, Charlotte?"

Charlotte answers, "Yup. Although now that you mention it, I think I saw Theodore at the Senior Center last month. He came in, picked up some books from our free library, and left."

I didn't know my grandfather was going out at all, and I'm relieved he's doing something other than sitting around the house, ordering take-out.

After Charlotte and Marge wish me a good day and leave, I look around for the woman who took my order. She's nowhere to be found. Getting up, I walk toward the counter and call out, "Hello? Anyone here?"

"Just ... a ... minute ..." I hear from the back room. I'm suddenly tempted to get my own coffee cake when she comes back out. This time it's clear she's been crying.

"Are you okay?" I ask with concern. Also, I really want my coffee cake.

She pinches her lips tightly together and nods. Then she shoos me away.

It doesn't take her long to bring my food after that. She drops a plate on the table which causes the fork to slide to the floor. As she bends to pick it up, she inadvertently spills the pot of tea on my lap. "Ouch!" I jump to my feet in shock and pain.

"I'm so sorry!" she says. "I didn't mean to ... I didn't think ... I didn't ..." and then she bursts into tears.

"No, no, no. No problem. Maybe I could just get a towel or something."

Instead of getting a towel for me, she runs into the back room again. This isn't quite how I anticipated my snack break going. I'm about to get up and get my own towel when the bell over the door rings again.

CHAPTER FIVE

FAITH

Not only have I eaten a dozen cookies today, but now I've gone and spilled hot tea on a customer. I'm spiraling downhill at such an alarming rate, I can only predict I'm minutes away from walking into a bus or accidentally lighting my hair on fire, *again*. It took me months to grow out my 'do after the great Bunsen burner debacle from junior year in high school.

As my victim isn't familiar to me, he's probably a summer visitor from Chicago. Which means there's a better than decent chance he's going to sue for pain and suffering. And here I am without a good lawyer. I suppose I could always ask Chris to represent me, but I can no longer ask Astor. *The fiend.*

A new round of tears bubbles up and follows the path of their predecessors. I have got to get a hold of myself. Splashing some cold water on my face, I make the executive decision to stay in the kitchen long enough for the stranger to leave. It doesn't matter that he hasn't paid. God knows everything is on the house now—second-degree burns included.

After hearing the bell over the door a few times, I realize I need to go out there and take care of my other customers. Imagine my surprise when I peak out of the back room to find the man I scalded standing behind the counter, handing out baked goods.

"What are you doing?" I demand angrily.

Without looking at me, he places a final lemon bar into a plastic shell. "Someone has to take care of these people."

"Yes, well, that's my job," I tell him while retying my apron before pushing him out of the way.

"You don't seem to be too interested in working." *Is he being snippy with me?*

Looking down at his wet pants, I immediately feel contrite. "I'm sorry. I'm having a really hard day. I didn't mean to, you know …" I wave my hand toward his crotch.

"Don't worry about it," he says. "I know a thing or two about having a hard day."

I don't know what gets into me, but I ask, "Did your boyfriend cheat on you too?" I sound every ounce as bitter as I feel.

He cocks an eyebrow while nodding like a bobblehead on a dashboard. "As a matter of fact, yes, I've been cheated on."

Well crap, now I feel bad. "I shouldn't have asked that," I tell him. "It was too personal. The thing is, I just found out about my boyfriend a couple of days ago." I hurry to add, "And I thought we were about to get engaged."

He releases a long whistle. "That's rough. "I'm really sorry."

"We're standing up for our best friends when they get married next month. Anna thought it would be romantic for us to walk up the aisle together." I sigh like a balloon with a serious leak.

"Anna's the best friend?" he assumes correctly.

And then, as though she knew she was being talked about, the woman herself walks through the front door. Her dark box braids are wrapped around her head in a more formal style than she normally wears. She even has makeup on, which she never bothers with. As a self-professed Nubian goddess, she claims her dark skin is the only color she needs. She's not wrong. Anna is one of the most beautiful women I've ever known. Inside and out.

Her first words are, "I've been at the salon trying makeup and hairstyles for the wedding. I tried calling you, but you didn't pick up."

"I turned my phone off," I tell her. "You should have used the bakery line."

She glances at the man I've been talking to before asking me, "Are you okay?"

"Not great. I was just telling ..." I halt while gesturing toward my helper. I don't know his name.

"Teddy," he supplies.

"My name's Faith," I tell him before finishing my answer to Anna. "I was just telling Teddy what a good-for-nothing, scum-sucking worm Astor is."

"Really?" She sounds shocked. And rightly so, as I normally don't go around town telling strangers my deepest, darkest secrets. She asks Teddy, "Who are you?"

"Just a guy standing in front of a girl asking for a gingersnap." His smile is pure radiance and I'm suddenly stunned by how good looking he is. I'm more surprised that I'm only just noticing.

Anna's left eyebrow arches. "You're quoting Julia Roberts in *Notting Hill*?"

He nods. "My mom used to make me watch all the nineties rom-coms with her. She said it was the best way to learn every-thing I needed to know about love."

Anna nods her head slowly. "She's right about that."

I decide to jump into the conversation. "Who said, 'Nice boys don't kiss like that?'"

"Bridget Jones!" they both call out at the same time.

Anna asks, "How about, 'I wanted it to be you. I wanted it to be you so badly.'"

I stumble for a moment while Teddy answers, "Meg Ryan in *You've Got Mail*!"

"Wow, you really are good at this," I tell him. Then I add, "If you're not dating anyone, I could set you up with Nick. Talk about an encyclopedia of rom-com trivia."

"Is Nick short for Nicola?" he asks.

"Nicholas," I tell him.

Teddy's eyes open wide, and he appears to be stifling a smile. "I'm not really looking to get involved with anyone right now, but thank you."

"I don't blame you." Then I tell Anna, "Teddy's boyfriend cheated on him too."

"Poor thing." Anna pats his arm sympathetically before adding, "Those are some nice guns you've got there."

"Well, you know how it is, breakups require a lot of workouts to burn off the angst." He looks at me. "Am I right?"

"Um … yes?"

Anna starts to laugh. "Women sometimes mourn differently than men."

Teddy looks between us with a confused expression on his face, so I come clean. "For example, I eat. That's the reason we don't have any gingersnaps or chocolate chip cookies."

"You ate them all?" He sounds impressed. Horrified, but impressed.

"We only had five gingersnaps and six chocolate chip cookies left." I say this like I'm the poster child for self-restraint.

"I used to buy shoes," Anna confessed. "I amassed quite a wardrobe before meeting Chris."

"Well, there you have it," Teddy says. "I suppose we all deal with heartache in our own way." He smiles at me. "I don't suppose I could get another cup of tea from you."

"Oh … yes … I'm so sorry! Here I am blathering on about myself and I totally forgot about, well, you know." I point to his pants again.

"While you're getting Teddy his tea," Anna says, "would you mind putting on a cup for me? You are not going to believe what my mother suggested we serve at the wedding."

"Klondike bars again?" I ask. Anna's mom, Dawn, marches to her own tune. She's something of an artist, but she doesn't work in traditional mediums. She knots together a lot of macramé and then glues it to canvasses before painting over it. As the painted rope looks like intricate bondage ware, she calls them her colorful cages.

"Pot brownies," Anna tells me.

Teddy stops mid-step like he doesn't want to miss this.

"She claims that now that marijuana is legal in half the country, we should offer our guests a nice high during the reception."

I stifle a laugh. "I have no words ..."

"I do," Anna says. "Can you imagine Chris's parents being offered a pot brownie? His mother is already mad that the only Asian part of the meal are the tuna roll appetizers. Pot brownies would send her over the edge."

"Does your mom realize marijuana isn't legal in Wisconsin?" I ask. "I mean, I know it's allowed in the more liberal states, but I don't see it ever being an over-the-counter purchase here."

"She thinks that because it's a private party, no one ever has to know," Anna explains.

"Except you've invited the sheriff and his wife," I remind her.

My friend shakes her head and motions toward the glass case. "I need a pain au chocolate, stat."

I take one off the silver tray and hand it over to her. "Go sit down. I'll be right over with your tea."

I watch as she follows Teddy's path and sits at the table with him. Pouring hot water into two small teapots, I hear her ask, "So what's your story? You just visiting or are you new to Elk Lake?"

CHAPTER SIX

TEDDY

So, Faith and Anna think I'm gay. While I'm delighted homophobia doesn't seem to be an issue among the residents of Elk Lake, I'm still oddly hurt. In my eyes I'm superhero manly, at least since playing Alpha Dog. And while I want to set them straight—pun intended—and share that I do, in fact, like women, having them think I'm batting for the other team might work in my favor. Having said that, I don't want to be a liar.

"About my being gay…" I start to say but Faith cuts me off.

"I should have known you were."

"How's that?" I ask nervously.

"Because you're nice, and you jumped right in to lend a hand. A straight guy would have sat on his butt and watched all those customers in need without helping."

"I'm sure there are some straight gays who would have stepped up." Of course, I'm speaking of myself.

"Please," Faith says. "Do not try to come to the aid of the enemy."

I certainly don't want to be thought of as the enemy, so I

decide there can't be any harm in letting her think what she wants. It's not like I'm going to see her that often, or after the summer for that matter.

Over the next half-hour, most of what I tell them about myself is true. I'm in the arts, I'm visiting my grandfather for a few months, and I'd like to do some woodwork while I'm here. I tell them about the abandoned gazebo in my grandpa's back yard.

"My mom knows your grandfather," Anna says. "Or rather, knows of him. She owns a couple of chairs he carved while he was here about twenty years ago."

"Theo Fischer is a big name in artisan furniture," I tell them proudly.

"He used to make pieces while he was in Elk Lake and only charged a fraction of what he could have gotten in Chicago or New York," Anna says. "That's how my mom was able to afford them." While the galleries who sold his stuff did charge a fortune, they charge even more now that he's no longer making anything new. Existing works fetch a premium.

"I loved watching Theo work," I tell them. "He used to say that each piece of wood had a shape it was meant to be in, and he waited until it talked to him before he started cutting it."

Faith giggles. "My grandmother used to take a pound of butter out of the refrigerator and wait for it to tell her what it wanted to be turned into."

"I wonder if our grandparents know each other," I say. "My grandmother used to bring me in here all the time when I was a kid."

"How about that," Anna interjects. "You two probably crossed paths a thousand times before today."

"I think I'd remember if we did," Faith says, making me think she might not be totally immune to my visage.

"Maybe not," I tell her. "I looked a lot different as a kid."

"Didn't we all," Anna says. "I mean, God help us if we never grew out of the awkwardness of our pre-teenage years." Anna doesn't appear to be the kind of woman who had an awkward minute, let alone a year, but I don't say that.

Faith, on the other hand, looks like she might have struggled. It's not that she's not pretty. She's certainly that, it's just that she seems to wear her emotions openly. And from what I remember from adolescence, that kind of transparency can work against you.

Bringing the subject back around, Faith asks, "What was so different about you back then?"

"Well, for starters," I tell her, "I was pretty skinny. I also had acne, braces ..." I pause for a beat before adding, "And *really* big feet."

Both women look down at my feet. "You know what they say about men with big feet ..." Anna declares.

Faith laughs. "I know what Julia Roberts said in *Notting Hill.* 'Big feet, big shoes ...'" she quotes.

"It's true," I tell them with mock seriousness.

Anna winks at me. "You're going to make some man very happy someday."

And we're back to my supposed gayness. As uncomfortable as lying makes me, if it helps me keep my anonymity, so be it. I stand up and tell them, "My grandfather is expecting me, so I'd better get going."

Faith jumps to her feet and hurries to the counter where she fills a bag with treats. "For you and Theo, on the house."

"That's not necessary," I tell her.

Before I can pull out my wallet to pay, she asks, "Are you going to sue me?"

"I hadn't planned on it."

"Then it's necessary," she says. "I can't properly welcome you to Elk Creek with nothing more than burns on your, well ... you know ..."

"My thigh," I finish the sentence for her.

She appears highly relieved I didn't say something else. "Thank God." Then she tips her head to the side and smiles genuinely. "I hope you'll come in again some time."

"Most definitely," I assure her. And while I'm not about to make a move on Faith, especially as she's currently heartbroken, I do like her. She's refreshing and unexpected. She's funny and vulnerable. It's an intriguing blend of traits that I will most definitely make a point to resist. "Hey ..." I start to say before thinking better of it.

"Yes?" She bats her beautiful blue eyes rapidly.

Shoot, now I have to say something. Nervously shifting from foot to foot, I finally blurt out, "I was going to ask you if you'd like me to take you to Anna's wedding. You know, so you don't have to face Astor all by yourself." *So much for my not seeing her often.*

"You'd do that for me?" She sounds touched which makes me happy I didn't chicken out.

I smile sheepishly. "We poor cheated-on souls need to stick together, don't we?"

Faith calls across the room to Anna. "Teddy is going to be my date to your wedding. Is that okay?"

The look on Anna's face is comical as her expression morphs from surprise to delight to concern. "Does this mean Astor gets to bring a date, too?" she wants to know.

"No!" Faith shouts, at the same time I ask, "Why not?"

"Why *not*?" Faith demands. "I think the more pertinent question would be *why*?"

"Because if you show up with a date and he doesn't, it'll seem like you planned it that way. Like you're trying to make him jealous." I continue, "But if he brings a date too, everyone will assume you're totally over him and couldn't care less."

"But I'd have to see *Tiffany* ..." She says the woman's name like she's referencing the bubonic plague. Which is certainly how I used to feel about the man Lindsey left me for.

"What will that matter? You'll be with me." I put my sack of treats on the counter and give her my manliest pose.

Laughingly, she says, "If only we were going on a real date."

"Hey, it could be a real date ..." I start to say but immediately stop when she gives me a disbelieving look. "I might be bi," I tell her, embarrassed that my macho self can't handle her thinking of me as gay.

"Are you?" she wants to know.

I shake my head, figuring I might as well stick to the truth on this one. "No."

She picks up a pen and writes her phone number down on a scrap of paper before handing it to me. "You're a life saver, Teddy. Thank you." Before I can respond, she adds, "And for what it's worth, I'm glad you're gay."

"Really, why?"

She tips her head to the side before saying, "Because you're really cute, and I'd be tempted to flirt with you if you were straight. All I need right now is a good friend."

If she's telling me she *needs* me to be gay, then I suppose I don't have to feel bad about letting her believe that I am. That's what I'm telling myself anyway. "I'm always happy to have a friend," I tell her.

Due to total devastation, I haven't dated much since Lindsey. After *Alpha Dog*, my heartbreak morphed into suspicion when I discovered the women who wanted to go out with me seemed more interested in my fame than me.

Even though nothing is going to romantically occur with Faith, I find that I'm looking forward to spending an evening with her. There's something about her that makes me want to be her champion.

With a wave, I turn to leave. That's when my lack of ballet training comes in and my feet get tangled up in each other. I wind up performing a dramatic multi-trip that nearly knocks me into the wall. Righting myself only adds to the absurdity.

There is no way I can leave without saying something more, so I turn toward my new friends and bow. "I always like to leave the people with something to remember me by."

Faith claps her hands. "It's those big feet you're so proud of!"

Anna hazes, "Clown shoes are so hard to walk in."

"Okay, then." I wave again and this time make it out the door without incident. The bell chimes overhead and I have the sensation I'm leaving Luke's Diner in Stars Hollow. Faith would be Luke in this scenario, so that would make me Lorelai. Boy, I *really* am switching things up here.

As I drive through the picturesque streets that lead me to my grandfather's house, I almost feel like I've fallen through time and that when I get to his cottage my grandmother will be there to greet me. Within minutes, we'd be heading to the lake for some fun.

Not only did I go tubing on Elk Lake, but I learned to water ski here, and I kissed my first girl at a beach party. I found myself in this town and it's making my return feel oddly sweet and melancholy at the same time.

As the blocks go by, I feel a yearning so powerful it's all I can do not to pull over to the side of the road and cry like a baby. I like my life. I have a great career, great friends, and a house full of potential. But none of that puts a dent in what I used to have here. My summers were magical, and it's almost physically painful that that time is over.

Double checking the address my grandfather sent me, I realize I've arrived at my destination. Gram and Theo stayed all over this lake when I was little, but the house they bought for their retirement is the epitome of perfection. It's not big, but it's charm on top of charm. It's painted white with a wraparound deck that looks out onto the lake. The windows are sporting flower boxes that I'm sure would have been full of bright blooms had my grandmother been alive. As it is, they're full of plants that died God knows how long ago.

My grandfather is sitting on one of the rocking chairs on the back porch, staring out at the water. He's so still I wonder if he's among the land of the living or if he died of a broken heart and all that's left is this shell of the man he used to be.

He turns his head so slowly it's as if he's moving through

molasses. He raises a hand to wave before pushing himself up into a standing position. I watch as he takes one wobbly step after another.

The only thought in my head is *thank God I'm here*. Theo needs me and there's no place in this world I'd rather be.

CHAPTER SEVEN

FAITH

"What a nice guy," Anna says after Teddy walks out of the bakery.

"I know, right? I mean, how many strangers do you know who would save my bacon by taking me to your wedding? And that's *after* I gave him second-degree burns."

"I'm guessing one, and he just walked out the door." Anna takes a sip of her tea before getting serious. "How are you doing anyway?"

I put a slice of sour cream coffee cake on a plate and carry it back to our table. "Not good. I'm seriously questioning everything that ever happened between Astor and me." I enumerate, "Did he ever like me? Was he cheating all along? Was I just some weekend fun?"

Instead of answering my questions, Anna looks at my plate. "A dozen cookies *and* coffee cake, huh? I might have to check into getting you a bigger bridesmaid dress."

"Don't fat shame me." I cut off a large chunk of cake and put it in my mouth. "It's not like I expected this to happen," I say as crumbs fly.

"I'm not fat shaming you, I'm saving you from yourself."

Anna pulls the plate away from me and places it on a table next to us. "Not only do you want Astor to see that you're over him, you want to show him what he's missing,"

My eyes well with tears and my nose fills with snot. With a quivering upper lip, I confess, "But I'm not over him."

"I know, Faithy. I could just wring Chris's neck for telling you about Tiffany."

"He didn't know I was listening," I remind her. "I wasn't supposed to be listening."

She shrugs her shoulders. "Still."

I lean toward the table until my forehead is resting on it. Reaching across to the table next to us, I make a grab for my plate, moaning, "Coffee cake is the only way I'm going to get through this."

Anna's hand comes down sharply, impeding my efforts. "I hate that what was supposed to be a fun day is going to be such agony for you." She offers, "Do you want me to hire a hit on Astor?"

"Yes, please," I whine pitifully.

"Should I see if I can get a twofer and knock Tiffany off while I'm at it?" Anna always knows the perfect thing to say, even when she's keeping me from my treat.

I release a small giggle. "Only if Chris agrees to represent us in the murder trial."

She shakes her head slowly. "I don't think a real estate lawyer is going to be able to keep us out of prison." After a beat, she adds, "That's not to say it wouldn't still be worth it."

An onslaught of sadness washes over me, and I release an actual whimper. "What am I going to do? I really thought Astor was the one."

"You're going to do what every other woman has done in the same situation since the dawn of time," she says. "You're going to pull up your big girl panties and fight back."

"Short of taking the train to Chicago and burning down his apartment building, I have no idea how to go about doing that."

Reaching across the table to take my hands in hers, Anna says, "You're going to stop eating everything in sight, and you're going to shine like the star you are at my wedding. You're going to show that *ass turd* this breakup means nothing to you. That you're riding a new horse named Teddy Fischer."

I smile at Astor's new nickname, before releasing a melodramatic sigh. "Leave it to a gay guy to be my knight in shining armor."

"At least someone is. I can't imagine how horrible it would be if you and Astor were both at the wedding alone. It would be open warfare."

Pulling my hands back from hers, I pick up a paper napkin and blow my nose, then tell her, "It could have been fun to make him look bad in front of everyone."

Anna tips her head from side to side. "That's not exactly how I want to remember my big day."

"I guess." A genius thought pops into my head. "I could still get the staff to put Visine into his water, couldn't I?" Anna and I learned this trick in college. When a guy was getting too handsy, all you had to do was squeeze a few eyedrops into his drink. His attention would turn away from amorous pursuits to his raging bowels.

"I really don't want any of my guests to be plagued with explosive diarrhea," she says. "It's not that Astor doesn't deserve it, but remember Haydn Barker ..."

Haydn Barker had already passed out from too many shots when his revenge hit. He wound up pooping his pants and making such a stink, the party ended early so his friends could throw him in the shower and fumigate. The next time we went to that frat house, there was a new sofa and Haydn was uncharacteristically well-behaved.

"Then maybe your mom is onto something with the pot brownies." I arch an eyebrow in question.

"Not going to happen, my friend. As it is, I've had to talk my dad off the ledge for wanting to catch all the fish we serve at the reception. Thank God he's not a hunter or the local cows would be in jeopardy, too."

"Why would he want to put that kind of pressure on himself?" I ask in surprise. "I mean, your dad is a great fisherman, but that could get a little crazy."

"To save money. Why else?" Anna rolls her eyes.

"I thought you and Chris were paying for the wedding."

"My dad doesn't care whose money he's saving. He lives for the opportunity to keep it out of the hands of the establishment."

I love Anna and her family so much. They're wonderful, interesting characters who bring such joy to my life. "Do you remember the time your dad tried to talk us into wearing our school shoes to the homecoming dance because new dress shoes wouldn't be worth the cost? He even offered to spray paint them for us." Mine, hot pink, and Anna's orange. We both declined.

"Why do you think I started working as early as I did? He used to tell me I only needed new jeans every two years. Can you imagine?"

"I'm just trying to picture the looks on the faces of the staff at the country club if your dad showed up with a trunk full of large-mouth bass on the day of the wedding."

Anna glances around at the empty shop. "Why don't you leave early today? We could go for a nice long walk or something."

"A nice long walk to the pub?" I ask hopefully. "I'd be happy to trade eating for some good, old-fashioned drinking."

"No, ma'am. I'm not interested in getting you tanked. If you want to feel better, you need some endorphins to kick in. Nature's high."

"I'd rather just finish my coffee cake," I tell her seriously.

"So when you sit down at the reception all your seams will give way and your dress will split down the back?"

I look at her in horror. "You're mean!"

She stands up and walks to the front door and turns the open sign over to closed. "I'm not mean. I love you and I want to help you get through this in a way that you won't regret."

"Then go down to Stark's Café and get me a large order of fries," I suggest. "I've never regretted their fries."

She takes me by the hand and drags me into the kitchen. "Put your tennis shoes on while I turn off the lights."

Anna has always been able to bully me into doing things I don't want to, and today is no exception. I sit down on the bench by the back door and kick off my kitchen clogs before putting on my tennis shoes. I'm going to have to walk a hundred miles if there's any hope of changing my current mood.

As Anna strides back into the kitchen, she looks down at my feet in approval. "Good girl. Now, let's go."

We're about to walk out the back door when my phone pings. I pull it out of my pocket to see that it's a text from Astor.

Astor: Faith, we need to talk. Please call me as soon as you get this.

I show the text to Anna, and she takes the phone. She promptly changes his name to Ass Turd. "Not bloody likely, loser," she grumbles while hitting the save button.

"He's already broken up with me. What could he possibly want?" I demand.

CHAPTER EIGHT

TEDDY

"Hey, Grandpa," I call out while exiting the car. The expression on his face causes my heart to clench. He looks old and worn out, like his inner light has been snuffed.

"Teddy." He makes an attempt to sound excited, but it doesn't work. After taking a couple of steps toward the stairs he stops and waits for me to come to him.

I get my suitcase out of the trunk before crossing the driveway. It dead ends at a cobblestone path that leads up to the back porch. Taking the stairs two at a time, I reach out and pull him into my arms. "You look great!" I lie.

"Great for a corpse," he mumbles with his mouth pressed against my shoulder.

I lighten my grip on him. "You're not dead yet."

"Is that why you're here?" He sounds angry. "To remind me that I'm not dead?"

"No, sir," I tell him. "I'm here because I love you and I miss you and I want us to spend another summer together, just like old times."

"Nothing's like it used to be." He pulls away from me and totters back to his chair.

"While I don't know what it's like to lose a spouse, I do know what it's like to lose a father," I remind him.

He looks chagrined as he says, "I know you do, son. And while I'm sorrier than I can say Brett died so young, it's still different. Abigail was my constant companion for most of my life. I don't know who I am without her."

Following along, I tell him, "I miss her, too." Then I sit down next to him. "But we're still here, so I say we make the most of it."

He turns to me and his gaze narrows. "You haven't spent a whole summer here since you left for college."

"I haven't," I agree. "And I've missed it."

"It's not the same," he says again. "Nothing is."

"That's the thing with life, isn't it?" I ask. "It's always changing and we're not always ready."

"What do you have to be complaining about?" he asks. "You're just starting your life. All the good times are ahead of you."

"I agree," I tell him. "But that doesn't mean it's always been easy."

"Ah." He rubs his hands together as though trying to warm them. "I'm guessing you're talking about Lindsey."

"Yes and no. I mean, I'm over her, but she certainly caused some damage."

"You need to meet yourself a nice normal girl," Grandpa says. "Someone who isn't busy clawing her way to the top."

"I liked that Lindsey had ambition," I tell him. "I just wish she'd trusted her own talent and wasn't convinced she needed someone to be successful with her."

"Your grandmother always worried about that one," he says cryptically.

"How so?"

He jabs a finger in my direction. "She pegged her for a user."

"I didn't have anything for her to use me for," I tell him.

"You do now." He doesn't say anything else; he just gets back onto his feet and slowly walks toward the back door.

Once we're inside, he sits at the kitchen table. "How long are you planning to stay?"

I look at the wreckage around us and approach the sink. Turning on the hot water, I fill the basin so I can get busy rinsing off dishes. The oatmeal pan is so crusted over it's probably been drying for days.

"Most of the summer," I tell him. "I have to go to Canada for a week in August to shoot my part in an indie film I signed on to do before *Alpha Dog* came out, but I'm coming right back here after that."

"So you can keep bossing me around?" Isolation combined with grief has made him grumpy.

"I already told you why I'm here. I miss you and I want to help you get through this tough period." I work in silence for several minutes before putting a cleaning pod into the dishwasher. I close the door and start it up.

"Your grandmother and I were married for sixty years. I'm not sure that's something you get over." He sounds so sad I don't know how to respond.

"I don't think you're supposed to get over her. You just have to find a way to live without her. For now."

"You mean until I drop dead, too?" Before I can answer, he adds, "If I weren't such a baby, I'd go for a swim in the lake and forget to hold my breath when I went under."

He can't possibly be talking about killing himself, can he? "How about if we finish Gram's gazebo instead?"

"Why? She's not here to enjoy it." As he pushes himself up, he leans to the side like he's about to fall over. I run over and offer him my arm, but he smacks it away.

"I bet she's here," I tell him. "She probably visits you all the time and is sad by what's become of you." I'm not sure guilting him is the best course of action, but I do know my grandfather would hate for Gram to see him like this.

He slowly starts to walk into the living room. "If she's here then she knows how badly I miss her." He removes a pile of newspapers from his recliner before sitting down.

I turn on a couple of lights and discover his lack of housekeeping has not been confined to the kitchen. "When's the last time you cleaned?" I run a finger over the thick layer of dust on the coffee table.

"I don't clean," he answers gruffly.

"Okay. When's the last time *anyone* cleaned?"

He shrugs his shoulders looking like a schoolboy who's just been sent to the principal's office. "That was probably your mother when she was here a few months back."

"Grandpa, this isn't healthy." I start to pile loose mail into a stack.

"Being that I'm not concerned about staying healthy," he says, "I don't suppose it's the big problem you're making it out to be."

"Okay," I tell him sternly. "Tomorrow is the first day of the rest of your life."

He rolls his eyes but doesn't say anything.

I put one finger up. "We're going to get you out of the house every day for some fresh air and exercise." I keep the fingers going. "We're going to get somebody in here to deep clean for you, and we're going to get you some proper food. A man cannot live on canned soup alone."

"You can't push me around, boy," he says. "I'm nearly three times your age. Show some respect."

"I respect the hell out of you," I tell him. "Which is why I'm not going to let you keep spiraling down into a pit of depression."

"You go through what I've been through and then you can tell me how to live my life." He seems to rethink his sternness because he adds, "I haven't forgotten about your dad, son. I think of him often and wish that you never lost him." My dad died in a car crash when I was sixteen. It was the defining moment of my life. It was also the time my grandfather stepped into his shoes as much as possible and became an even bigger presence in my life.

Theo picks a newspaper off the stack on the floor and makes a show out of opening it up. I know this maneuver well. He's telling me he's done talking.

"I'm going to take my bag upstairs," I tell him. "Which room do you want me to stay in?"

"Whichever room you want as long as it isn't mine."

"I love you, Grandpa. I'm happy to be here," I tell him again. He doesn't respond.

As I climb to the second floor, I wonder how he can get up and down the stairs. At his age, he should live all on one level. But if I know my grandmother, she probably told him climbing stairs was critical to good heart health. The irony is not lost on me that she died from a heart attack.

It's clear by the state of the house that my grandparents were planning to renovate. They loved a project and being older wouldn't be an excuse they would ever use to get out of one. I start a mental list of things that need to be done. The first is a deep cleaning; the second is new paint and carpet. I'll need to get someone out to take care of the yard and trim some trees back. And while I'm at it, I'd better get someone to check the dock.

Peeking around the rooms upstairs, I find they're all still full of boxes. No wonder my grandfather isn't taking care of things. The house probably doesn't even feel like his home yet.

I put my suitcase in the corner of the guest room and begin to look around for sheets to make the bed. There's a set in the closet but they smell as dusty as everything else, so I opt to go without tonight. Sitting down on the old mattress, I pull out my phone and call Terri.

"Teddy Bear!" she greets enthusiastically. "How was your trip? How's Elk Lake? How's Theo?"

I exhale loudly before telling her, "The trip was fine. Although I was recognized at the car kiosk and wound up spending extra time signing autographs before I could get on the road."

"Poor baby," she says dramatically. "That must have been so hard on you."

"You know I don't mind," I tell her. "I was just excited to get to Elk Lake."

"And now that you're there?"

"My grandfather is in worse shape than I expected."

"You didn't expect much," she says. "So it must be bad."

"It is. No one has cleaned in months, and from what I can tell the Campbell soup company is the only reason there's still any meat on his bones."

"Sounds like it's time for you to turn superhero again," she teases. "Where are you going to start?"

"I'm going to hire people to get everything done so I can focus on getting his weight up. I think I'll make him walk to town every morning. We can get muffins at Rosemary's Bakery to give him energy and calories." I pause, wondering if I should tell Terri about meeting Faith and offering to take her to her friend's wedding.

The problem is that Terri is a total busybody when it comes to my personal life and if I tell her something like this, she might start pushing me to date Faith for real. Which is not going to happen. Not only do I not want to be her rebound guy, but I'm not a predator. I'm not into taking advantage of someone's grief.

"What aren't you telling me?" Did I mention that Terri also claims to have inherited her mother's psychic tendencies? On occasion I've been inclined to agree with her. This is one of those times.

"Nothing."

"Teddy ..." she says warningly, like if I don't answer she's going to take my phone away and withhold my allowance for a week.

"Fine. I met a girl, but nothing is going to happen with her, so don't get pushy."

"What's her name?" She sounds intrigued and excited at the same time. A dangerous combination if there ever was one.

"Faith Reynolds. She works at Rosemary's Bakery. Rosemary is her grandmother."

"And?"

"I told her I'd take her to her friend's wedding next month to help make her ex jealous."

"Does she know who you are?"

"She thinks my name is Teddy Fischer," I confess.

"You mean she doesn't recognize you?"

"My only big role has been Alpha Dog, and I wore so much makeup to become him, it's not that surprising. She's probably not even into superhero movies."

"Everyone's into superhero movies. I mean, you were recognized at the airport ..." she says.

I fluff up a pillow and sneeze when a cloud of dust whooshes out of it. "The counter girl recognized my name, not my face."

"You've been in enough magazines and on enough episodes of *TMZ* that people under a certain age should know who you are."

"People in the Midwest aren't as hungry for Hollywood gossip as people in LA," I tell her. "Also, no one here expects to see a movie star in their midst."

"Hasn't your grandfather told everyone about you?"

"He barely leaves the house," I remind her. "Plus, it would be way more my grandmother's thing to brag about me. And she died before she had the opportunity."

"So, Faith ..." Terri lets the sentence hang for me to finish.

"Her boyfriend just broke up with her and they're going to be in the same wedding."

"And you offered to help."

"That's all I did. Nothing more," I tell her.

"Because ..."

"Because I know what it feels like to be cheated on, and I want to help her get revenge."

"What are you going to do, tie the guy up and put him in a pair of cement boots before taking him for a swim?"

I laugh. "I'm going to accompany her to the wedding and help her show this Astor that the breakup isn't upsetting her."

"Astor?" she laughs. "He sounds like an uptight asshole."

"I don't know how uptight he is, but his actions have certainly confirmed your other assumption."

"Okay, have fun," she says. "I'll want a full report after the fact."

"Why?"

"Call it an inkling," she says mysteriously.

"Don't get your hopes up, Terri," I tell her. "I'm doing a good deed and that's all."

"Sure thing, boss. You're just a boy scout at heart."

"Terri," I caution.

"Gotta run, Bear! I'm meeting Kay at that new sushi place on Wilshire."

"Happy Sushi?" I ask.

"I don't know how happy it is, but it's supposed to be delicious." Before hanging up, she adds, "Don't be afraid to take a chance, Teddy. You deserve a happy ending as much as the next guy."

She clicks off before I can tell her not to hold her breath. I know I deserve a happy ending, and I'm sure as heck hoping I get one someday, but as much as I hate to admit this, I'm still not fully over my own breakup. To clarify, I'm over Lindsey, I'm just not sure I'm prepared to hand my heart to someone else.

CHAPTER NINE

FAITH

It's Saturday, which means I'm supposed to be in Chicago. Instead, I'm sitting in my house crying. My eyes are nearly swollen shut as a result, making me look like a prize fighter who's gone around the ring five too many times. *Note to self: The post-boxing-match look does not look good on you …*

I'm tempted to go into the bakery and tell GG the news about Astor. GG is Rosemary's abbreviation for Gorgeous Grandma, which she insists on being called by her grandchildren. The only problem is there's no going back once I tell her. And part of me is still holding out hope that Astor might come crawling back to me.

Obviously, I'd make him grovel and beg for forgiveness. He'd have to swear that Tiffany drugged him and took advantage of him. There would, of course, need to be regular flower deliveries, and he'd have to start coming to Elk Lake instead of me schlepping to Chicago. But if all that happens, maybe, just maybe, we aren't through.

That would not be the case if GG knew what had gone down. She'd bring the cheating up every time she saw Astor, and he would never be able to get out from under her suspicions. Not that he would deserve to. The truth is, I might secretly want him to beg me to take him back just so I can make the rest of his life a living hell. Although, I'm not quite ready to admit to that. I'd like to think my intentions are pure, and we could live a beautiful life together.

I pick up my phone to call him, but quickly have second thoughts. There's no way I can talk to him right now without spectacularly losing it. Which would negate my plan to make him jealous at Anna's wedding.

After turning my phone off, I pull my tennis shoes out of the hall closet so I can get my food shopping done for the week. I normally go on Mondays after getting back from Chicago, but now that I'm not leaving town, I need some staples.

I start to feel a little bit better on the way to the market. That is until I flip on the radio and Whitney Houston's version of "I Will Always Love You" comes on. Astor sang that to me the night he told me he loved me for the first time. It was a cringingly bad performance, but who cares? When the man of your dreams is declaring his love, there aren't enough flat notes in the world to mess that up.

I park in the back of the lot, hoping a longer walk will snap me out of my current malaise. It helps a little as I'm not a complete basket case when I walk in. Grabbing a cart, I start my regular path through produce before hitting the cereal aisle and beyond. I grab a few apples, a couple of bananas, and a bag of greens before stopping dead in front of the dragon fruit display. I gasp before bursting into another uncontrollable sob fest. Astor told me we should plan a trip to Costa Rica so I could eat freshly picked dragon fruit. He claims the stuff we get tastes nothing like it should.

Picking up one of the hot pink fruits, I hold it to my nose. There will be no trip to Costa Rica now. Astor will probably take Tiffany, and they'll stroll hand in hand on the beach while eating their body weight in exotic fruit. Hopefully it has the same effect on them as prunes. That would certainly ruin all chances of romance.

"Excuse me, ma'am. Can you tell me if you have any ripe avocados in stock?" The voice is too close for the man not to be talking to me.

As I turn around, I demand, "Why would I know about avocados?" I'm staring right at Teddy.

"Oh, hey, Faith. How are you?" Before I can lie and tell him I'm fine, he says, "I thought you worked here. You know ..."—he motions toward my outfit—"you're wearing the same thing the employees are."

Is it any wonder Astor cheated on me? I look down and confirm that yes, I am wearing khaki pants and a light green shirt. I have no fashion sense whatsoever. I open my mouth to tell Teddy he should forget his ridiculous plan to help me make Astor jealous. There's clearly no way that can ever happen. But as my lips part, no words come out. Instead, I hiccup loudly.

"Oh, Faith, no." Teddy steps away from his cart and puts his arms around me. "I was hoping you might be feeling a little better."

"This *is* better." I rub my nose against his shoulder hoping not to leave a snot trail. *It feels so nice to be held in someone's arms. I hope he never lets me go.*

"Have you talked to him yet?" Teddy starts to gingerly pat me on the back. *What is he doing, burping me?*

"No. If I'm going to convince him I'm unmoved by our breakup, I can't talk to him like this."

"What are you doing for supper?" he wants to know. "I'm making carnitas for my grandfather. You could come eat with us if you want."

I step out of his arms and look up at him. "Why are you being so nice to me?"

"You're a likable person." He sounds sincere.

"How do you know that?" I demand. "I've done nothing but

burn you, cry on you, and moan about my sorry love life. Surely, you can see the writing on the wall. I'm a total loser."

"You're not a loser, Faith. You're just going through a rough patch. You should have seen me right after my breakup. I was way worse." He smiles so kindly I want to beg him to stop being gay so he can be my real boyfriend. I cringe even thinking something like that. It's not that he's making a choice, it's who he is.

"You'd really make me supper?" I ask.

"I really would. In fact, you can help me finish shopping and we can drive over to my grandfather's house together."

"I've got my car."

"You don't seem to be in any shape to drive," he says. "If you're feeling better after supper, I'll bring you back here. If not, we can get it tomorrow."

"Can we drink tequila?" I ask hopefully. "I love tequila." There go any plans for driving myself.

"If you think that will help, sure." I know he's placating me, and while I'm not sure tequila is the answer, unconsciousness sounds like a great idea.

Abandoning my cart, I walk next to him. Teddy is so tall and strong looking, he makes me feel like a delicate flower in comparison. Astor was only a couple inches taller than my five eight, and he was on the slim side. The combination motivated me to try to lose weight, so I didn't outweigh him.

"How long did it take you to get over being dumped?" I ask with no tact whatsoever.

He stops walking like he's concentrating on solving a calculous problem. "It's hard to say. I mean, it's a process. I started feeling a little better after a couple of months though."

"When did you start dating again?" Talk about none of my business, but there's something about Teddy that's caught me off guard. It's like I have no defenses around him. No game.

"I sort of threw myself into my work after it happened, and then I bought a house, and I threw myself into that ..." And we're walking again.

"Teddy," I say with a good amount of disbelief. "Are you saying you haven't started dating yet? How long has it been?"

Instead of answering, he shrugs his shoulders.

"Teddy …"

"It's been a while." He finally confesses, "Over two years since I've had a second date. But it's not like I'm still in love. It's more of a once bitten, twice shy kind of scenario."

My heart sinks into my stomach. "My God, if a guy who looks as good as you do can't bounce back, there's no hope for me."

He looks at me kindly. "Don't say that. You're lovely." He's got to be lying, but he sounds so sincere. I'm thinking the time for glasses may have arrived.

Teddy stops his cart in front of the citrus section, and inexplicably reaches for an orange from the bottom of the pyramid. Within seconds, the whole formation starts to crumble and the orange balls bounce to the floor. Unflappably, he begins to restack them.

"I'm wearing the same outfit as the grocery store employees," I remind him. Then I point to my head. "My hair is a complete wreck, and I haven't stopped crying in three days. I am not lovely."

"You are too," he says kindly. "You're just grieving. I predict that once you show Astor you're over him, you'll be back to your old self in no time." He concludes his sermon with, "There's nothing like some well-placed revenge to help a person heal."

"Is that what you did?"

He shakes his head. "No, but things are going to be different for you."

"How do you know that?" I pull a plastic bag off the roll next to the limes and fill it.

Smiling sweetly, he says, "Because you've got me, and I'm going to make sure Astor regrets ever cheating on you."

"Why can't you be straight?" I surprise myself by asking out loud. "I'm sorry, I should have never said that." *But darn it, why can't he be straight?*

"Would you be interested in me if I were?"

"I'd drop down on one knee and propose to you." I feel the heat in my face intensify as I offer Teddy a shy smile.

"It's not every day a man gets proposed to ..." I can tell he's trying to make light of what could be an uncomfortable situation. I mean seriously, how pathetic am I, making a play for a man who could never be into me?

But there's something about the expression on his face that makes me wonder if maybe he isn't just the tiniest bit flattered.

CHAPTER TEN

TEDDY

Shopping with Faith is like giving a toddler free range to buy whatever they want. So far, she's added three kinds of sugary cereal to the cart, along with kettle corn, dry-roasted peanuts, fruit jerky, a jar of black olives, and a can of spray whipped cream. When she throws in a family-size package of bologna, I have to ask, "Do you normally eat like this?"

"Gross, no. But when I'm sad, I crave all the things I used to love when I was a kid. You know, like bologna can magically whisk me back to a carefree time when my heart wasn't broken."

On impulse, I toss a package of salami into the cart. My dad used to make fried salami sandwiches. He even made me one for breakfast on the day of his accident. I haven't allowed myself to eat one since, as though the sandwich was the reason that semi hit him from behind.

Once we get into the checkout line, I spy a tabloid with my picture on the cover. The headline reads "Alpha Dog Teddy Helms is on the Prowl!" Oh. My. God. They're using a picture of me thumping melons at the farmers' market. It's so suggestive I can't help but grimace.

As I step between the magazine rack and Faith, so she doesn't see it, a kid standing behind us tries to bodily move me out of the way to get to the bubble gum display.

When I don't budge, he says, "Dude, what's your problem? I need a Hubba Bubba." Faith grabs a pack and hands it to him. Taking it, he offers a reluctant, "Thanks." Then he gets back in line while giving me an odd look. I can't tell if it's because he recognizes me or he thinks I'm a jerk for not moving. Either way, it leaves me on edge.

"I used to love Bazooka bubble gum," Faith says. "It was wrapped in those silly comics, but that always made it feel extra special, you know?"

"I loved it too, but it's hard to come by these days," I tell her.

"They carry it at the Purple Cow down the street." She picks up several packages of fruit-flavored Tic Tacs and puts them on the conveyer belt with her order.

I start to unload the cart. "My grandfather used to take me there for grape soda floats. I can't believe it's still around."

"You'd be surprised how many places are still here from our childhood. Once people open a business in Elk Lake, they rarely close it."

"Summers are still pretty busy then?" I ask.

Putting the extra-large bottle of Cuervo Gold behind her Tic Tacs, she answers, "Oh, yeah. Now that there are all those websites that rent places by the night or week, there's a steady traffic of new faces everywhere you look."

"My grandparents used to rent by the month," I tell her. "They'd come at the end of May and leave after Labor Day."

"How long did you stay?" she asks.

"I was usually here from mid-June to mid-August. I wanted to have some time at home with my friends."

"Where did you grow up?"

"Scottsdale. That made leaving during the summer months extra enticing." I tell her, "I'm not a fan of a-hundred-and-twenty-degree days. Our poor dog had to pee inside, so he didn't burn his paws."

"Did you have a lot of summer friends in Elk Lake?" she wants to know.

I push the cart forward in line. "A few. But honestly, I was here to spend time with my grandparents." She looks at me oddly. "I bet that makes me sound like a real dork, huh?"

"I think it makes you sound like a nice guy. I love my grandparents too, and I don't know what I would have done without them."

As the cashier starts to ring up our purchases, I ask, "Are they still alive?"

"My grandmother is, but Gramps died over ten years ago."

"How's your grandmother doing with that?" I ask.

"It was a tough transition at first, but she went back to work so that helped fill some of her time."

The cashier gives Faith an odd look as she rings up her order before asking, "Break-up?"

Faith nods her head. "What gave it away?"

"The lack of tampons," the older woman says. "When I used to shop like this, it was either my period or a breakup."

Faith doesn't seem at all insulted by this personal information being bandied about. Instead, she asks, "Are you happily married now?"

"No way. Honey, I realized twenty years ago that the only man I needed was Tom Selleck. He does more for me on the television screen than any real man has ever done in person."

Sliding her credit card into the payment machine, Faith tells her, "If only I didn't want kids."

"Cats are a very viable alternative," the checker tells Faith. Then she eyes me before asking her, "This isn't the loser who broke your heart is it?" Her hand hovers above the "This Line Closed" sign like she's going to refuse me service if I am.

"Not at all," Faith assures her. "This guy is the best friend a girl could ask for."

I'm honored by her comment. I'm also relieved that I won't have to put my groceries back into the cart and wait in another line.

On the way out of the store, I ask Faith, "So, how long do fourteen packs of Tic Tacs usually last you?" She continued to add more as her order was being rung up.

She shrugs. "Given the current state of my life, I may be back for more in two days." The look of shock on my face has her explaining, "But according to the label there are no calories in them."

"How can that be?"

"A serving size is one. I'm guessing there's less than half a calorie in that, so they don't count it."

"How many servings in a container?"

"Fifty. And before you judge me for eating seven hundred Tic Tacs in two days, that's only three hundred and fifty calories—if they're only a half a calorie each—which they might not be."

Thank goodness I'm pushing the cart because once again I trip over my foot. Hopefully Faith didn't notice. But even so, why have I become such a klutz all of a sudden? "I would never judge you, Faith," I tell her while clicking the key fob to open the trunk of my SUV.

She whistles when she sees where we're headed. "Nice wheels."

"I'm renting," I tell her, like that somehow makes it less nice.

"Why in the world would you rent that for just you and your grandfather? You must be paying a fortune."

"I got a great deal on it." After unloading into the back hatch, I hold the passenger side door open. "Milady."

She giggles before getting in. Once I'm situated behind the steering wheel, she starts pushing buttons to arrange her seat the way she wants it. When she's finally settled, she leans her head back and says, "Thank you."

"For what, renting a car with all the options?" I ask.

Her mouth turns up slightly at the edges. It's not so much a smile as a look of pure contentment. "For everything," she says. "I've barely known you two days, but I already know we're going to be great friends."

"You can never have too many friends," I tell her while backing out of my space. As we drive toward the lake, I ask, "Where do you live?"

"I'm about a mile away. My parents moved to Florida a few years ago. I live in their house."

As we near my grandfather's place, she points. "That's me, right there."

Turning into my grandfather's driveway, I tell her, "We're neighbors!"

"I've been meaning to stop over and see who the new owners are," she says, "but I never see any activity so I thought it might still be vacant."

"Theo does little more than sit on the back porch," I tell her. "He's become somewhat of a hermit since my grandmother died."

"Poor guy." She hops out of the car and meets me at the back. I hand over her bag of groceries before picking up the other two. "You can put your bologna in my fridge to keep it fresh."

"There are so many nitrates and nitrites in that stuff, I could probably leave it on the counter for a week and it would still be safe to eat." *Yuck.*

"Don't take it personally if Theo's not friendly," I tell her. "He's a bit annoyed that I'm upsetting his apple cart by trying to bring him back into the land of the living."

"Don't worry about me," she says. "I spend time volunteering at my grandmother's retirement home one afternoon a week. I'm used to grumpy old folks."

After leading the way up the back steps, I put one bag down so I can open the back door for Faith. She walks in ahead of me. Once we put our purchases on the counter, she looks around. "What a nice house."

Disbelievingly, I ask, "By that, you mean outdated and in need of fixing up?" Most people our age are into everything being new.

She shrugs. "No. I mean it's sweet. A bit old-fashioned, but totally delightful. I much prefer houses with character to the soulless McMansions of the world."

My kind of girl.

My grandfather hears us and calls out, "Who did you bring back with you, Teddy?"

"My friend Faith." I motion for her to follow me into the living room where my grandfather is sitting on his chair with his eyeglasses perched on top of his head.

When we get there, I add, "Faith, this is my grandfather, Theo."

He looks up and squints. "How in the world have you made a friend so quickly?"

"Faith works at Rosemary's Bakery," I tell him. "She's the one who sent that bag of cookies and muffins home with me yesterday."

My grandfather puts his glasses on his face to get a better look at our guest. He immediately says, "You're a pretty one, aren't you?"

Faith starts to laugh. "I think you might need to get your prescription updated."

"Nonsense," he tells her. "I like the color of your hair and those glasses really give you some pizzazz. All you need is a little lipstick."

"Grandpa …" I start to say, but he cuts me off.

"Your grandmother always said that the only thing she needed to feel like herself was her lipstick."

"I could definitely use some," Faith agrees, which helps to take some of the tension out of the air. She surprises me by confessing, "My boyfriend just dumped me, so I really didn't feel like going to the effort."

"He must not have any taste," Theo says. After a beat, he adds, "You should date Teddy."

"Grandpa …" I should have never brought Faith over here. Even though my grandfather knows I'm staying under the radar, he doesn't know I'm pretending to be gay. I'm still not quite sure how Faith decided I was.

Faith winks at me while saying, "I'll keep Teddy in mind when I start dating again."

"Teddy got dumped too," my grandfather feels the need to share. "That Lindsey dared to think she could do better."

Faith must assume that Grandpa has never met Lindsey. It's clear she still thinks I'm in the closet with him because she doesn't so much as flinch that he calls Lindsey *her*. "Then she's not very smart, is she?" Faith asks.

"Can I get both of you something to drink?" I interrupt, hoping to change the subject.

"Yes, please." Faith sits on the couch next to my grandfather's chair. "I'll have a margarita on the rocks with extra lime and no salt, please."

My grandfather groans. "I'd love the same, but I can't mix alcohol with my medication." He looks up at me with one finger in the air. "Make mine without any tequila but show it the bottle so it can absorb some fumes."

I'm a bit worried about leaving them alone. I don't want Grandpa to tell Faith anything more about my social life. But maybe if I hurry … I practically sprint out of the room to make their drinks before he can get me into any trouble.

When I come back into the room, Faith is sitting by herself. "Where's Theo?"

"He said he wanted to take a nap before supper." She smiles conspiratorially before whispering, "I think he's leaving us alone."

"Ah, that could be."

"He doesn't know you're gay, huh? That must be rough."

I'm not sure how to answer her question. I was about to tell Faith I was straight in the bakery, but she literally told me she was happy I was gay. In order to be the friend she wants me to be, I need to keep up the lie. At least for now. "He doesn't think I'm gay."

"Lindsey isn't a common name for a man, is it?" she asks.

Thinking fast on my feet, I answer, "There's Lindsey Buckingham from Fleetwood Mac."

"I totally forgot about him." She takes a long sip of her drink. "Can I help you cook?"

"That would be nice." I lead the way back into the kitchen.

Once we have our aprons on, I hand Faith a head of lettuce, tomatoes, and a red onion. "Why don't you cut those up for our toppings." She gets right to work while I chop the skirt steak and peppers for the carnitas.

"I always wondered what it was like for the summer kids who came here," she says. "They always looked like they were having so much fun."

"Weren't you having fun, too?" I ask. "I mean, you got to live here full time."

As she peels back the outer leaves of the lettuce head, she answers, "You summer kids had a way of making Elk Lake feel like it was a glamorous destination spot. I assure you that in the middle of the winter, it was anything but."

"I guess I can see that." Working side-by-side with Faith feels delightfully domestic, I once again wonder why any man would ever choose to leave her. Her unassuming beauty and vulnerability are such an intoxicating combination, I can only conclude that Astor is a total idiot.

Once the carnitas are made, and the toppings are ready to go, I tell Faith, "I'm going to go call Theo. Why don't you fix your plate and get yourself settled at the table?"

Her smile momentarily stops me dead in my tracks. How is it that I feel like I already know her when I only just met her? Before I can try to sort out this strange sensation, my grandfather joins us in the kitchen. He stretches and says, "I'm so hungry I could eat a bear."

"It's a good thing we used bear meat then," Faith teases him.

Theo smiles at her as he picks up his plate and starts to

assemble his carnitas. "Abigail would have liked you. You're sassy."

"I'll take that as a compliment," she tells him with a wink. "I come from a long line of sassy women."

"Some men can't handle it, you know?" he says. "It threatens them."

"But you're not threatened, are you?" she asks him playfully.

As we carry our plates to the kitchen table he says, "No, ma'am. I'm one of the lucky men who fell in love with a spunky gal. I've never wanted anything less."

Conversation flows smoothly and easily while we eat, and I proceed to have the best evening I can remember sharing with a woman. We laugh and talk about all kinds of things. The list includes Faith's favorite places to eat, shop, and fish. I'm hoping to have the opportunity to do some of those things with her while I'm here.

Once we're sitting with empty plates, my grandfather excuses himself and goes to bed. That's when I tell Faith a little bit more about my life. I stay as close to the truth as possible without sharing everything. For instance, I share that I just bought a new house and that I work for a movie studio. She might have gotten the impression I'm a set builder.

"It sounds like you lead a pretty glamorous life," she says. *If she only knew.*

"Glamour isn't all it's cracked up to be."

"I suppose that's true. Can you imagine all those poor movie stars?" she asks. Before I can answer, she adds, "I have no sympathy for the media-whore reality show people, but I do feel sorry for actors who just want a normal life. They're never left alone." She couldn't be more on the money.

By the time we're sipping our margaritas on the back porch, I'm left thinking that if Faith weren't on the rebound and I was looking, she might just make the perfect girlfriend.

But of course, neither one of us is in the right place for that to happen.

CHAPTER ELEVEN

FAITH

Dinner with Teddy and Theo is just what the doctor ordered. The evening is as near perfect as I could have hoped for. Not only is the company outstanding, but I eat six delicious carnitas, savoring every bite. It's probably four too many, but I remind Teddy I'm currently eating my feelings, so he takes it in stride.

After finishing my third margarita, I get up from the porch swing and announce, "I should be getting home, but I'm definitely not up for driving."

"I'll walk you," he says.

"You don't have to. I'm literally two houses away."

"I'm still going to." He picks up a jacket from the back of a chair and hands it to me. "It's gotten a little cool out."

I slip into his jean jacket and immediately savor the warmth. "You really are the perfect guy, aren't you? Are you sure you don't want me to introduce you to Nick?"

"I'm only here for a short time, and I don't want to get involved with anyone. It could make things messy." *Especially as Nick is definitely not my type.*

"Two months should be long enough to know if someone has lasting power."

"Yeah, but I still live in LA. No sense making things unnecessarily complicated."

"Let me know if you change your mind." As we start to walk down the stairs, I add, "Please tell Theo goodbye for me. And let him know that I look forward to seeing him again."

"Does that mean you'll come back for dinner some time?" he asks as we walk up the driveway.

"I'm cooking for the two of you next," I tell him.

"That sounds like an offer we'd never pass up."

We're quiet the short time it takes to get to my house. The whole while I secretly wish this were a date, and Teddy was going to kiss me goodnight at the door. Not only could I use the boost to my self-confidence, but the truth is I really like him. Once again, I take a moment to chastise myself for wishing he was something he isn't.

When we reach my front door, he puts his hand out for me to shake. "Let me know when you're ready to go into town tomorrow to get your car."

"After everything I ate tonight," I tell him, "I should probably walk. Anna's making noise that my bridesmaid's dress is going to be too tight if I keep going on the way I have been the last few days."

"I'm going to make my grandfather start walking, too. Maybe we'll see you."

Once the front door is open, I watch as Teddy walks back down the sidewalk. He is not the kind of guy you'd kick out of bed for eating crackers, that's for sure. In fact, I have yet to discern any unflattering characteristics about the man.

When I get inside, I pull my phone out and find another message from Astor.

Ass Turd: Chris told me you were bringing a date to the wedding. I guess that means it's okay for me to do the same?

Suddenly feeling a bit stronger than I have. I type back: *Of course.*

The ellipses on the phone immediately start to flash, alerting me that he's responding.

Ass Turd: You're taking this well. I was worried you'd be more upset.

Me: I guess, like you, I didn't think we were that serious.

Ass Turd: I thought we were serious. I just didn't expect to meet someone like Tiffany. She took me totally by surprise. I'm really sorry, Faith.

I'm not sure how he thinks that's supposed to make me feel better. *I really liked you, but not enough to resist temptation and stay faithful.* The jerk.

Me: Don't worry about it. I'm dating a lovely man who I would have never agreed to go out with had we still been together.

As in, *I'm* not a cheater. How's that for passive aggressive? I can't help but add:

Me: In fact, I know it's early days, but I think Teddy could really be the one.

This feels so good.

Ass Turd: Wow. Where did you meet him?

I'm not ready to chitchat with Astor about how I've moved on. Especially, as that's a fabrication on my part.

Me: Oh, you know how these things are. Sometimes you just bump into the person you're destined to be with.

Ass Turd: So you just bumped into him? Where? On the street corner?

Clearly, he doesn't like the idea of me stepping out on him. Well, two can play at that game, mister.

Me: We met a couple of weeks ago. I only agreed to go out with him once I found out about you and Tiffany.

I leave his last text on unread, but I still see it.

Ass Turd: A couple of weeks?

No one will enjoy this text thread as much as Anna, so I give her a call. Even though Chris is in town, I'm sure she'll spare me a few minutes.

Her phone rings once before she answers in a breathy voice, "Hey."

"Hey yourself," I say. "You'll never guess who I was just texting with."

"Astor?" she whispers.

"How do you know that?" I ask.

"He just called Chris, and I'm trying to listen in on their conversation."

"Can you walk over to him and put the phone down so I can hear, too?" *How exciting!* Astor really must be upset if he called Chris right after texting with me.

The next thing I hear is a thump—the phone being put down —and then Chris saying, "Hey man, I didn't know she was seeing someone else, but why should it matter? You're with Tiffany now."

As Astor isn't on speaker phone, I only hear Chris's side of the conversation. "Yeah, you should bring her. Anna said it was okay."

I make a face like I'm about to vomit.

"You'd better hurry up and get a hotel room now that you won't be staying with Faith. Things in Elk Creek book up pretty fast over the summer, especially because there's a professional pickle ball tournament in town next weekend." He pauses for a beat. "It's sort of a cross between ping pong and tennis."

I can only imagine Astor's reaction to that. He's a tennis player who looks down on people who play what he calls "pedestrian sports." In truth, Astor's a bit of a snob.

I hear scratching on the other end which I assume is Anna retrieving her phone. I have confirmation when I hear her say, "You told him you'd already started seeing someone?"

"Teddy," I tell her. "I had supper with him and his grandfather tonight. We had a great time."

"But he's …"

"Gay, I know. But Astor doesn't know that. Nor will he ever. He was really put out when I told him I've known Teddy for two weeks."

Anna sighs loudly. "I should be relieved you've communicated with him but I'm more nervous than ever."

"So long as I can keep from ripping every hair out of Tiffany's head, everything should be fine." I hurry to warn, "I wouldn't put any money down on that bet though."

Oozing sarcasm, she responds, "That makes me feel better, thanks."

"Don't worry. I'm feeling more optimistic than I have," I tell her. "I wasn't doing very well today but then I ran into Teddy, and I'm feeling a lot better."

"That's good, Faithy." I hear Chris calling Anna in the background. "I've gotta go," she says. "I'll call you in the morning and let you know if I find out anything else."

"Love you like a sister, Anna. Thanks for everything."

"I love you, too. We're going to get you through this. I promise."

I hang up feeling almost like myself again. Even though I'm still horribly sad, I'm the tiniest bit less depressed. Hopefully that will be a continuing trend and by next month, I'll be able to pass for a woman who wasn't dumped. Fingers crossed.

CHAPTER TWELVE

TEDDY

"Let's go, Grandpa!" I shout up the stairs.

He comes down slowly while grumbling, "Why can't we just eat here? I have some instant oatmeal in the cabinet."

"Because we could both use the fresh air and exercise," I tell him.

"You mean *I* could use the fresh air and exercise."

Instead of confirming his suspicion, I tell him, "Think about the sticky bun waiting for you at Rosemary's when we get there."

He picks up a sweater and puts it over his head. I lend him a hand as he struggles to find the head and arm holes. "I'll probably pull out a filling," he mutters.

Getting old is a lot like being little. Belligerence, tantrums, and confusion seem to be the name of the game. "Come on," I tell him while leading the way to the front door. "We're going to have a great day."

Once we hit the sidewalk it becomes clear it might take us the entire day to get into town. Grandpa is neither a fast nor a steady walker. Without saying anything, I offer him my arm. I smile when he takes it.

As we near Faith's house, I look for signs of activity. I tell my grandfather, "That's where Faith lives." In the daylight it's easier to appreciate the pretty two-story yellow cottage with the white picket fence and swing on the front porch. It's the exact kind of place I used to dream of living in when I was a kid.

"You should date her," Grandpa says plainly.

"So you mentioned last night. In front of her." There's more than a bit of censure in my tone.

"It's called killing two birds with one stone." He stops walking. "If I tell you both where I stand, then there won't be any confusion about my feelings on the matter."

"She's a very nice girl," I say. "But I live in LA, and I'm not interested in long distance dating."

"You're not interested in dating, period. But it's *your* life, not mine." He's obviously trying to make a point.

"If you think that sentiment is going to keep me off your back, you're wrong. It may be your life, Grandpa, but I'm not going to let you throw it away."

"Sounds to me like we're at a standstill." He glares at me.

As we're literally not moving, he's right. "Do your worst, old man."

"Consider that gauntlet picked up," he threatens. I don't know why he's so determined to pick a fight with me.

Giving up, I ask, "Can we walk into town now?"

"I'm already worn out." He sounds every minute of his eighty-four years. "I want to go home."

"Are you really tired or are you just being ornery?" He leans against me, and I know he's exhausted. "Come on, I'll take you home and then I'll drive into town for sticky buns."

"I've been thinking, Teddy," he says as we retrace our steps.

"What have you been thinking, Grandpa?"

"I think it's time for me to move into an assisted care facility."

"A nursing home?" I'm shocked. My grandfather has always been the most capable man I've ever known. This current picture of him is the farthest thing from that. I feel like he's simply given up.

"Surely there's no shame in needing some help at my age. I'm almost eighty-five."

I immediately feel horrible for making him feel bad. "If that's what you want, I'll look into it."

Instead of answering, he simply nods his head. It takes us another five minutes to get home, and once I open the door, he goes straight to his chair and closes his eyes. A wave of sadness hits me hard. It's been tough enough losing my grandmother, but what in the world am I going to do without both of my grandparents? They've always been more like a second mom and dad to me. In fact, Theo has been my only father figure since my dad died. Talk of him moving into a facility makes me feel like my life is sliding completely off-center.

Walking out the back door to my SUV, I toy with the idea of seeing if Faith wants a ride into town. I'm still undecided by the time I get to her house, but good sense tells me to keep moving. Then I see her on the sidewalk a half mile down the road and I can't help myself. I stop.

Rolling down the passenger window, I call out, "Hey, stranger! You want a lift?"

She's wearing a cute light blue sundress with white daisies all over it. The skirt ends above her knees which gives me a nice glimpse of her legs. Stepping down from the curb, she grabs the door handle and says, "Yes, please."

Once she's settled, I tell her, "Theo walked as far as your house, but he had to turn back. He was too wiped out to keep going."

Out of my peripheral vision, I see a look of understanding cross her face. "It's hard watching them get old, isn't it?"

"Is your grandmother slowing down, too?" I ask.

"Oh, yeah. She's started forgetting things. The doctor says it's an early sign of dementia."

"What does she forget?" I ask.

"Nothing big, yet. One Saturday last month she was in charge of making the brownies, but she neglected to put the cocoa in. They're not brownies without the cocoa," she tells me.

"What did you do?"

She shrugs. "I was in Chicago. Nick said he told people they were blondies and he sold them anyway. Either way, she's not as sharp as she's always been, and she knows it, too."

Turning left on Main Street, I ask, "Is she still living on her own?"

"No. She fell two years ago and broke her leg. I offered to bring her to my house, but she said she'd rather rehab at Vista Pines. That's the retirement home on the lake." She adds, "After she was back to normal, she said she was having so much fun, she wanted to stay."

"My grandfather told me this morning that he's ready to investigate assisted living. It knocked the wind right out of me." She puts her hand on my arm and gives it a squeeze. The act seems so natural and yet so intimate at the same time, it's hard to believe we haven't always known each other.

As I pull into the grocery store parking lot, Faith says, "It's a nice place. There's always tons of stuff going on, so the people who live there have things to do other than sitting around watching TV. My grandmother plays bridge with a group of ladies and is even taking a dance class. She's having a blast. But more importantly, she has people watching out for her."

"Vista Pines sounds like the perfect place." I ask, "Which car is yours?"

She points to the far end of the parking lot. "The white Honda. It's equal amounts rust and white paint, but it's all mine."

"Not having a car payment is nothing to scoff at," I say seriously. I drove something similar before getting cast as Alpha Dog.

"You're telling me. We're using the proceeds from the sale of GG's house to pay for her care, but that's not going to last as long as we'd hoped. We have enough for maybe five more years, and then my parents and I will have to cover it."

"Is it weird living in your parents' house without them?" I ask. "For instance, my mom, who still lives in Arizona, has a thing for strawberries, and they're a huge part of her décor. I would be very uncomfortable living full-time amongst her strawberry patch."

"My mom and dad took the stuff they liked with them, and I've been turning the house into my own ever since. Not a strawberry in sight."

"I'll look forward to seeing it, then," I tease.

As I pull in the spot next to her car, she asks, "How about Thursday night? I can cook for you."

"I'd love that," I tell her. "It's been a long time since I've had dinner at a friend's house." Lest she think I'm a hermit, I explain, "We eat out a lot in LA."

"No one knows how to cook, huh?" I can't tell if she's teasing or not.

"More like everyone wants to be out and part of the action."

"You, too?"

"I like to cook, but the kitchen in my new house currently pays homage to the avocado green appliances from the seventies, and they're not working like they once did." I hurry to tell her, "But when my reno is done, my house will be the entertainment hub for my friends."

"Renovating a kitchen costs a fortune," she says. "I've looked into it and believe me when I tell you, a new oven is about all I can afford."

Not wanting to divulge my current income bracket, I tell her, "Which is why I'm taking things a step at a time."

When Faith gets out of the car, she says, "Don't be a stranger until Thursday. I'm at the bakery Monday through Friday."

"I'll see you soon," I tell her, suddenly very much looking forward to our next interaction. Faith Reynolds is an unexpected boon to my summer in Elk Lake and I'm eagerly anticipating seeing her as much as possible.

CHAPTER THIRTEEN

FAITH

Talking to Teddy about my grandmother has gotten me to wondering how she's doing at the bakery, so I decide to stop in. Esmé and Nick say she's a lot of fun, and while I don't doubt that, I'm concerned that working weekends might be getting to be too much for her.

As I drive down Main Street, I spot a line out the door of Rosemary's. A line is pretty standard this time of year, which is a good thing. The summer months are what carry us through the non-tourist season.

I hurry to park and then bypass the people waiting on the sidewalk. As I walk into the bakery, I spot Anna's mom at the counter talking to GG. She's wearing her standard long, hippy skirt and loose white blouse. Her dreads are hanging down her back like a beaded curtain. Walking up behind her, I say, "Hey, Dawn, are you getting excited about the wedding?"

She turns around enthusiastically. "Faithy!" She motions toward GG. "Rosemary and I were just talking about some special brownies for the reception." *Oh, dear.*

"What are you doing here, hon?" GG wants to know. "I

thought you were in Chicago until tonight." She's wearing a red floral print dress, and her white hair is up in a bun. She looks very pretty.

"I came home early." I'm going to have to fess up to the truth about what happened with Astor before the wedding. Because once she sees me with Teddy, she's going to know something's up. "Let's talk later," I say, before shooing her and Dawn off to the side to discuss their illicit treats.

Meanwhile, I go behind the counter and start taking orders to keep the line moving. After thirty minutes, I find myself staring at Teddy. "Hey, you. I didn't know you were coming in here today."

"I told my grandfather I'd get some sticky buns. I don't suppose you have any left?" he asks hopefully.

I put the last four into a bag and hand them over to him. "Tell him I hope he's feeling better."

"I'm paying this time." He gives me a twenty-dollar bill.

Meanwhile, Nick walks up beside me, his spiky blue hair standing on end thanks to the gallon of hair gel he must use every day. He stares at Teddy like he's seen a ghost. Seriously, his mouth is open, and his eyes look like they're about to pop out of his head. "Nick," I say, "this is my friend Teddy. Teddy, this is Nick, the guy I was telling you about."

Teddy smiles politely. "Pleased to meet you, Nick."

Nick doesn't make any move to respond, so I admonish, "Nick, say hello to Teddy."

He shakes his head in bewilderment and demands, "How do you know Teddy Helms?"

"I don't know who Teddy Helms is," I tell him. "This is Teddy Fischer."

He shakes his head more firmly this time, and yet the spikes still don't move. "No. This is Teddy Helms." Then to Teddy, he gushes, "I'm a huge fan. Honestly, I didn't even like superhero movies until *Alpha Dog*. I mean, you were just ... so ... so ... alpha." *Is that drool at the corner of his mouth?*

I briefly wonder if Dawn gave Nick one of her special

brownies to sample. But one glance at Teddy makes me realize my counter guy isn't the one who's gotten it wrong. "Teddy?" I ask, more than a bit confused.

He looks around like he's worried he's being surveilled by the FBI, or you know, a mob of teenage girls. "Can we talk somewhere?" To Nick, he says, "I'd appreciate it if you didn't tell anyone about this."

"Your secret's safe with me." Nick bats his eyes repeatedly.

I motion for Teddy to come behind the counter and then lead the way into the kitchen. Esmé is busy making cookie dough and doesn't even look up as we pass by on our way out the back door. As soon as we're standing in the alley, I demand, "Why didn't you tell me you were a famous actor?"

With an aw-shucks kind of smirk, he answers, "I was hoping for a quiet summer with Theo. That would be easier if people didn't know who I was."

"Teddy," I tell him, "we may be Wisconsinites, but we're not morons." He gives me a questioning look, so I add, "Fine, maybe I'm a moron, but most others aren't."

"You're not a moron. You just don't watch superhero movies … I'm guessing."

I shake my head. "I've seen every movie Marvel has come out with at least twice. Four times in the cases of *Black Panther* and *Avengers: Endgame*."

"Ah, you're one of those Marvel snobs who doesn't see Wonder movies then?"

"I saw *Alpha Dog*," I tell him. I don't mention I was so busy making out with Astor that I have no idea what the movie was about.

"And you didn't recognize me at all?" He sounds hurt. I can understand he didn't want people to know who he was, but I thought we were becoming friends.

"Sorry," I tell him. "I guess I'm just not that observant."

"Alpha Dog had a lot of facial hair," he says hopefully, as though needing a reason for my obliviousness.

I stare at his gorgeous face and try to remember him from the movie. I got nothing. "Okay, fine. I was busy making out with Astor and didn't really pay attention to the movie." Then something else dawns on me. "Why in the world would you invite me to a wedding if you're trying to stay below the radar?" I demand.

"Because I wanted to help you."

"What if someone recognizes you?" I ask before saying, "Oh my God, and here I gave you a hard time about renting such a fancy car. What an idiot."

"You're not an idiot. I really, truly, just wanted a quiet summer. I'm sorry I lied to you."

"That's just it though. You didn't really lie to me, did you? You just didn't offer the truth."

"Correct," he says with his head hanging low. "But I can see where you might have thought it was a lie of omission." He shifts nervously from foot to foot.

I consider his words for a moment before declaring, "I've never had a famous friend."

"Well, you do now. If you'll keep me on, that is." He smiles so enticingly I feel my pique begin to melt. If I can't be Teddy's girlfriend, I'll take friendship as a booby prize any day of the week. I shake my head like I'm trying to disengage an earwig. *I have got to stop thinking about him like that.*

"Do people know you're gay?" I ask.

He shakes his head. "No one thinks I'm gay."

"That might make it kind of hard to sell you as Alpha Dog, huh?"

"Only to bigoted people."

"Yeah, but remember when Rupert Everett from *My Best Friend's Wedding* came out? He never got to play a leading man again," I tell him.

"In that case," he suggests, "maybe we can keep my supposed sexuality under wraps as well."

"Supposed? Next thing I know you'll be telling me you're not gay." Before he can respond, my phone pings. It's a text from Nick.

Nick: Holy shit! You know Teddy Helms!

Me: Nick, you can't tell anyone.

Nick: It might be too late.

Me: Who could you have already told?

Nick: Hypothetically, my mother, brother, cousin, and the guy who lives down the street from me.

Crap.

I look up at Teddy. "Don't get your hopes up about Nick staying quiet. It appears the temptation to out you has been too great."

"He's already said something?"

"Looks that way," I tell him. "I'm sorry."

He shrugs his shoulders. "What can you do?" Before I can answer, he says, "I'd appreciate it if you could keep the location of my grandfather's house a secret. I don't need any reporters knocking on the door for a story."

"Sure," I tell him, suddenly feeling nervous around him for the first time since meeting him. Here I thought he was just a nice normal guy, but I now know there's nothing normal about him.

CHAPTER FOURTEEN

TEDDY

"I hear Vista Pines is a great place," I tell my grandfather while handing him the bag of sticky buns.

"Who told you that?" He pulls one out and puts it up to his nose before inhaling it like it's an exotic perfume.

"Faith. Her grandmother lives there."

He arches one eyebrow which makes him look like an interrogator at a murder trial. "You've already seen her today, have you?"

"Don't get any ideas. She was at the bakery this morning." I walk into the kitchen and pour two cups of coffee before coming back out to the living room. Handing him one, I ask, "What do you say we stop by and take a tour?"

"Today?" He sounds surprised. "I've already been out today."

"I'm not sure walking two houses away constitutes an outing." I take the bag of sticky buns from him and pull one out.

With a voice full of exasperation, he says, "You can't just blow in here and expect me to be the same man you remember from when you were little. I've changed, Teddy."

"You're not even the same man I remember from the *Alpha Dog* premiere," I retort. "You had a lot more spunk then and that was only three months after Gram died." I don't know why I'm suddenly so mad at him. I'm guessing if I still had my dad, it might be easier to deal with Theo aging.

"You got your acting talent from somewhere, boy. I wasn't going to show up to your big event and be a downer."

"Fine, let's go tomorrow. Today we can go out to the gazebo and see what needs to be done to finish it."

"We should just tear it down," he says with a mouthful of sticky bun.

"No, sir. You started Gram's gazebo and we're going to finish it." It was the one thing I thought we could do together this summer and I do not want to let go of that dream.

"Why? If whoever buys this place doesn't even know it was supposed to be here, they'll never miss it."

"What if they knew it was supposed to be here?" He looks confused, so I tell him, "I've always wanted to own a house in Elk Lake. If you sell this one, I'm your buyer."

"You're kidding."

"Why would I kid about that? Some of the best memories of my life took place in this town. I found myself here, and that's not something a guy forgets."

"Yeah, but you make movies now," he says like I've forgotten what my job is. "You live in LA."

"I can make movies while living anywhere I want. Plus, it's not like I'm going to be here full-time. I'll still keep my house in LA."

"I've never thought about you living here, even part-time."

"Will you help me finish the gazebo now?" I ask.

His head starts to move up and down slowly. "You bet I will."

And just like that, we have a plan for the day.

While he finishes his bun, I run upstairs to put on some work clothes. I briefly look at my phone for messages, but there aren't any. The start of a perfect summer is at hand.

My grandfather is sleeping in his chair by the time I come back down, so I decide to go outside by myself and take a tour of the property. I didn't come here planning to buy a house, but when an opportunity like this arises, who am I to turn my back on it? It might be fanciful, but I feel the hand of my grandmother and dad in this.

From what I've seen, the places on this side of the lake are older and have more character. The view from the back porch indicates the houses across the lake are bigger and showier. They're not my speed at all.

The land between the house and the water is full of mature oak and maple trees, making me guess the autumn view is spectacular. While there's a lot of coverage, I wouldn't quite classify it as a forest. There's plenty of room to set up a volleyball net or build a basketball court—which I think I might do—while still being able to string up hammocks between the trees.

Pulling my phone out of my pocket, I hit Terri's number on impulse.

"What's up, Teddy Bear?" She sounds like she's in a blender.

"Where are you?" I demand. "I can barely hear you."

"Oh." She pauses a second before asking, "Is that better?"

"A little."

"I'm at the car wash, but I also had some vintage Zeppelin cranked. I turned it down."

"Are you ready for some interesting news?" I ask.

"Good interesting, or end-of-your-career interesting?" She sounds nervous.

"What in the world would you classify as end-of-my-career interesting?"

She thinks for a moment before saying, "Alien abduction, for one."

"I believe in aliens."

"So do I, but you don't go blabbing that stuff to the press or you're going to look like a lunatic."

"Why *is* that?" I completely segue from the point of my call. "According to NASA, there are billions of habitable planets in the

Milky Way Galaxy alone and they estimate there are billions of other galaxies out there. How in the world could any sane person think that earth is it?"

"Solid question," she says. "And while you and I are sketchy on the intelligence of earthlings, most people think we've really got it going on."

"Don't get me started."

"So, you're not calling to tell me that you've been abducted by some exotic extraterrestrial life form ..." she prompts.

"Nope."

"Are you calling to tell me you've fallen in love with a goat and are planning a very public and lavish commitment ceremony?"

"Also, no." I can't help but laugh at that one.

"Perhaps you've decided to take up yodeling and are going to display your talent at the Oscars this year?"

This kind of banter is yet another reason I love Terri so much. Not only is she funny, but she thinks outside the box. "No yodeling," I tell her. "Do you give up?"

"I've got one more. You've fallen for that girl you told me you weren't going to fall for."

"I'm still blissfully single." Even though I like Faith more and more every time I see her, I'm still not going to date her. Nope, I've just got a new friend, which is pretty great news in itself.

"Fine, tell me."

"I'm buying my grandfather's house in Elk Lake. He wants to move into an assisted living place." The dead air on the other end of the line makes me think we got disconnected. "Terri?"

"No."

"What's wrong? This is good news," I tell her. "And definitely *not* career breaking."

"You're going to make me come out there and visit, and you'll probably even force me to fish for my supper."

"That's a given but wait until you see how magical it is here. You and Kay will be looking for a vacation house in no time."

"You seem to think people in Wisconsin would welcome an openly married lesbian couple."

"Of course they would. It's Wisconsin, not nineteen fifty," I tell her. "In fact, Faith thinks I'm gay, and she hasn't said a thing about it."

"She thinks you're *gay*? How? Why?"

"When we met, she told me her boyfriend had broken up with her. Then she asked if my boyfriend had ever cheated on me. I said yes, I had been cheated on."

"I love you like a brother, Teddy. And as a gay person, I'm all for being here, queer, and out of the damn closet, but as an already heterosexual man, I don't think you should be putting yourself into a closet so you can come out of it. It might confuse your fanbase. Also, it's kind of a dick move."

"I'm not telling people I'm gay. I'm just not telling them I'm not," I explain.

"Teddy, my friend, just date the girl. I've never seen anyone go to such lengths to avoid someone they clearly already like."

"I like her like a friend." I'm lying through my teeth. Friends don't think about friends the way I think about Faith, but I'm not going to tell Terri that. She'd never let it go if I told her even a fraction of the things I find so attractive about Faith—her kindness, her honesty, her seriously gorgeous curves …

"Fine, be friends. Don't be friends. But for the love of God, please quit pretending to be something you aren't. Take it from me, it's hard work faking being into guys when you're not."

"Again, I'm not trolling for dudes, I'm just not setting the record straight. I like to think of it as playing a part. Faith isn't ready for more—not that I want a relationship with her—but this way, we can still hang out in a non-threatening kind of way." Switching back to the original topic, I ask, "So when are you and Kay coming for a visit?"

"Once the deed to the house is officially in your hands, and you've made sure there's indoor plumbing. I'm not doing my business in an outhouse, and I'm not bathing in a lake."

"Wisconsin isn't located on the set of *Little House on the Prairie*. Not only is there indoor plumbing, but we have refrigerators instead of ice boxes; milk is no longer delivered to your door and, wait for it, the mayor of Elk Creek is Black." At least according to the political sign in the neighbor's yard.

She sighs loudly. "It sounds too good to be true."

"It's my favorite place in the whole world, and you're going to love it here," I tell her.

"Will you introduce me to Faith?"

"Of course. All my friends should know each other." Hopefully she takes the hint that Faith is, and will only ever be, a friend.

"You know I love you, Teddy …"

"Yeah."

"But you're not that quick on the uptake." Before I can take up for myself, she adds, "Go buy your house, and I'll break the news to Kay."

After she hangs up, I put my phone back into my pocket and stare out onto the lake. I have never felt as at home as I do at this moment. I feel it in the center of my bones that my life is about to take an incredible turn.

CHAPTER FIFTEEN

FAITH

"Nope, I'm not kidding," I say while handing Anna a gingersnap. I felt like the Teddy news was something that should be shared in person.

"Teddy *Helms*, though? He's *huge* right now."

"I know." I pull two cookies out of the bakery case for myself and lead the way to a table. Once we're sitting down, I tell her, "He was hoping to stay under the radar, but Nick outed him."

Anna's eyes pop wide open. "Astor is going to be so jealous!"

A slow smile crosses my face. "You know the whole time we were together he always expected people to treat him like he was special. It didn't matter if it was a server at a restaurant or a checkout clerk at the market, his whole demeanor made it clear that he thought he was fabulous and so should everyone else. It will be nice to show him that I found someone who actually merits that kind of attention."

Anna lowers her voice perceptibly. "I was actually surprised when you decided to date Astor."

"What are you talking about? *You* introduced us."

She offers a casual shrug. "Chris thought you might be a good fit. Not me."

"Then why did you go along with it?" I demand. "You're supposed to have my back. You're my best friend!"

"I do, and I am, but I also wanted to prove to my fiancé that I was willing to listen to his instincts once in a while."

"Chris has no instincts. He's the type of guy who thinks he can rollerblade on the pier in a tornado and nothing bad will happen to him," I remind her.

"In his defense, that tornado came out of nowhere."

"He got carried out into Lake Michigan and had to be rescued by the Coast Guard," I remind her.

"That doesn't mean he doesn't have good dating instincts. He picked me, didn't he?" She sits up taller and uses her hands to spokesmodel the air around her.

"Still, you never let on that you didn't see us together."

"It wasn't my place. I got to pick my own guy and you get to pick yours. It's in the best friend rule book."

After swallowing the bite of cookie in my mouth, I remind her, "But you picked a great guy."

"None of us expected Astor to be a cheater," she says. "And, while I didn't think he was right for you, I used to at least think he had integrity."

"Is he really bringing Tiffany to your wedding? It seems an unnecessarily cruel thing to do, if you ask me."

"He's bringing her. But just so you know, I'm not going to be nice to her."

"She ought to have a great time then," I say sarcastically. "Seriously, why would she even come, knowing that I'm going to be there?"

Anna wipes some cappuccino foam off her lip. "If I had to guess, I'd say it's a territory thing. She wants to make it clear that Astor belongs to her now."

"What's she gonna do, pee a circle around him?" I giggle as that very image pops into my head.

"Also," Anna continues, "she might not trust Astor not to cheat *with you*."

"Cheat with *me*?" While I've toyed with the idea of wanting him back, I would never do anything while he's with Tiffany. I suddenly ask, "What would you say if we got back together?"

"Are you kidding me right now?" Anna has gone from cookie content to outraged in record time. She's clearly not a fan of the idea. "When someone tells you who they are, Faith, believe them. Astor has made it clear he's not a man to be trusted."

Exhaling loudly, I remind her, "Yet we had ten great months together …"

"You had nine, if that. Remember he was cheating on you during the tenth."

"It's just that the thought of starting all over again is so over-whelming …"

Pushing away from the table, she crosses one leg over the other. "You get to relive the excitement of a first kiss all over again. Will he? Won't he?" She makes a hand motion like she's pulling an invisible rope in a game of tug of war.

"I get to go out with fourteen guys who claim to be gentlemen only to have to fist fight them when they try to get me into bed on the first date." I teasingly remind her, "You know my rule, no sexy stuff until I know his middle name, his mother's maiden name, and the pin number on his bank card."

"Dating isn't easy," she agrees. "But it's better than divorce."

"You really don't have any hope things could work between us?" I don't really want to get back with him, but the idea of being on my own again is daunting.

"Ass Turd is a cheater. He was already unfaithful once, that we know of." Her eyes bore into mine so deeply I suspect she can see the back of my head. "Do not fool yourself into thinking you want him back," she cautions.

"You're right, but I'm going to enjoy taunting him with Teddy." I don't tell Anna that I'm seriously starting to have feelings for the guy. I do not need to see that look of pity.

"Absolutely," Anna says. "In fact, see if Teddy is up for a little PDA. Even though you're not his type, you're very pretty and I bet he could fake it convincingly. I've heard he's a decent actor."

My lips curl in response. "It's flattering you think he'll need to use his acting skills."

Ignoring my comment, she reaches over and takes the last cookie off my plate. She shoves the whole thing into her mouth. Standing up, she orders, "Go put your tennis shoes on. You need to work off that cookie."

"Me? I only had one to your two."

"Fine. Go put your tennis shoes on and we'll both get some exercise."

"I'll meet you out front in a few."

As I walk back into the kitchen I run straight into GG. "You said you wanted to talk to me," she reminds me.

"Oh, yeah, I did." I look back out into the bakery and see that Anna is tying her shoelaces. Putting my arm around my grandmother, I tell her, "I have some bad news."

"You're moving to Boca to be with your parents?" Holding onto my arm tightly, she adds, "I've been worried that might happen. Honey, I don't want you to go."

"I'm not moving to Boca," I tell her, totally unaware that she was concerned I would ever do that. "Astor and I have broken up."

"Who?"

"Astor. The man I've been going to see in Chicago all these months."

"Oh, him."

"That's all you have to say? We were together for ten months."

She shrugs her bony shoulders. "Why did you break up?"

"He was ..." I stumble over my words. "That is to say, he ... well ..."

"Let his horse out of the barn with the wrong filly?" she asks. *What an odd euphemism.* "Yes. That."

"Then good riddance to bad rubbish," she says. "Time to saddle up and find yourself a new mount."

"What's with all the horse comparisons, GG?" I ask. "I've never known you to be interested in equestrian pursuits."

She lifts one eyebrow. "There are horses and there are stallions."

"Meaning?" She can't possibly mean that to sound the way it does.

"I've never been interested in riding horses, but there's nothing wrong with hopping on a stallion of a man."

Dear God. Desperate to change the subject, I tell her, "I'm taking my friend Teddy to the wedding instead."

"Do I know him?" She tilts her head to the side in a confused manner.

"No, ma'am, but I'll introduce you to him. He's a nice guy and I just know you're going to like him."

"Don't get your hopes up, dear. I plan on being very protective of you now that what's his name has stepped out on you."

"Teddy is just a friend, GG." I don't plan on sharing why that is. My grandmother is open-minded, but I think Nick is the only gay person she actually knows. And while she's nice to him, she's from a generation not known for their open-mindedness.

Not to mention, I don't want her to slip up and make some inappropriate comment.

"I'm off to walk with Anna," I tell her. "I'll stop by the home and see you tomorrow if you're up for a visit."

"I've got line dancing tomorrow," she says with an odd little shimmy. "I should be available before ten and after two though."

"It's a four-hour class?" I ask in surprise.

"One hour, but then there's lunch and my after-lunch siesta. I keep a full schedule." She reaches out and gives me a hug before walking away.

That went much better than I expected. Now all I have to do is forget that I ever felt anything for Astor, and everything should be smooth sailing. More than anything, I was kind of in awe that someone as smooth and polished as him would have anything to do with someone like me. Yet, Teddy is a thousand times more impressive than my ex, and I truly feel he likes me for myself. In all honesty, that's probably because he doesn't want to get into my pants, but still, it's kind of a stunning realization to be liked without prejudice.

Out of nowhere, a chill of something that feels like a warning starts at the base of my neck and makes its way down my back.

What the heck is that all about?

CHAPTER SIXTEEN

TEDDY

My grandfather and I have been hard at work on the gazebo all afternoon and we're both in need of a break. When my phone rings, I signal to him that I'm going to take this call. "Red alert!" Terri says as soon as I answer.

Sitting down on the ground by our project, I ask, "What in the world has you in such a panic?"

"Lindsey."

"What about her?" While neither of us particularly care for my ex, she's never been the cause of a red alert before.

"She just called and said she desperately needs to talk to you. She mentioned her calls aren't going through."

"That's because I blocked her. I figured it was the only way she was going to accept that I didn't want to talk to her."

"Yes, well, she wants to know where you live. Apparently, she's already been to the guest house in Santa Monica and found out you're no longer there."

Running my hand through my hair, I ask, "What's wrong with that woman? She needs to take a hint already."

"Are you really asking for a list? Because I'm prepared to give you one. Fair warning, I'll still be going strong in a few hours."

"No, I don't want a list. I just want her to leave me alone."

Terri clears her throat loudly before suggesting, "Perhaps if you started seeing someone else, the tabloids would get wind of it, and she'd clue in that you've moved on."

"Except I'm currently trying to stay out of the papers."

"That's a bad strategy all around," she says. "We live in a world where celebrities need to stay visible, or they're forgotten."

"Have they forgotten about Al Pacino and Robert De Niro?" I ask with some heat. "Neither of them has ever courted the press's attention and they've both had bigger success than I could ever dream of."

"Teddy, those two are older than the internet. They're dinosaurs. It's a whole new world, man."

I know this lecture well, and while I'm prepared to do my part to stay relevant, I really did want this summer to myself. "I'll think about it," I tell her. "In the meantime, do not give Lindsey my address, and definitely don't tell her I'm in Wisconsin."

"She's not stupid," Terri says. "If she's called me, she's probably contacted every mutual friend the two of you share."

"Like every other broken up couple in the history of couple-dom, we've already divided the friends. Mine aren't going to give her anything, and I don't keep in touch with hers."

"Just be on your toes," she says. After a brief pause, she adds, "I was just about to ask you to come by for dinner tonight. I must be going senile."

I laugh. "I'd love to have dinner, but by the time you get to the airport and fly here, it'll be the middle of the night." I ask, "Did you talk to Kay about coming out?"

"I talked to her."

"And?"

"She's up for a trip. She seems to have already heard Wisconsin has kept up with the times."

"Shoot," I joke. "There goes my plan to pick you up at the airport in a horse and buggy."

"I'm hanging up now," Terri says. And sure enough, she does.

"Who was that?" my grandpa asks as he hobbles in my direction, taking extra care as he crosses the lawn.

"Terri. She and Kay are planning a trip to visit us soon."

"I like that girl," he says. "She's a real ball buster. Takes no prisoners, you know?"

Boy, do I. I was terrified of her for the first year she repped me, but she slowly let down her guard, and I got to see what an amazing person she is. She's the most loyal friend I could ever hope to have.

Staring at the gazebo, my grandfather says, "I've been thinking that instead of doing the two-tiered pagoda on top, we should make it a single."

"Why?"

"Less work," he explains.

"Is that what Gram wanted?" I ask pointedly.

"It doesn't matter what she wanted because she's not here to enjoy it." Spittle flies out of his mouth.

"I want what she wanted." I know I'm being difficult, but even if it takes us all summer to finish this thing, there's no downside to us spending time together. That's what this whole trip is about.

"I need a nap." He drops the dowel he's been sanding and starts a slow march to the house.

"What do you want for supper?" I ask him. "I'll get busy preparing it while you rest."

"I don't care. We can have leftovers if there are any."

I hurry to his side to offer support while he climbs the back stairs. "We don't. Faith was pretty hungry last night." I smile remembering how much she put away. It was a pleasure to see her enjoy her food. When I was with Lindsey, she barely ate enough to keep a cat alive.

"I like that girl, too," my grandpa says. "My motto in life is that you can't trust a woman who won't eat."

"*That's* your motto?" I ask. "I thought your motto was, 'If you can't build it, it's not worth having.'"

He glances at me out of the corner of his eye. "Mottos change according to topic, Teddy. Pay attention."

"I could make scrambled eggs and bacon," I suggest.

As we reach the top step, he inhales deeply before releasing his breath. "If you're offering breakfast for supper, why not pancakes? I think I have some sausages in the freezer. We could have pigs in the blanket."

"That sounds really good," I tell him as I lead him through the house to his chair. Once he's settled, I go into the kitchen to make sure I have all the ingredients I need. The only thing missing is baking powder. Luckily, my neighbor is a baker, so maybe I can avoid a trip to the market.

As I walk out of the house in the direction of Faith's, I feel a sense of contentment having a friend so close. I hope she's as excited as I am that I'm going to buy my grandfather's house.

When I get to her front door, I see some movement through one of her windows. Peeking in, I watch her slow dance around her living room. She's wearing a bath towel and singing into her balled-up fist. There's a reason they say dance like nobody is watching. It's a mesmerizing performance and I can't look away.

But then Faith spots me and lets out a blood curdling scream. She throws her hands up into the air like she's being held up, and her towel hits the ground. Even though I should look away, and fully intend to do so, I don't. The image is too perfect not to enjoy. It's like seeing the *Venus de Milo* at the Louvre. Such works of art as Faith and *Venus* beg to be appreciated.

Faith hurriedly bends down and picks up her towel. Moments later her front door opens, and she demands, "What are you doing here?"

I give her what I think is my most endearing smile, hoping she won't hang onto any anger at being spied upon. "Looking for baking powder."

"Excuse me?" I can see where she might find my comment confusing.

"I'm making pancakes for supper, and we don't have any

baking powder." I do my best not to gape, but it's hard.

"You scared the hell out of me!" she yells. "I thought you were a creeper."

Shaking my head, I tell her, "Just a neighbor looking for baking supplies."

She steps aside to let me in. "Well, you've come to the right place, even though you've just taken years off my life." She stops at the front closet and pulls out a trench coat to put on.

As she pulls the sash tightly, I tease, "Who's the creeper now?"

"Hahaha." She's not really laughing. "I'm lucky you're, you know ..."

"Devastatingly handsome and talented?"

She cocks an eyebrow before saying, "Gay. I'd be mortified right now if you weren't."

"Why?" I follow her into the kitchen. *I'd only embarrass her if I told her the truth now.*

"Because I can count on one hand the number of men who have seen me naked and believe me, I'm not looking to increase that number any time soon." She opens the cabinet above her stove.

"I'm still a man," I tell her. "And as such, I can certainly appreciate a woman's nude form." *And boy, did I.*

"You know what I mean." She hands me the baking powder before asking, "Do you have enough ingredients to cook for three? I think you owe me after scaring the life out of me, and pancakes sound good."

"You're on," I tell her. "Everything will be ready in a half-hour, unless of course you want to come as you are." I shrug my eyebrows comically.

"I'll see you in a half-hour." Instead of walking me to the front door, she turns to climb the stairs at the back of the kitchen. "You can let yourself out."

I do so with a smile on my face. My new neighbor is certainly easy on the eyes, and I look forward to seeing a lot more of her. I don't bother analyzing that thought, I just enjoy it.

CHAPTER SEVENTEEN

FAITH

My heart is still in my throat as I look through my closet for a loose summer dress. I want to eat without worrying I'll cut off my circulation.

I truly did think Teddy was some kind of Peeping Tom. I'm usually comfortable living on my own, but moments like that make me wonder how safe it really is.

Before he scared the life out of me, I had been imagining I was dancing at Anna's wedding to GG's favorite song, "Unchained Melody" by the Righteous Brothers. As I swayed to the tune in my head, I began to sing the words out loud. They're so full of yearning I felt ripples of anticipation and raw hunger flow through me like molten lava. Then I opened my eyes and thought it was all over.

Thank God it was Teddy, but still … I'll never admit this out loud, it was Teddy I was pretending I was dancing with. I know, I know, I'm pitiful, wishing he was someone other than he is, but still, there's something about him that makes me dream he was straight. But we're only friends, and I'm totally cool with that.

This weird attraction I'm feeling is probably because I'm super vulnerable right now and will take any sign of male attention as hope that I'm not the loser Astor has made me feel like.

Once I'm dressed, I run a brush through my damp hair and then put on a pair of stud earrings. As far as making myself look good, it isn't even the bare minimum, but it's all I can muster.

When I get to Theo's house, I knock on the door and wait for what feels like an eternity before it's answered. Theo finally opens the door. "Faith, come on in. Teddy's in the kitchen burning supper."

"I'm not burning anything!" I hear the man himself shout. "I just like my sausages crispy."

"Crispy, burnt …"—he shrugs his shoulders—"tomatoes, tomahtoes, am I right?"

"Are you one of those people who likes limp bacon?" I ask while joining him in the living room.

Sitting in his chair, he answers, "I like to know that if my bacon drops on the floor, it won't shatter," he says.

Nodding my head, I tell him, "My grandmother always says that if it isn't chewy, it isn't bacon."

"Smart woman."

I feel the need to share, "I like mine nearly burnt."

He shakes his head. "Your generation is lazy." He immediately seems contrite. "I'm sorry, that wasn't nice."

"You're forgiven," I tell him. "You've had a tough time of it lately, Theo. I can't imagine how hard it is to lose your wife after so many years together." Tipping my head to the side so my ear is almost touching my shoulder, I add, "I can't even imagine what it would be like to be married."

He waves his hand in front of him. "True love will come in its own time. And once it does, it will be hard to remember what it was like before it did."

"About that," I lean back against the sofa and kick my feet out. "I'm not sure I'm fully out of love with the guy who just broke up with me." *Although, I would be stupid if I wasn't. Astor puts himself first on all occasions. From what I know about Teddy, he puts everyone else ahead of himself.* My thoughts are about to wax poetic on how Teddy would be the perfect man, if only he was straight, when Theo says, "Love can feel a lot like food poisoning. When it's fresh, you feel like you'll never be the same, but once the raging nausea passes, you slowly recover."

"I hope you never get into the greeting card business, Theo."

"Too graphic?" he asks innocently.

"Too horrible. Is that what being in love felt like to you?"

"After I met Abigail that summer in Elk Creek, I couldn't eat or sleep, I was so consumed by thoughts of her. But the more time we spent together, the more those feelings grew, and they changed me. I was no longer boring old Theodore Fischer. I was a man who was loved by the most perfect woman in the world."

An unexpected tear slides down my cheek. "I'm sorry she died," I tell him. "You sound like you were the perfect couple."

He scoffs. "Don't get me wrong, we didn't always see eye to eye. We had disagreements and arguments, but that's just what happens when two people act as one. There are bound to be growing pains. Inevitably compromises must be made on both sides."

"What was the biggest compromise you ever made?" I boldly ask. I'm talking to Theo like I've known him my whole life, but that's kind of how it feels right now. Both he and Teddy just feel like they fit into my life—like they've always been there.

He thinks about my question for several moments before answering. "The biggest compromise was at the end." He takes a moment to clear the emotion out of his throat. "After the paramedics took Abigail to the hospital, they wanted to know what her end-of-life wishes were. You know, was she okay with being on life support and all that."

"Oh." I think I know where this is going.

"She didn't want it," he says quietly. "In fact, she was adamantly opposed to it. But when faced with letting her go, I almost went against her wishes."

"Oh, Theo." I stand up and move over so I can take him into

my arms. "You did the right thing. I know it's no comfort, but I'm sure Abigail was very proud of you." I hold onto him tighter when he lays his head on my shoulder.

Teddy walks into the living room, and jokes, "Oh, hey, I didn't mean to interrupt anything." I give him a sad face, so he knows this isn't the time.

Theo, however, takes the bait. "If you're not going to woo this girl, then I am." He leans back and shoots me a wink.

"That's right," I decide to play along. "Theo and I are thinking about eloping. You're missing out, buddy."

Teddy walks across the room and reaches his hand out to mine. I consider not taking it, but I eventually do. "Don't be greedy, Grandpa," he says.

"So, you're going to declare yourself, are you?" Theo asks him.

Teddy jokingly gets down on one knee. "I say we fly to Vegas tonight and make it official."

Why couldn't Astor have been more fun like this? Why couldn't he have really loved me? A wave of emotion washes over me and tears spring to my eyes. "Uh-oh," Teddy says. "I was just kidding, I'm sorry." He stands up and starts to shift around nervously before backing into the coffee table.

I'm so embarrassed I want to run out of the room, but I don't. I just stand there feeling awkward and sad.

Theo saves the day by standing up. "I'm starving. I hope you didn't burn everything."

Teddy looks at me as though trying to discern if I'm all right. I force a smile before saying, "Yeah, I hope you didn't ruin supper, Teddy." He smiles, seemingly relieved I'm not on the verge of yet another emotional display.

Everything goes back to normal once we're sitting at the kitchen table dishing up our food. I put four pancakes rolled around sausages on my plate and then add a giant scoop of maple butter. Theo tells Teddy, "This one's a keeper. Not afraid to eat."

It's nice that someone is appreciative of my appetite. I'm tempted to have Theo call Anna and explain that my ability to eat in the face of heartache is nothing to worry about. As I put the first bite into my mouth, Teddy announces, "I have news."

"It's a whopper too," Theo says. "The best news I've heard all year."

I swallow the food in my mouth and demand, "What is it?"

"I'm buying a house in Elk Lake." He looks as excited as if he'd just found out he won the lottery.

I'm not quite sure how to respond, so I go with, "Really?" Then hurry to add, "Where is it?" First of all, I love the idea of seeing Teddy all the time, but what would happen if I didn't get over this silly infatuation I've started to feel for him?

"Right here," he says. "I'm buying my grandfather's house. We're going to be neighbors!"

Confusion fills my brain. "But I thought you lived in LA."

"I do, and I will some of the time, but I'll be here just as much, I hope."

"Wow." I don't sound overly excited which he clearly picks up on.

"I thought you'd be happy."

"Oh, I am, really. This is such great news." I sound as excited as I'd be about a flu epidemic. What if Teddy moves to Elk Lake, and I fall head over heels in love with him? What then? My pulse starts to flutter, and I feel lightheaded like I'm about to faint. I grab ahold of the edge of the table to steady myself.

"Faith ..." he says with meaning. "What's wrong?"

I can't tell him. Even though I'm trying to chalk my crush up to part of the mourning process for Astor, I know what I am beginning to feel for Teddy has nothing to do with my ex. Teddy is sweet and sympathetic, and oh boy, that wavy dark hair is screaming for me to run my fingers through it.

To make matters worse, he's easy to talk to, and he loves his grandfather. Summing it up, he's the perfect man, except for one giant glaring problem. His love for other men.

I put another bite of food into my mouth to avoid talking but the problem is I'm not sure I can swallow it without choking.

CHAPTER EIGHTEEN

TEDDY

My grandfather goes to bed after we're done eating, which leaves Faith and me to do the dishes. You'd think I was at the front of the line for Space Mountain instead of performing such a mundane chore. That's how much I enjoy being with her.

"Why aren't you excited that I'm moving to Elk Lake?" I ask without making eye contact. "I expected you to be doing a dance." After all, how can I be so happy to be near her without her sharing my feelings?

"Oh, I'm dancing," she says. "But it's an internal sort of dance."

I'm not buying it.

"I expected the lambada," I tell her jokingly.

She looks at me in horror. "I've seen *Dancing with the Stars* and the lambada would put me in traction."

"I saw some of your dance moves earlier tonight," I remind her. "It didn't look to me like you were in jeopardy of hurting yourself."

Her eyes widen in alarm. "No, but you're going to be hurting if you ever mention that again."

We're clearly not at the point where we can joke about it, so I change the subject. "What kind of dancing lessons is your grandmother taking at Vista Pines?"

"Line dancing. They use it as a teaching aid to help the old folks keep their balance."

"I imagine swing dancing is beyond most of them at this point."

"Swing dancing is beyond me, and I'm not even thirty." She suddenly drops her dishtowel on the counter. "Will you make me a cup of tea?"

"Would you rather have a margarita?" I offer. "You don't have to drive home, you know. Another bonus to having a good friend like me in the neighborhood." *Seriously, if I'm not enough to make her happy, the least she can do is appreciate the free booze.*

She walks across the kitchen to the back door. "I would rather have a margarita, but after eating four pigs in the blanket, I feel like I have to show some self-restraint." As she walks out the door, she says, "I'll meet you on the swing."

Porch swings seem to be an oddly Midwestern thing. I don't recall ever seeing one in Southern California or Arizona. And believe me when I say, those folks don't know what they're missing. Staring out onto a scenic view while gently lulling yourself into a meditative stupor is my idea of heaven.

While the kettle heats up, I pull two mugs out of the cabinet and put a peppermint tea bag into each. Then I add just a touch of honey. When the water is heated, I pour it into the cups and carry them outside. "You don't see a lot of people our age drinking tea," I say as I hand Faith her cup.

"Says who?"

Sitting down next to her, I rephrase my comment. "Do you see a lot of people our age drinking tea?"

"Who cares if they drink tea or not?" Someone's in a mood.

Using my foot to kick off the porch, I put the swing into motion. "Is something going on I should know about?"

She scoffs loudly. "I might have mentioned that my boyfriend just broke up with me and we're going to be in the same wedding?" Before I can comment, she adds, "*And* he's bringing his new girlfriend. You know, the one he cheated on me with?"

"I can't wait to see what kind of loser passed up a life with you." I nudge her gently and remind her, "Plus, you'll always have me."

Instead of being pleased by my comment, it seems to make her angrier. "Quit saying things like that."

"Why? I'm trying to be supportive."

"And while I appreciate that, I ..." She doesn't finish her sentence.

"You, what?" *What is going on with her?*

"You shouldn't be flirting with me. My heart has recently been broken, and I'm liable to take it the wrong way." Now would be the perfect time to tell her I'm not gay, but I don't trust myself to sit with her on this moonlit night and not make a play for her. Letting her think I'm batting for the other team is the only thing keeping me in check. It's the only thing keeping me from breaking her heart.

"Faith," I start to say.

She holds up a hand. "Don't talk. Just drink your tea."

We sit for nearly thirty minutes not saying anything at all. The crickets chirp and the bullfrogs croak, but we stay quiet. When Faith puts her empty cup onto the deck, I finally ask, "Want another cup?"

She shakes her head. "I should get going. I need to be at the bakery early tomorrow. I'm making a prototype of Anna's cake to see if there's any way I can make it more special."

"What kind of cake?" I ask. If small talk is all that she's offering, I'll happily take it.

"Black Forest. It's been Anna's favorite for as long as I can remember."

"Isn't that the one with cherry liquor?"

She nods her head. "Cherry brandy. Kirschwasser. I'm going to make dark chocolate bark to surround the various cakes, and then display them all at different levels. It's a very dramatic presentation."

"I'm sure Anna will love it. You two go back a long time, don't you?" Faith's relationship with Anna is a lot like mine with Terri. You cannot underrate the importance of a best friend.

"It was love at first sight ever since preschool," she says. "I ran up to her and touched her hair and declared it the coolest thing I'd ever seen." She glances at me sideways. "My mom was mortified."

"Why?"

"It was the early two thousands and we were all supposed to act like there were no differences between people's skin color. She felt that by my saying something I might be offending Anna and her mom."

"Were they offended?"

"Not in the least. Dawn told me that if I wanted, she'd give me a thousand little braids in my hair someday, too. Anna said she wished she had silky hair like mine. Kids have a way of taking things in stride without feeling insulted."

Forgetting myself, I tell her, "I want at least five kids."

She turns to me and opens and closes her mouth several times without saying anything. She finally asks, "Are you going to wait until you find Mr. Right, or are you going to do this thing on your own?"

"I suppose it depends how long it takes me to find love." Yet again, neither confirming nor denying her misconceptions. *It's better this way,* I tell myself. Though I'm having trouble remembering why at this point.

"But you're not even looking," she accuses. "You told me it's been two years since your breakup, and you're still not seeing anyone."

"You don't always have to search for love," I tell her quietly while resisting the temptation to tuck an errant lock of hair behind her ear. "Sometimes it just finds you."

Several tense moments follow while we simply stare into each other's eyes. I want so badly to pull Faith into my arms and kiss her. But there are so many reasons not to. She's fresh off a breakup, and I'm, well … only going to be living here part time … I don't want to ruin our friendship by starting something that couldn't possibly work out.

Faith looks away first and abruptly stands up. "Thanks for the pancakes."

As she turns toward the back stairs, I say, "Wait up. I'll walk you home."

She slows down just enough for me to know she's okay for me to tag along. As we stroll up the driveway, I stumble over what I'm sure must be a renegade pinecone. *This is getting ridiculous.* "You know what we need?" I ask, trying to divert her attention from my lack of grace. She arches an eyebrow in question, so I tell her, "We need to practice dancing together so we can show Astor how perfect our chemistry is."

"You want *us* to practice dancing together." Her tone indicates that I suggested we take an underwater basketweaving class. Naked.

"Why not?"

"Because we only have a few weeks?" She points to my feet and adds, "And you have such big feet you can barely walk without falling over?" *Crap, she saw that.*

"There was a rock in my way," I tell her. If only that were so. The truth is that Faith makes me nervous, and my natural dexterity seems to hit the skids when I'm with her. "Come on. I saw a dance studio on Main Street. Let's see if they can fit us in for some last-minute lessons."

"Teddy …" She opens and closes her mouth again.

"Faith …" I counter.

A smile overtakes any hesitation on her face. "It *would* be fun to rub his face in it."

"I'll stop by tomorrow and see what they can do for us." I don't really want to learn how to dance, and I don't really care what Astor thinks of us. I just want to have a reason to hold Faith in my arms.

"I don't want to go for something big, like where you lift me up over your head and spin me around," she warns. "I might throw up."

"No dirty dancing then," I agree. "How about something where I spin you around on the ground and then end it with a big dip?"

She appears to consider my suggestion closely. "I could be up for that."

By the time we arrive at her front door, her mood has turned for the better. It makes me feel like a kid on Christmas morning, full of excitement and possibility. "I'll stop by the bakery tomorrow and let you know what I find out."

Instead of offering my hand to shake, this time I give her a hug. She leans into it for the briefest moment before pulling back like she's been burned. "Good night," she says. Then she turns and walks into her house.

Once she's inside, I just stand there like we've been tied together by an invisible string and there's not enough length for me to go anywhere. *What was I doing suggesting we take dancing lessons?* No good can come from that and yet I find that I don't care. All I want to do is hold Faith and never let her go.

CHAPTER NINETEEN

FAITH

"Why are there so many people out there already?" I ask Nick while staring out the front window. It's only six and we have yet to unlock the doors for the day.

He shrugs his shoulders and mumbles, "Don't know."

"Nick." I stop him in his tracks as he turns to go into the kitchen.

"Yes?" He doesn't turn around.

"Come here." Four steps later, my blue-haired friend is standing in front of me. "What have you done?"

He hems and haws before confessing, "I might have mentioned to a few people that Teddy Helms likes to come in here in the mornings."

"But he doesn't. Why would you say that?"

"He's been in twice that I know of, and according to you, he's only been in town for a few days. That's most mornings. Plus," he adds, "it's good for business. And by business, I mean it's good for tips."

"Ah, so you've outed him for mercenary reasons." Shaking my

head, I add, "I would have appreciated a little notice, so I could've had more baked goods on hand."

"Don't you have emergency stuff in the freezer?" he asks. "I'll just go take some out." He turns and walks away.

Meanwhile, I unlock the front door and prepare myself for the onslaught of early morning business. Our first customers are usually elderly people who get up before dawn because they go to bed right after the early bird special at the diner. This morning's crowd is oddly young and almost entirely female.

A girl I recognize steps forward and demands, "Is Teddy Helms coming in this morning?"

"I don't know," I tell her.

"What's his favorite thing to eat here?" another girl wants to know.

I look over at the pastry case to see what I have the most of. "He loves the coffee cake." We sell out of coffee cake in our first hour open.

When things slow down out front, I go back into the kitchen to give Esmé a hand. She's scooping macaroon dough onto several large sheet pans. "You should have seen the crowd out there this morning," I tell her.

Esmé is about half my size and twice as talented. She's five years younger than me, and she's saving her money to go to Paris so she can intern at one of the patisseries there. After that, she wants to come back to the States and work at a restaurant in New York City. "Nick has been broadcasting the news about Teddy Helms to anyone who will listen," she says.

"What about you?" I ask. "Are you excited he's here?" Most women between ten and fifty would be.

"What difference does it make to my life?" Esmé is also one cool cucumber. She always wears her pale blonde hair in a chignon at the base of her neck, and the expression on her face is practically regal.

I point to the front of the bakery. "There are about twenty girls out there who would trip their own sister at the Grand Canyon for a chance to date that man."

"Are you one of them?" she wants to know.

"Ah, no." That's a bald-faced lie if there ever was one, but I'm never going to tell anyone the truth. I look pathetic enough as it is. "I've just been broken up with and I need some time to lick my wounds before putting myself on the market again."

Thank God, I never told Nick I wanted to set him up with Teddy. If he knew that, he'd have been hard-pressed not to out him for real.

Esmé stares at me as though contemplating her next words carefully. "Astor was never good enough for you."

"Why would you say that?" If anything, in my mind, I was never good enough for *him*. He's crazy good-looking, super successful, and borderline snobby. I always assumed people thought he could do much better than me.

"He always walked around like he had a stick up his butt. You're …"—she waves her hand in my direction—"fun and fresh. You're a total catch."

"I appreciate you saying that more than you will ever know," I tell her. "Seriously, thank you. Even if you're lying to my face, it's exactly what I need to hear right now."

While washing her scooper off in the sink, she says, "Tell me the story about Teddy taking you to Anna's wedding."

"How did you hear about that?" I know the answer even before the question is out of my mouth. Nick's inability to keep any Teddy Helms news to himself makes me assume he's the culprit.

Instead of confirming my suspicions, Esmé says, "I would love to be a fly on the wall to see how Astor reacts to seeing you there with a mega Hollywood star."

"Why don't you hang around the reception after setting up the cake." I secretly love the idea of a bunch of people shooting Astor the evil eye.

"Do you think Anna will mind?" She suddenly seems excited.

"Anna will supply you with a bucket of eggs to throw at him if you ask." Even though my friend claims not to want a scene at her wedding, she would relish anything that would cause Astor discomfort.

"I'll bring my own eggs," Esmé says with a twinkle in her eye.

As I open the refrigerator to take out a new batch of lemon curd that we serve with the ginger and lemon scones, the swinging door slams open. Nick blows through it declaring, "Teddy Helms is in the building!"

Oh dear, he's probably being swarmed. "Bring him back here, Nick."

"Right away? Shouldn't we let the ladies enjoy him for a little while first?"

I point to the door. "Now, Nick."

He returns moments later with a shell-shocked Teddy trailing behind him. "What's going on out there?" he asks.

"Nick apparently took an ad out in the *Elk Lake Gazette* telling everyone you're in town, and that you love to eat here."

Teddy glances nervously at Nick before saying, "I thought you were going to keep my secret."

"I wanted to," Nick tells him. "I really did, but ultimately, I couldn't."

"Why?" Teddy wants to know.

"It's like this, Teddy. You're the biggest deal that's ever happened to Elk Lake, which makes the person who breaks the news a pretty big deal." He points to himself before adding, "I'm not such a big deal on my own, so I kind of jumped at the chance to grab onto your coattails. I'm truly sorry, but there really was no way I could pass up the opportunity."

Teddy visibly bristles. "I appreciate your candor, but remind me to never tell you any of my secrets."

Nick bows slightly to Teddy. "I think I might have it out of my system now, so if you ever feel like sharing anything else, I'll probably come through for you."

"Nick," I say warningly. "Go!"

I turn to introduce Teddy to Esmé but she's gone into the walk-in. So I tell Teddy, "You're here early. Have you been to the dance studio already?"

He nods his head excitedly. "I have, and I've met a lovely older lady who introduced herself as Madam Bernadette. She can give us our first lesson in ten minutes. Any chance you can get away?"

"Ten minutes?" I weigh the odds of leaving Esmé and Nick in the weeds here with my desire to get even with Astor. Untying my apron, I tell him, "You bet I can!"

CHAPTER TWENTY

TEDDY

As we walk out of the bakery, Faith says, "Madam Bernadette taught me ballet for six years when I was a kid."

"Why didn't you continue?" I ask.

"Madam told me I wasn't designed for ballet and that I might enjoy hip hop or tap dancing more. I wasn't particularly interested in either of those."

"What does that mean, not designed for ballet?"

"At the time, I thought she was telling me I was too tall. In retrospect, I'm inclined to think she might have been referring to my weight."

"Were you a heavy kid?" Faith is curvy in all the right places, but she doesn't strike me as someone who was ever overweight.

She shrugs her shoulders. "I've always been sort of like I am now. Not fat, not thin, but if you had to choose which direction I might turn, I don't think anyone would guess there would be a run on size fours."

In LA, I'm surrounded by Hollywood's standard of beauty, and it's not one I share. There's something wrong with an ideal that requires starving yourself only to have other parts augmented. "I think you're perfect," I tell her. She is, too. She's curvaceous and womanly and just, well … the ideal female form.

"Thank you, but I've recently lost fifteen pounds, so this isn't exactly my norm." She laughs without meeting my gaze. "Give me a couple of weeks and I should be back to my fighting weight."

"You wouldn't believe the diet I was on to prepare for shooting *Alpha Dog*. I wasn't allowed any carbs, and I ate so much chicken I'm not sure I'll be able to eat it again in this lifetime."

"I can't imagine you looking any better than you do now." She immediately appears to regret her words because her body tenses perceptibly as her chin juts forward and her shoulders square off.

"Thank you," I tell her. "I've signed on for another *Alpha Dog* though, which is why I'm determined to enjoy all the sweets you can bake for me until I go back into training."

When we get to the dance studio, I open the door for Faith. After following her inside, I wave to Madam Bernadette, and announce, "We're here for our lesson."

Madam is average height and quite stocky in build, which makes it odd that she would have had any issue with Faith's size. She walks across the room with a huge smile on her sixty-something face. Clapping her hands enthusiastically, she greets, "Faith Reynolds, you're back to dance!"

Faith shrinks slightly in her presence. "Yes, Madam. I hope that's okay."

"It's more than okay. It's marvelous!"

"Oh." Faith seems to consider her next words carefully. "I just thought that when you kicked me out of ballet, you might have been happy to be done with me."

Madam looks confused. "I kicked you out of ballet? That doesn't sound like me."

"You told me I'd be better suited to hip hop or tap," Faith reminds her.

The wheels appear to turn in Madam's head as she tries to

remember. She suddenly says, "Faith, I would have been happy to have kept you in ballet, but you always went through your moves so quickly, I thought you'd really thrive with a dance that was more vigorous and lively. Ballet is a lot of wonderful things, but it's not what I'd call lively."

"Really?" Faith sounds dumbfounded.

"Really," Madam tells her. Then, getting down to business, she asks, "What kind of dance are the two of you looking to learn for Anna's wedding? We don't have a lot of time."

"I was thinking a waltz," I tell her. "I already know a few of the basics and I'm guessing with Faith's dancing background, she'll pick it up quickly as well."

"I know how to waltz," Faith says as though affronted that I assumed she didn't. "My dad taught me when I was little."

"Well, then!" Madam Bernadette claps her hands. "I say we go with the waltz and if you both remember what you're doing, then we can add to it."

She turns around and strolls over to an ancient-looking record player before pulling an album off the shelf. She puts it on the turntable while motioning for us to move to the center of the dance floor. "I need to see what you can do before we start."

The opening strains of Norah Jones' "Come Away with Me" fill the room. I open my arms to Faith and watch as she tentatively walks toward me. Our eyes are glued to each other, and time seems to stop moving. Five seconds or an hour pass, I couldn't say which. When our hands finally touch, we move effortlessly. Forward together, right together, back together … We glide across the floor like we're one person being pulled by the invisible strings of the melody. Where it goes, we go. I've never felt this connected to anyone in my whole life.

I hold Faith so close I swear I can feel her heart beating against my own. Then I spin her out and pull her back again. The only reason I learned to dance was for a part in a film, but waltzing with Faith makes me think I should dance every day. As long as I'm doing it with her.

When the song ends, Madam Bernadette takes the needle off the record and declares, "I don't know what you two need me for. You've got this down pat."

Faith's eyes are fixed on the floor, and mine are glued to the top of her head. "Wow," I tell her. "You're really good."

She finally looks up. "*I'm* good? I think you're the one who's good. In fact, you're so good you make me look passable."

"You were both wonderful!" Madam interjects. "I suggest we try the waltz to a couple more modern songs to make sure you can increase and decrease the tempo at will, but after that, we might be able to add some interesting moves to your repertoire."

"Interesting moves?" Faith asks nervously. "What do you have in mind?"

Madam waves her hand in front of her. "Just some dips and lifts. Nothing too challenging."

Faith turns to me and declares, "There will be no lifting unless I'm lifting you."

I start to laugh. "Are you saying you don't think I could pick you up?" I take one step toward her while she takes one step back.

"I don't want you to try. I'd feel horrible if you pulled a muscle in your back or something."

"Now you're saying I'm not strong enough?" I advance toward her again. "I was Alpha Dog, you know. You can't possibly think Alpha Dog can't lift a woman."

"I'm sure he could." She backs into the mirrored wall. "I'm sure *you* could. I just don't want to be lifted, that's all."

I reach out to Faith and pull her toward me, but instead of it being effortless, she lets her body go limp so I'm pulling dead weight. "Faith," I warn her. "I'm going to pick you up and prove to you that I'm a big, strong man."

"Please, Teddy," she begs while doing her best to sit on the floor.

As I have every intention of winning this battle of wills, I tell her, "You're hurting my male pride."

"I'm saving your back."

I bend down so that I'm eye to eye with her. "Faith, I can bench press two hundred and eighty pounds. Do you weigh anything close to that?"

"No."

"Then why don't you let me pick you up?"

"What if you trip and drop me?"

"Ouch." Yet she might be on to something. Faith has certainly messed with my equilibrium.

She smiles sheepishly and her body seems to relax a little. "Two hundred and eighty, huh?"

I nod my head slowly. "Yes, ma'am."

She reaches her hand out for me to help her up. "Okay."

I pull her to her feet and put my arms under her knees. As I lift her up, I tell her, "You're as light as a feather. I could carry you around all day."

She buries her face into my chest and laughs. "I should make you do it, too, after all that bragging."

"I'd love nothing more," I assure her. But it turns out holding onto her like this is wreaking havoc with my willpower to only be her friend. Ever so gently, I lower her to the ground. Against my better judgment I make sure our bodies are touching the whole time.

Once she's on her feet, Madam asks, "Faith, how limber are you? Do you think you can do the splits?"

"The splits?" Her voice cracks in what I'm guessing is panic. "I'm pretty sure I haven't even tried in twenty years."

Madam points to the ballet bar. "You know what to do. Go stretch and then we'll put you to the test."

"You don't want me to do the splits, too?" I ask nervously. I'm afraid if I tried, I might pull a muscle that I'd never recover from.

"No, young man." She runs her hand up my arm flirtatiously. "A big strong fella like you is needed for other things."

I watch while Faith lifts one foot to the bar and begins a series of stretches. She occasionally lets out a groan of pain. "Keep going!" Madam encourages her. "You've got this, Faith!"

After several minutes, Faith walks back to us. Actually, it's more of a hobble. Madam claps her hands excitedly and declares, "I'm going to teach you a split lift."

"I thought we were going to practice the waltz a few more times," Faith says nervously.

"You two can waltz on your own. If the goal here is to impress at Anna's wedding, I think we can safely focus on a couple of lifts."

Madam instructs us how to stand and where to put our arms, and then orders, "Now, plié together and on the way up, Faith, you jump and Teddy will lift you up."

We practice this a couple of times before she tells Faith, "On the lift, I want you to kick one leg up and let it carry you over the top of Teddy. In the air, your legs will be in the splits, and you'll land on the leg you kicked up with." Then she looks at me. "Do you follow that?"

I nod my head. The first time we try it, I almost drop Faith. But not because she's too heavy. More like because she tries some ninja moves up there instead of a simple split. The second time, we both fall to the ground, but the third time is perfect. Okay, not perfect, but no one gets hurt.

Once Faith is on her feet, I pick her up and spin her around in celebration. "We did it!" Turning to Madam, I ask, "That was great, wasn't it?"

"No, Teddy. That was not great, but if you work hard, there's a chance it will be by the day of the wedding."

I put Faith back onto the ground to find her beaming from ear to ear. "That was fun!"

She nods her head slowly. "It really was."

"And we're going to do it again and again until it's perfect, aren't we?"

Instead of answering, she asks, "You're pushy, do you know that?"

"Only when I really want something."

"And what you want is to dance with me?" She doesn't sound convinced.

"Dancing with you is the only thing I want." I don't mention the rest for fear that it will scare her away.

CHAPTER TWENTY-ONE

FAITH

The next couple of weeks pass like I'm living in a dream. I barely even think about Astor, and I see Teddy almost every day. He either stops by the bakery—usually wearing a baseball hat and sunglasses to avoid his adoring public—or he comes by my house to practice dancing. I don't want to jinx us, but we're turning into a fabulous dancing duo.

In addition to becoming the next Fred Astaire and Ginger Rogers—I know these names because GG is a huge fan of vintage movies—we share all kinds of things with each other. Like one night over tacos, I told Teddy about the time Anna and I were cat sitting for the Andrettis and Anna thought it would be fun to try on Mrs. Andretti's clothes—the woman had seriously gorgeous dresses. I was adamant that we weren't going to do that, yet somehow in my next memory, we're standing in the Andrettis' living room wearing vintage Oscar de La Renta and being chewed out by my old neighbor.

Among a slew of funny anecdotes, Teddy told me all about the day his dad died. I know what he ate for breakfast that morning—a fried salami sandwich; I know the last thing he said to his dad—

"No way you're gonna make me do that!" That was in reference to his father encouraging him to try out for the school play. His dad thought he'd love it, and Teddy thought he'd be ridiculed by his football teammates. Long story short, his dad was killed in a horrible car accident, and he tried out for the play. That day irrevocably changed his life.

I like Teddy more and more every day, meaning it's quite possible he's going to break my heart. He is the perfect man who has no idea he's reeling me in like a largemouth bass on a fishing line.

As we don't have any plans to see each other today, I've decided to wax my legs for the wedding. If I do it now, they won't be bumpy on the big day. I'm currently sitting on my back patio with a pot of wax, baby powder, cloth strips, and a pack of Tic Tacs. I pop two in my mouth every time I pull off a strip.

I'm just unscrewing the baby powder lid, when I hear, "Faith? You there?"

"What are you doing here?" I ask Teddy and he climbs the back stairs. "I thought you were working on the gazebo today."

"We finished it!" he says excitedly. "I can't wait for you to see it. I put two Adirondack chairs under it so we can sit and watch the sunset." I don't know if the chairs are for him and me or him and Theo. I decide to play it safe, and say, "I'm sure your grandfather will love that."

He looks down at my waxing paraphernalia. "Are you getting ready to terrorize the villagers or something? That looks like some kind of medieval torture."

"It is," I assure him. "The lengths women will go to in order to look pretty are truly insane." I ask him, "Ever been waxed?"

His face screws up in a look of sheer horror. "Never."

Now's my chance to have some fun with him. "I bet you couldn't handle it."

He doesn't bite. "I bet you're right." He pulls a chair out from under the patio table and sits down.

"It hurts like hell," I tell him. "Men don't genetically possess the level of pain tolerance needed to handle it."

He takes the bait. "Are you saying that *I* couldn't handle it?"

I nod my head. "Pretty much."

I can see the wheels turning in his head and have to restrain my laughter while I wait for his response. He finally asks, "What do I get if I let you wax something on me?"

"What do you want?"

"If it's up to me, then I get to choose what I want *after* I win."

"That's not fair," I tell him. "I need to know the prize doesn't exceed the pain."

"How about this? How about I get to pick what I win, but you have final approval. Does that sound like something you can get behind?"

"Only if I get to do both legs," I tell him.

He hems and haws and bounces his head around like he's trying to decide between going on the moon shuttle or jumping into a fiery volcano. He finally says, "If you can do it, I can do it."

I clap my hands together. "That's the spirit!" Then I tell him, "Come over here and sit by me."

He doesn't budge. "I want to see you do it to yourself first."

"I've been doing this for years, Teddy. You don't trust me?"

"No." I laugh at his expression.

"Fine." I lightly dust baby powder onto my calves, then I use the wooden stick that came with the kit and liberally apply an inch-wide strip of wax. I immediately press a piece of waxing cloth on that part. Once one whole calf is done, I tell him, "Now I remove the strips, and my legs will be perfectly smooth."

I rip the first one off, forcing myself not to scream a litany of vulgarities. Then I ask Teddy, "Do you want to try to pull one off?"

He's a little more excited than I think he should be, as he promptly declares, "You bet I do!" I show him how to do it, and before you know it, he's ripping one after another off my legs. The good news is that he goes fast, so there's a lot less pain for me.

Doing my own waxing causes me to go slower than I should because I know it's going to hurt.

When he's done, I pour most of the Tic Tacs directly into my mouth before saying, "It's your turn."

He actually groans when I rub baby powder on his legs. "That feels good." When the wax goes on, he adds, "It's so nice and warm." When I press the strips onto the wax, he says, "It's like a massage."

When I'm all done with both legs, I ask, "Do you want to pull your own strips, or do you want me to do it?"

"I did yours, so you can do mine," he says confidently. *The poor guy has no idea what he's in for.*

"Okay." I edge my fingernail under the first strip to get a good hold on it before asking, "Are you sure?"

"Yeah," he says assuredly, although he's starting to look a little nervous.

"I'll count to three," I warn him. "One ..." Instead of going to three though, I rip that sucker off on two. It's a technique Anna taught me. She claims it's less painful when you don't know it's coming.

Poor Teddy doesn't know what hit him. The first thing he does is jump to his feet while screaming, "Mother of GOD, that's horrible!" That's followed with, "What kind of masochistic monster came up with this torture?" Then he looks down at all the strips on his legs and looks like he's going to cry. "That can't be the only way to get these off."

"I told you it wasn't something men can handle." The truth is that his legs are way hairier than mine have ever been, and I'm a veteran of waxing, so I've built up a tolerance. I cannot begin to imagine how much pain the poor guy is in.

"Oh, I can handle it ..." He reaches down to pull off a strip on his own, but he can't quite seem to bring himself to pull it. "You do it," he says. "Go fast."

As he doesn't bring himself back toward me, I scoot in his direction. "Honestly, Teddy, if it's too much just say so."

"So there *is* another way to get these off?" He sounds so hopeful.

"No," I tell him.

"Then what good could come from me saying it's too much?" he demands angrily.

"No good for you, but I would certainly feel vindicated." He does not seem to appreciate my attempt at levity. I begin ripping one strip off after another while Teddy screams, cries out, and threatens to find and kill the person who invented waxing.

By the time I'm done, his face is pale and rivulets of sweat are running down his face. "I thought we were friends." He sounds betrayed.

"We are friends," I tell him. "Which is why I won't suggest we wax your chest."

He grabs ahold of his pecs as though protecting them. "How do you do that to yourself?"

I shrug, "It's about a tenth as expensive as having someone else do it."

"Are your legs the only place you wax?" he wants to know.

"Are you asking me if I have a Brazilian?" I tease.

"Do you?" He suddenly sounds a little too interested in the answer, so I tell him, "I also wax my mustache."

He looks at me closely. "You don't have a mustache."

"That's because I wax it," I tell him. "You want to wax my mustache?" I decide to let him extract a little revenge on me for the dirty trick I played on him. After all, I knew what he was in for and there's no way he could have guessed at the kind of agony coming his way.

He reaches up and pulls me down so that I'm practically sitting on his lap. "Yes," he says. "I'll do your mustache."

"Don't forget the baby powder first or you'll pull the skin right off my face."

He puts a small amount of baby powder in the palm of his hand and then ever so gently dabs it on my upper lip. He looks closely and says, "There's hardly anything there. Why bother?"

"Because I'm newly single and I'll never catch a man while sporting a 'stache." My tone is light, but the truth is I'm going to have to be better about my upkeep now that I'm going back into the dating pond.

"But what if the guy you fall for loves a woman with facial hair? Then you'll be doing this for nothing."

"That's a risk I'm willing to take." My face is so close to his, I could lean forward and kiss him. And boy do I want to kiss him. These last couple weeks with Teddy have been a divine torture of their own.

Teddy eventually looks away before putting a dab of wax on the stick. He ever so gently runs it across my upper lip. How this feels like an erotic experience is beyond me, but it really does. When he presses the strip to the wax, I'm ready to throw caution to the wind and profess my devotion. Thank God he chooses that moment to rip it off.

"Yow!" I jump back. "I'm going to have to put some ice on that."

"Does ice make it feel better?" Suddenly he's on his feet making a mad dash to my kitchen.

"It numbs it for sure," I tell him while following along.

After filling a plastic bowl with ice cubes, we return to the patio to start running them across our freshly waxed skin. Teddy takes two big handfuls and is rubbing them all over his legs when he says, "This isn't the most fun we've ever had together, is it?"

I shake my head. "Not even close. But the good news is that friends who wax together are friends for life." I look at him closely and ask, "Do you think we're going to be friends for life, Teddy?"

"I sure hope so, Faith. You're unlike any other woman I've ever known, and I'd hate to lose you."

While it's not a declaration of love, it's pretty darn sweet, and I'll take it.

For now, anyway.

CHAPTER TWENTY-TWO

TEDDY

When I leave Faith's after the waxing fiasco, I'm tempted to go straight down to the lake for a swim to cool off. The only thing that stops me is the thought of someone taking a picture of me and selling it to a tabloid. I couldn't care less if anyone thought I waxed my legs, but I currently look like something much worse has occurred—like I've been beaten by a pack of Lilliputians.

As I walk home, I think about how Theo keeps canceling our visits to Vista Pines. One day he had a headache, the next he's too tired. I finally sat him down at breakfast this morning and asked, "What's going on? I thought you wanted to move to an assisted living place."

He nodded his head slowly before saying, "I wanted to get the gazebo done before taking the next step."

"The offer to hire someone to come here still stands," I told him, in case that wasn't the reason.

He was quiet for ages before answering, "I need to be somewhere where your grandmother wasn't. In this house, I have the constant reminder that she's gone. I can go to Vista Pines this afternoon if you're available." I told him I was game and we could leave when I got back.

So as soon as I get home, I put on a pair of long pants and search him out. I find him sitting inside the gazebo, staring out at the water. Before I can say anything, he announces, "Abigail would have loved this. Thank you for making me finish it."

"You can come over all the time," I tell him.

He nods his head before pushing up to his feet. "I'm sure that will be nice."

I reach out and offer him my arm, "Let's go, Grandpa. We've got a new step to take."

As we're walking up the sidewalk to Vista Pines, I tell him, "It's almost like a resort." The two-story main building is flanked by two single-level wings. The grounds are heavily populated by pine trees as well as other types of greenery.

He slowly puts one foot in front of the other while leaning heavily on my arm. "So far so good." He doesn't sound overly enthused, but neither does he sound upset.

The doors open automatically as we step on the front mat that runs the length of the entrance. I lead us in the direction of the front desk.

The woman behind the glass doesn't look like she's much younger than the residents here. Her name tag says *Millie*. "Hi, Millie," I say in a friendly manner. "My grandfather and I were hoping to take a tour of your facility."

She types away at her keyboard for a moment before making eye contact and smiling brightly. "I can have Jocelyn show you around in a few minutes. You can wait over there." She points to a sofa a few feet away.

We do as she suggests and pass the time watching people come and go. Everyone seems upbeat and happy, which makes me feel better about being here. After a few minutes a woman, about my age, walks toward us. She's wearing a skirt with a short-sleeved T-shirt, and she has a bounce to her step. "Hi there! I'm Jocelyn. I hear you two are looking for a tour."

I stand up and stretch out my hand. "Hi, Jocelyn. I'm Teddy. My grandfather is interested in finding out more about your facility." It's clear by her expression that she recognizes me—darn Nick for opening his mouth—but happily, Jocelyn is very professional and doesn't say anything. Instead, she turns her attention to my grandfather.

Theo seems to perk up in her company. He stands with a bit of difficulty, but once he's on his feet, he tells her, "The name is Theo Fischer. I'm happy to meet you, Jocelyn."

Jocelyn offers him her arm. "You barely look old enough to live here." She clearly knows what to say to make her charges feel good.

My grandfather's chest puffs out proudly. "My wife died a year ago, and I think it's time to simplify." He points at me. "My grandson is going to buy my house, so I'll still have the opportunity to go visit it."

"That sounds like the best of both worlds, if you ask me," she says.

Interested in getting down to the nitty gritty, I ask, "What kind of accommodations do you offer?"

"Like most retirement facilities, we have different levels of care. We have an independent living wing that's more like apartments. They're all one bedroom, with one bath, but they have a small kitchenette which allows tenants to make their own meals if they don't want to come down to the dining room." She leans toward my grandfather like she's going to tell him a secret. "The food is so good here; people rarely cook for themselves."

"What kind of assisted living do you offer?" I ask next.

"We have two levels. One, where your medication is brought to you every day by a nurse. They'll take your blood pressure and vitals and make sure you don't have any concerns about your health. The second is for bed-bound patients. That's more along the lines of hospital care."

My grandfather smiles as he asks, "Do you call the second level, 'heaven's waiting room?'"

"We don't," Jocelyn says. "But it's kind of accurate. The truth is, once you reach the second level of care, you rarely go back to the first." I like that she's talking straight with him. It shows a degree of respect that I want for him.

"That's kind of the name of the game with nursing homes, isn't it?"

"Not at Vista Pines," she says enthusiastically. "We have some people who have been here for over fifteen years. I think they're having too much fun to die."

My grandfather squints his eyes skeptically. "What kind of fun?"

"We offer all kinds of dance and art classes. There's a bingo night, poker night, Mahjong, and canasta clubs. We have a group who play charades regularly, and we even have several book clubs, depending on the genre you like to read. Oh, and there's a pool for rehab and water aerobics."

"Huh." My grandfather doesn't appear to have any comeback. In fact, he seems intrigued.

Our tour starts at the cafeteria. "You're more than welcome to stop by here for lunch afterward. That way you'll know what you're getting into," Jocelyn says good-naturedly.

"It smells good," I tell her. And it really does. Like a combination of maple syrup and tacos. Which is an oddly enticing pairing.

After we leave the cafeteria, she shows us the social rooms. They appear to be full of happy people, which causes my grandfather to ask, "What are they all smiling about?"

"If I had to guess," she says, "I'd say not having to mow the lawn or do their own laundry."

I like that Jocelyn has a sense of humor, so I tease, "That's almost enough to make *me* want to move in."

My grandfather looks between us and orders, "You'd better not be flirting with this young lady. Don't forget about Faith."

I don't comment on his persistent optimism about my future with Faith. Instead, I tell him, "I'm not flirting. I'm just being nice."

Jocelyn doesn't seem too concerned that I'm making a play for her. "I'm married with three little ones. Trust me, if you were flirting with me, I'd never know it. My mind is too full of *my* laundry and yard work." We all share a laugh.

"Do you have any apartments available?" I want to know. Even though my grandfather said he wanted to look into assisted care, I'm thinking he just wants to be near help should he need it.

"We have two," she tells us. "They're both in the same wing."

"Is there some kind of waiting list?" Theo asks.

"We have quite a list for assisted care, but not for the apartments. The good news is that once you have an apartment, should you need assisted care, you'll get bumped to the front of the line."

Jocelyn smiles and waves to several tenants as she leads the way down one of the residential hallways. She stops at room #114 and pulls out the key. Before she can even open the door, Theo says, "I'll take this one."

"Don't you want to see it first?" Jocelyn asks.

"Of course I want to see it, but this is the apartment I want." His eyes fill with tears as he explains, "My wedding anniversary is on November fourth."

"That's a sign if I ever heard one," Jocelyn says. "Your wife didn't happen to love hydrangeas, did she?"

"They were her favorite flower," I volunteer. "Why?"

"The patio off this apartment is surrounded by hydrangea bushes. The palest lilac and the lightest pink."

She leads the way into a snug but delightful space. Everything appears fresh and clean, and there's no sense that it ever belonged to anyone else.

Jocelyn says, "We paint between tenants, and re-carpet every five years whether it needs it or not. We want everyone to feel like their apartment is theirs, so we don't have them furnished, but we do have some beds and dressers if you prefer not to bring anything."

While my grandfather looks around, I iron out the details with Jocelyn. After finding out the prices, I tell her, "I'll talk to my grandfather, but I'd like to make sure he gets this apartment. I'll give you whatever kind of deposit you need."

When I look around for Theo, I find him standing at the railing on the patio. It's small but certainly big enough for a table and a couple of chairs. "Penny for your thoughts," I say.

"I'm thinking that your grandmother would like it here. I can almost feel her."

"That, and the apartment number being the same as your wedding date, makes me think we should sign you up." As I'm still not ready for him to leave the house, I add, "We can move you in slowly."

He nods his head. "Okay, let's do it."

And just like that, my grandfather enters a new phase of life that both relieves me—that he isn't alone—but also makes me sad. Hopefully, he'll be like the tenants Jocelyn told us about. The ones who are having too much fun to die.

CHAPTER TWENTY-THREE

FAITH

Two days before Anna's wedding, I tell her, "I can't believe I'm going to admit this to you, but I'm starting to have feelings for Teddy."

"What kind of feelings?" she asks as she inspects a bouquet of pale pink peonies. We're shopping for flowers for her rehearsal BBQ.

"I like him," I tell her plainly.

"I like him, too." She's missing the point entirely.

"No, Anna, I like him, like him."

She puts the flowers down and turns to face me. "Like you want to jump his bones?"

"Shhh." I look to see if anyone in the florist shop heard her. Surprisingly, they don't seem to have noticed. "Yes, Anna. I want to jump his bones. Now, please keep your voice down."

"Oh, Faithy, no. I thought you learned your lesson with Trevor in college."

"Yes." I can't keep the snippy tone out of my voice. "But I didn't know Trevor was gay so you can't hold that over my head."

"But you know Teddy is," she reminds me.

I tip my chin up until I'm looking up at the ceiling. "He's just so nice, and caring, and helpful ..."

"And smokin' hot ..." Anna contributes.

"Why can't he just be straight?" I moan.

"Because then he probably wouldn't be so nice and caring and helpful. I know we're all supposed to be so enlightened now and no longer give credence to the stereotype of gay bestie—rest in pieces, *My Best Friend's Wedding.*" She's referencing the giant back-lash one of our favorite rom-coms was subjected to.

I agree with her. "The stereotypes exist for a reason. And regardless of what people say, it's my profound opinion that gay men make fabulous girlfriends."

"Amen, sister!" Anna raises her hands for a fist bump.

"You should see how Teddy dances." And just like that I'm back to my favorite topic. "He picks me up like I don't weigh anything at all."

Anna points to the peony bucket while calling out to the sales-clerk, "I need ten individual vases of these with five peonies each." Then she tells me, "Maybe you just think you like him because you need a boost after Ass Turd."

"Is that really what you think, Professor Freud?" Sarcasm oozes out of me. "Obviously that's what's going on."

"You know what my mom always says." She holds up a finger like the mother of all great advice is forthcoming. "The best way to get over one man is to get under another." She shrugs her eyebrows up and down for comedic effect.

"That sounds like something GG would say, and I'm not going to be getting under anyone for a very long time." I add, "But truthfully, Teddy has really gotten my mind off Astor. I barely think about the breakup anymore."

"I don't think Astor is having the same success," she says mysteriously. "According to Chris, he's full of questions about you and your new boyfriend."

"What an egomaniac," I practically yell. "He doesn't want me, but can't stand the idea of anyone else having me either. What did I ever see in that guy?"

Anna opens the shop door for us to leave while remarking, "Astor has some decent qualities if you're willing to look over the fact that he's a stuck-up cheater. Which, as of a few weeks ago, it seemed like you were willing to do." She gives me a pointed look.

"Not anymore," I assure her. "I'm now on the lookout for a straight man who treats me like Teddy does." I release a long sigh. "I'll probably still be single in fifty years."

"Maybe you two could be friends without benefits." She laughs at her poor attempt at a joke.

"You mean like we already are?" I don't let her answer before asking, "When does Astor get into town?"

"Tomorrow morning. He and Tiffany are staying at the Trout Lodge." She doesn't even try to suppress her giggle.

"Ew, why there?" No one stays at the Trout Lodge who isn't in town to fish. The whole place smells sketchy.

"Because Astor planned to stay with you and the only vacancy in town is at the Trout Lodge."

"That ought to be romantic," I joke. "Can you imagine the look on his face when he checks in?"

"Can you imagine the look on Tiffany's?" She barks with laughter. "I think karma is going right to work on Astor Hill."

"Let's hope he's smart enough to realize it."

When we reach the corner, Anna says, "I'm going to the church to make sure everything is ready. You want to come along?"

"I can't," I tell her. "I'm meeting Teddy at Madame Bernadette's to put the finishing touches on our dance."

"You two should be ready to turn pro by now," she jokes.

I shrug with one shoulder. "Just because I'm over Astor doesn't mean I don't want to rub his nose in what he's missing. And to do that, Teddy and I need to tear it up on the dance floor."

"I'm just worried about that tender heart of yours," she says.

"Me too. But Teddy leaves in a few weeks for Canada. I figure if I can make it until then, I can convince myself to stop falling in love with him."

"I thought he was staying for the whole summer," Anna says.

"He'll only be gone for a week and then he's coming back."

"I'll get busy putting together a list of guys I think might be good for you. Hopefully, by the time he's back you'll have focused your attention elsewhere."

I want to beg her not to try to set me up, but she might be onto something. "Fine," I tell her, "but no lawyers. I'm done with lawyers. And no one in Chicago. I'm not commuting for love ever again."

"Yes, ma'am," she says with a salute. "I need to hustle. I'll see you later this afternoon when we pick up our dresses."

"If my dress doesn't fit, I'll fast until the wedding," I promise.

"I'm not worried about the dress, Faithy, just about my best friend who will be wearing it."

After we hug goodbye, she goes her way and I go mine. As I walk along the park, the little hairs on my arm stand at attention, like that premonition of doom returning. *Not this again.*

The very last thing I need right now is bad energy.

Teddy and I nail our rehearsal. Not only does he flip me over his head in a split lift, but we've added two twirls and three dips. We could totally win the Mirrorball trophy with this performance. Teddy's only complaint was that his legs were still on fire and that he's pretty sure I removed a couple layers of skin during the waxing. I told him he was lucky he didn't aspire to be a drag queen because he'd never make it.

After our rehearsal is over, he walks me to Bride's Paradise. When we stop out front, he asks, "Can I come in and see the dress?"

"No way!" I tell him. "Haven't you heard that it's bad luck to see the maid of honor's dress before the wedding?"

"I heard it was the bride's dress," he says. "But now that you mention it, I suppose the maid of honor is equally important."

"Darn straight she is." I give him a friendly hug goodbye before walking into the dress shop.

Missy Corner calls out, "She's in the back, Faith."

"Thanks, Missy." I look closely at my old classmate and realize she's looking kind of rough—like she hasn't had a good night's sleep in a while. Missy was cute in high school, but things appear to be taking a turn. Her dress is matronly, and her hair looks kind of dull. I stop at the closest mirror to give myself a once over. I don't know if I'm just in denial, but I still think I look pretty good.

As I walk back into the changing rooms, I call out to Anna, "Where are you?"

"Back here!" I follow the sound of her voice to the curtained area at the end of the corridor.

"I'm ready to find out if I still fit into my dress." I sound about as excited as I feel. I'll probably have to buy Spanx in two sizes. The first as an under-layer to suck me in enough to get the smaller pair on. I won't be able to breathe or eat, but I suppose that's the price I'll have to pay for my folly.

Anna pulls aside the curtain. "It's in here. I'll come out while you change." She emerges in her formfitting mermaid tail dress with the keyhole neckline.

I release a low whistle. "You look like a million bucks!" And she does. The fabric is barely off-white which makes her skin positively glow. "Seriously, Anna, you've never looked more beautiful."

She scoots me toward the changing stall. "You're going to look beautiful, too. Go."

Why didn't I get a larger size dress? Of course, I didn't expect Astor to dump me right before the wedding. After putting my purse on a hook, I turn around but my dress isn't there. Instead, there's one that's the same color but not the same design. This one is a silvery chiffon with a form-fitting bodice and flowing tea-length skirt.

"Where's my dress?" I call out to Anna.

"Surprise!" Anna throws the curtain back. "I figured you'd be hard-pressed to waltz in the other one so I asked Missy to find something else that still looks like it belongs with the rest of the wedding party."

I've been so preoccupied with worry about fitting into the sheath, I hadn't even considered the functionality of it. There would be no split lift in that without my whole dress splitting. I hold the new gown up in front of me in the mirror. "You're the best, Anna. You think of everything."

"Just imagine spinning around the dance floor in this! You'd better wear some nice underwear because I'm guessing this skirt is going to fly up." She claps her hands together enthusiastically.

I hurry to slip off my shorts and t-shirt before putting my new dress on. Once it's over my head, Anna zips it up the back. "It's a tiny bit big," I tell her. "How is that even possible?"

"I got it in a size up. I didn't want you to feel uncomfortable."

Missy calls out, "I still have time to take it in if you want." That girl must have bionic hearing.

"Let me walk around in it a bit," I tell her.

Missy's eyes bug out when she gets a load of me. "Oh, Faith, you look gorgeous. Really. This one is so much more your style than the other."

I watch my reflection as I glide down the short aisle that leads to the large trifold mirrors. I'm so stunning, I'm speechless. As though reading my mind, Anna says, "Wait until your hair and makeup are done. Astor won't be able to keep his eyes off you and Tiffany is going to want to rip your hair out."

I briefly wonder what Teddy will think, but I don't say anything. While my fondest wish can never come true, my runner-up dream is that he'll use all his acting skills and pretend to be blown away by my gorgeousness.

I'm not yet ready to take the dress off, so I walk out of the changing room and spin around the store a few times. Then I sit down on a stuffed pincushion seat to see how it feels. "I don't think I want it taken in, Missy."

"It looks perfect just the way it is," Anna says before suggesting, "Being that you aren't going to have it altered, what do you say we go out for an ice cream cone?"

My eyes open excitedly at the prospect. "I have always found rum raisin to be a cure-all for whatever ails me."

"That's exactly how I feel about peanut butter fudge." She takes me by the hand and pulls me back into the changing room. "Maybe we can have an early dinner afterwards."

"Now you're talking." I change in record time, suddenly feeling very optimistic about the weekend ahead. Who knows? I might even have a great time.

As Anna and I walk out onto Main Street, I tell her, "You're the best friend a girl could ever hope to have, do you know that?"

She nods smugly. "It's true, I am." Then she reaches out and takes my hand. "But so are you, Faithy. I don't know what my life would have been without you, but I guarantee it wouldn't even be close to as great as it is now."

"I'm glad you're not moving back to Chicago," I tell her.

"No chance. You and I are small-town girls. We were made in Elk Lake, and we're meant to live here always."

My cell phone rings as we approach the Purple Cow. I check caller ID and see it's Teddy. "Hey, you. Want to join me and Anna for an ice cream cone? We just got done with our fitting."

Instead of answering my questions, he says, "Faith, my grandfather has fallen. The ambulance just came and took him to the hospital. I'm going to follow behind."

I stop dead in my tracks. "What? No! I'll come too."

"What happened?" Anna demands.

I whisper, "Teddy's grandfather fell. He's on his way to the hospital."

Anna turns around and starts walking back to our cars.

"Don't come yet," Teddy says. "They're not going to let you

back with him, and we don't know the extent of his injuries. There's no point in sitting in the waiting room doing nothing when you can be enjoying an ice cream cone." I hear the door on his SUV slam shut.

"I could be there in case you need anything. You know, like a cup of coffee or a bagel or something."

"I'm grateful for the offer, but you go ahead with your plans, and I'll keep you posted."

"If you're sure ..." I really feel like I should be at the hospital, but I don't want to be pushy.

"I'm sure," he says. "I'll call you as soon as I know something."

"The very second you know." I turn back toward the Purple Cow.

"Will do." He hangs up before I can say anything else.

"You're not going to the hospital?" Anna wants to know.

"Teddy doesn't want me to. He says they won't let me see Theo, so I might as well eat ice cream."

"He makes a good point."

We start to move toward our original destination when I once again stop dead in my tracks. "Anna ..."

When I don't finish my sentence right away, she prompts, "What?"

"What if Teddy can't come to the wedding?"

"Why wouldn't he be able to come?"

"What if Theo is hurt badly and Teddy needs to stay with him?"

Opening the door of the ice cream parlor, my best friends says, "Let's not burn that bridge before we come to it. I'm sure Theo will be fine."

Of course, that's my hope as well. Not only because I like Theo and I hate the idea of him being hurt, but my deep-down selfishness can't stand the thought of seeing Astor without my new friend by my side.

I offer up a silent prayer. *Please, God, let Theo be okay. I know it's* not a very Christian sentiment, but I've got some vengeance to deliver, and I need Teddy's help.

CHAPTER TWENTY-FOUR

TEDDY

As soon as I get out of the car at the emergency room parking lot, I realize I've parked like I'm drunk. I'm tempted to get back in and do a better job, but I'm technically in the lines, so I don't. Instead, I run to the ambulance entrance to look for my grandfather. I make it just in time to follow him in.

Keeping pace with the EMT, I ask, "How's he doing?"

"He's definitely broken something. They'll have to do some x-rays to know the extent of the damage."

"How are you doing, Grandpa?" I ask him. "Can I get you anything?"

"How about a fifth of bourbon and a bottle of pills?" His mouth is contorted in pain. "Those damns steps. I told your grandmother one of us was going to fall down them and kill ourselves."

"The good news is you didn't die." I pat him on the arm in what I hope is a comforting manner. I've clearly missed the mark as he slaps my hand away.

"That's good news?" he demands. "Good news would have been death on impact, then I wouldn't have to go through whatever hellish healing process is ahead of me." He looks up at the EMT. "Can't you just push this thing into oncoming traffic and be done with it?"

"Sorry, sir, that would go against my job description."

As soon as we enter the hospital, a pair of double doors flies open, and my grandfather is wheeled into the triage area. The EMT waits for a doctor to arrive before wishing Theo good health and taking off.

The doctor, who is a slightly built Chinese woman, approaches my grandfather's side. While picking up the notes left by the EMT, she says, "I'm Dr. Wang, Mr. Fischer. Can you tell me what happened?"

"I fell down the damn stairs," he grumbles. "I'm pretty sure I've broken everything from the waist down, but my left elbow is pretty banged up too."

She turns to me and asks, "Are you related to Mr. Fischer?"

Nodding my head, I tell her, "I'm his grandson, Teddy Helms." It doesn't occur to me to lie about my name here.

"My son is a big fan," she says, not sounding all that impressed on her own behalf. "Were you with your grandfather when he fell?"

"I'd just walked through the back door when it happened. It sounded like the whole house was falling down."

I answer a few more questions before she announces, "We're going to need several X-rays before we know the full extent of his injuries."

"Will you admit him?" I want to know.

"Most definitely. We wouldn't send a man of Theodore's age home to recoup. When he leaves here, he'll most likely go to a rehab facility."

"I just signed him up at Vista Pines a couple of weeks ago," I tell her. "He hasn't moved into his apartment yet, but it's all his."

She nods her head. "They're a great facility." Then she turns and smiles at Theo. "Mr. Fischer, the radiology tech will be here in a couple of minutes. You hang tight, okay?"

"I'm hardly going to get up and leave." He seems to think better of his surly mood because he forces a smile and asks, "Can I please get something for the pain?"

"You bet," she tells him. "I'll have the nurse come in and give you something to take the edge off. We need to wait until we know the full extent of your injuries before we do more than that."

"I'll take whatever I can get," he says. "And thank you." In this moment, my grandfather looks like a scared old man, and it's breaking my heart. He was with me on three different trips to the emergency room when I was a kid. Once, when I dove off the dock and landed on a large rock. That one gave me a concussion. Then there was the time when I nearly cut my thumb off gutting a fish, and finally, after I kicked myself in the head with a water ski. That required some acrobatics I wasn't trained for. It also resulted in twenty stitches.

I pull a chair over to the side of his bed and sit down. Taking his hand, I say, "I'll be here with you the whole time. Don't worry about anything."

With a squeeze, he says, "I'm sorry if I'm being a bear. I'm just not feeling too good right now."

"Thank goodness we got you into Vista Pines, huh? According to Jocelyn, you get moved up to a priority spot with assisted care."

He nods his head. "I'm glad you're here. I can't even imagine what would have happened to me if I'd been on my own. They probably would have found me in a couple months all decaying and ..."

"I was there," I interrupt him. "And you're going to be fine, I promise."

When the radiology tech arrives, I ask if I can go with them, but that apparently isn't allowed. Grandpa says, "Go get a cup of coffee or something. I'll meet you back here when I'm done."

As he's pushed away, I feel a tightening in my chest. It's a combination of fear, anger, and relief. Fear, that I could have lost him; anger that he's getting older and frailer and there's nothing I can do about it; and finally, relief that I was there to help. I'm starting to think I'm going to need to spend as much time here as possible, even if that means leaving my home in California unoccupied. At the moment, I can't even see myself going back there.

After leaving the emergency room, I follow the signs to the cafeteria. Taking my phone out of my pocket, I call Faith. "Hey."

"How is he?" She sounds breathless with worry.

"I don't know. They've just taken him for x-rays. He's really shaken up, though."

"I bet!"

I wish I'd told Faith to come to the hospital. I'd really love to see her face. "Are you still at the Purple Cow?"

"Nope. I'm standing out front of the hospital with ice cream for you."

"Seriously?" A smile overtakes my face, and my heart starts to beat in overtime.

"I know you told me not to come, but I couldn't stay away. I can leave after I give you your ice cream, if you want." She sounds nervous that I'm going to send her packing.

"I'll meet you at the front entrance," I tell her while retracing my steps. Having Faith here feels like the right thing. In fact, I was tempted to drive by the Purple Cow and pick her up on my way, but I didn't want my grandfather to be kept waiting on his own.

When I see her, she's practically running through the waiting room doors. I open my arms wide and meet her halfway. Then like we're in some big rom-com movie, I pick her up, hugging her tightly. "Thank you for coming."

"I know you said not to ..."

"Forget what I said. I'm glad you're here. Thank you."

When I finally put her down, I notice the bag she's carrying. "How much ice cream did you bring?"

"Enough for a small army." She reaches into the bag and pulls out an ice cream scoop. "They packed it in cartons and gave me the cones on the side. That way everything would stay frozen longer."

I take the bag from her and then instinctively hold her hand. "Come on, I'll take you back there."

As I lead her through the hospital, I feel a very definite shift in how I view Faith. Yes, she's vulnerable from her recent breakup, and yes, I claim to not be interested in dating. But right now, I'm very interested in dating Faith.

All I have to do is figure out how to tell her that I'm not the gay man she thinks I am. I suddenly have an idea.

CHAPTER TWENTY-FIVE

FAITH

Having Teddy hug me made me feel like I was the most important person in the whole world to him. Holding his hand makes me feel like I'm sitting in a hot fudge whirlpool—warm, sweet, and utterly decadent.

As we walk down the hallway toward the emergency room, he says, "Theo probably won't be coming back to the house to live. Dr. Wang said he'll need rehab first, and after that, he'll most likely move right into his apartment at Vista Pines."

Even though I can feel the angst radiating off him, I say, "Thank goodness you got him in there. I know this is hard, Teddy. I've been there with my own grandmother, and it was really scary. But honestly, it's the best thing for them. Vista Pines certainly gave GG a second chance at enjoying life."

He inhales deeply but doesn't speak until after he blows his breath out. "It's weird that we're the ones taking care of our grandparents, and not our parents."

"My grandmother would go insane if my parents were still here. They didn't see eye to eye on most things which led to a definite power struggle. GG and I don't have that because obviously, I know my place and treat her like the queen she is."

"I guess I can see that," he says. "My mom was close with both of my grandparents, but she still works, so I can't really see her uprooting her life to move to Wisconsin."

"What does she do?" I ask.

"She owns an art gallery in Scottsdale. She used to sell a lot of my grandmother's paintings when she was alive." He pushes the large button that opens the double doors leading into the emergency wing.

"I didn't know your grandmother was a professional artist. You have quite a lineage, don't you?"

"I guess you could say that, but for me, it's just been my life, you know?"

The doctor is standing next to Theo's gurney when we walk in. "That was fast," Teddy says.

Consulting the chart in her hand, she relays, "Your grandfather broke his hip, so he'll be in the hospital for quite a while. The ball-joint was damaged, so he's going to need a full hip-replacement. The nurse just gave him a heavy-duty IV for pain which should hold him well into the night."

Theo opens his eyes and glances around the doctor. "Faith, you came."

"Of course I did, Theo. There's no way I was going to leave you in the hospital without some ice cream."

He waves his hand in front of him. "Give it to the nurses. It's been my experience that bribery is the way to go when you want people to pay attention to you."

"When have you ever had to bribe anyone?" Teddy asks, while walking toward his grandfather's gurney.

"I think the better question is, when haven't I?" His head relaxes to the side and it's clear he's gone to sleep.

"Can we go up to his room with him?" Teddy asks the doctor.

"Sure, but it's going to take us a few minutes to get him

settled. He's going to be in room 219 if you want to meet us up there in thirty minutes or so."

I have the feeling Teddy doesn't want to leave Theo's side. "Why don't we go sit in the waiting room and you can have some ice-cream?" I suggest.

"Why don't we send it up with Theo for his nurses?"

"Fine by me." I stand up and put the bag on the gurney next to Theo's feet. I ask the transport guy who just came in, "Could you tell Mr. Fischer's nurses this is for them?"

He nods his head once while releasing the brakes on Theo's bed. We follow them into the hallway, staying a short distance behind. "Depending on when surgery is," Teddy says, "I may have to miss Anna's rehearsal dinner." I'm guessing he sounds sad because of Theo and not because he's possibly missing an opportunity to eat his weight in BBQ bass.

"You can miss the wedding too if you need to," I tell him. "I mean it. Nothing is more important than Theo right now."

"And leave you on your own with Astor and Tiffany? I don't think so." He reaches out to take my hand again.

Tingles of awareness start a slow crawl up my arm. It's hot and prickly at first, leaving a trail of numbness in its wake. *Wait, am I having a stroke?* "When are you leaving for Canada again?" I ask, hoping to shake off this delicious attraction that keeps building. The sooner I get a break from Teddy, the sooner I can come to my senses and accept that nothing of a romantic nature can ever happen between us.

"Two weeks, why? Looking forward to getting rid of me?" He nudges me with his shoulder, causing another jolt of electricity. It's like I'm Ben Franklin holding a key up to a stormy sky and Teddy is the bolt of lightning.

"Don't be silly. I was just wondering."

There's not room for all of us, so Teddy and I wait for the next elevator.

I'm leaning slightly against his arm when I see Reba Simms a short distance away. Reba was the queen of the gossip mill in high school. "Faith, is that you?" she asks while picking up her pace to an outright trot.

"Hey, Reba." I wave with my free hand. "What are you doing here?"

"My mom is having some varicose veins tied off." She rolls her eyes before zoning her attention on Teddy. She looks at him like he's the first watermelon slushy of the season. "Hello, there ..."

"Hi." Teddy appears to be amused by her behavior.

"Reba," I say. "This is my friend Teddy."

She takes a step toward him, which has him taking a step back. "I heard you were in town." Her eyes glance down to where Teddy's and my hands are entwined before she looks up in shock. "You're dating Teddy Helms, Faith? When did this happen?"

"We're just friends ..." I start to say but Teddy interrupts me.

"We've been seeing each other since I came to town last month."

"What about that guy you were seeing from Chicago?" she demands. "I thought the two of you were on the verge of getting engaged."

"We broke up." I'm not about to tell her that Astor was cheating on me. She'd probably buy a Mr. Microphone and drive around town sharing the news. So I tell her, "He worked so much, I just didn't feel like he was making us a priority."

Reba looks confused. "But Teddy must work all the time. Plus, he lives in LA. I'm assuming ..." She looks at him for clarification.

"My grandfather lives in Elk Lake, and I plan on spending a lot of time here." He squeezes my hand.

"Wow," Reba says. "I mean, that's great, but wow. Elk Lake isn't exactly known as a hotbed of celebrities."

"Teddy's grandfather was just taken to his room," I tell her. "We should get going."

Reba pulls out her phone and practically jumps on Teddy. "Can I get a quick selfie first?"

"Um, yeah, sure. I guess." I can't imagine how uncomfortable it is having people constantly demand your attention like this.

Reba steps between me and Teddy and then boldly pushes me off to the side. I stumble before grabbing the wall to right myself. "Don't mind me ..." I mutter angrily.

"Sorry, Faith, but you know how it is." Throwing one arm around Teddy, she begins to fire off a series of shots. The first couple are pretty tame, but as she maneuvers around, she gets so close to him, she's practically on top of him.

"That's enough, Reba." I reach out to take Teddy's arm, but she's not having any of it.

"I'm not done."

She attempts to push me again, but Teddy intervenes. "We really do need to get going. It was nice meeting you, Reba." *As nice as showing up on the first day of school stark naked with braces and a shaved head—why was that always a recurring dream for me?*

Luckily the elevator door opens on cue. As we walk in, Reba tries to join us, but Teddy tells her, "We'd like some privacy, if you don't mind."

The look on her face is one of shock and awe, and not a small dose of irritation. *What in the world does she have to be annoyed about?* When the doors close, I tell him, "You shouldn't have told her we were seeing each other."

"Why?"

"Because I'm pretty sure she's about to share that news with everyone she's ever met."

"Nick is already telling everyone I'm in town. What could it possibly hurt for them to think we're dating, too?"

I offer a slight shrug. "It's one thing to have a Chicago lawyer break up with me, but I promise you it will be another thing entirely to have a movie star break up with me. People will really think I'm pitiful."

"Who says I'm breaking up with you?" he asks coyly.

"Teddy ..." My tone is full of warning.

"Seriously, what if you break my heart? Then all of Elk Lake will think you're the biggest catch in town."

"They'll think I'm a lunatic, is what they'll think," I murmur.

"What's that?" He leans his head down so that his ear is right in front of my mouth. I'm tempted to bite it.

"Nothing," I tell him.

When we get off the elevator on the second floor, we make quick work of finding Theo's room. A nurse meets us outside of the door. "We're just going to help Mr. Fischer into a hospital gown and into bed. We'll let you know when you can come in."

"Do you want to go sit in the waiting room?" I ask.

Teddy shakes his head. "Let's just wait here."

Life is such a vulnerable business. I wonder how it's possible that more of us don't go insane. How in the world do people get through the loss of parents, siblings or, God forbid, children? Right now, I'm not sure I ever want to put myself in another situation of being vulnerable. Maybe I should just join a convent and call it quits on men entirely.

But then I look up at Teddy and that idea slips away as easily as a ripe banana peel.

CHAPTER TWENTY-SIX

TEDDY

Faith stays at the hospital with me for two hours when I finally tell her, "There's nothing you can do here. Why don't you go home and enjoy the rest of the day?"

She looks at her watch quickly before answering, "I am supposed to help Anna set up tables for the rehearsal dinner tomorrow. But I don't want to leave you."

"Go. I'm probably not going to stay much longer, either. Theo is so out of it from the pain meds, he'll probably sleep through the rest of the day and night. They won't do surgery for another day or two."

Faith stands up and stretches, causing my eyes to linger at her midriff where her t-shirt rides up. *What a perv, huh?* "Call me if you need anything."

"I will." She gives me a quick hug before walking out the door. It's all I can do not to call her back and beg her to stay, but that would be ridiculous.

I'm about to sit back down and close my eyes when my phone rings. It's Terri. "Hey, what's up?"

"Who cares what's up with me? What's up with you? I hear Theo is in the hospital."

"How in the world do you know that already?" I ask.

"I've been fending off phone calls from reporters for the last half hour. It seems a photo of you and some girl named Reba is in the process of going viral."

Absently scratching my head with my free hand, I ask, "Why would anyone care that I'm in a hospital in Wisconsin?"

"The caption on the photo this girl posted to social media reads, 'Hanging with my sweetheart Teddy at Elk Lake Hospital, while we wait to hear the news …' All of Instagram and Twitter are speculating that you're dying."

"How in the world could they have gotten that from what Reba said? Also, she's not my sweetheart."

"I figured that, dummy. If she was your special lady, her name would have been Faith."

I don't take the bait.

"If that's what the photo said, how did you find out about Theo?" I ask.

"I made an educated guess it had something to do with him, so I called the hospital and asked for his room number. When they gave it to me, I realized I'd hit the nail on the head."

"He fell down the stairs," I tell her. "God, Terri, it was so scary. By the time I got to him, I thought he was dead."

"What are his injuries?"

"A broken hip and two broken ribs. He's going to need a hip replacement."

"Well, thank goodness that's all it is," she says. "Meanwhile, I have a slew of reporters wanting to know the scoop. What do you want me to tell them?"

"The truth, I guess. Tell them I'm hanging out to make sure he's okay."

"They'll find you now, you know?"

"At least I had a few weeks of anonymity." I think about the scene at Rosemary's Bakery and realize that's about to play out again and again. While viral photos are everyone's dream publicity, this one is going to be more of a nightmare for me.

"Tell Theo hello for me," Terri says. "I'll send him some of those cookies he liked so much when he came out for the *Alpha Dog* premiere."

"I'm sure he'll love that." Before she hangs up, I say, "Terri …"

"Yes, Teddy?"

"Thanks for being my friend." Most actors have agents who will do everything in their power to make sure their clients' names stay in the press—which often includes making up rumors about them and then tipping off the media themselves. While Terri encourages me to show up at different events, she respects my need for privacy.

"I'll always be your friend. Now let me go so I can feed the vultures while simultaneously requesting they give you your space."

"Love you," I tell her.

"Of course you do. I'll call later to see if there's any update."

After hanging up, I open my phone and type my name into a search engine. The photo Reba posted was not one I would have ever chosen. It's one of those mid-expression shots where I look like I've been partying for a week and am about to throw up. She appears to be comforting me by way of wrapping her limbs around me like a boa constrictor.

I send Faith a quick text.

Me: *Your friend Reba just outed me to the world.*

Faith: *She told everyone you're gay? How did she know? OMG, she probably thought you'd have to be gay to be seen with me. That bitch.*

Me: *She didn't tell people I was gay, she told them I was at the Elk Lake Hospital.*

*Faith: Oh. Well, how bad could that be? I mean Nick has already
told the whole town you're here.*

Before I can respond, there's a knock on the door and a nurse
pops her head in. "Mr. Helms?"

"Yes." I put my phone in my pocket.

"There's a bit of excitement going on downstairs. We were
hoping you might address it."

She doesn't have to spell it out. The press has found me.
"Sure," I tell her. "I'll head down in just a few minutes."

"Thank you, and I'm sorry to ask it of you, but we're just a
small-town hospital and we simply aren't equipped to deal with
press matters."

I nod my head. "I understand."

Picking up my phone, I text Faith back.

*Me: Can you please meet me at the hospital and bring some kind
of disguise so I can get out of here without being seen?*

Faith: Sure. Where will you be?

*Me: I think it will be safest for you to meet me in Theo's room.
That way we can leave together, and you can become part of my
disguise.*

Faith: I'll be there in 30.

After putting my phone away, I look into the mirror and brush
my fingers through my hair in hopes of looking more presentable.

On my way down to the lobby, I try to imagine how big the
scene is. Surely no one from Chicago or farther away has had time
to get here.

When the elevator doors open, I'm bombarded by flashes of
light, making me realize things are worse than I had thought.

"Teddy!" a man in a seersucker suit calls out. "Are you sick?"

Someone else wants to know, "How long are you going to be staying in Elk Lake?"

I raise my hand and push my way through the throng of people. There aren't more than thirty of them, but that's probably way more than this hospital has ever seen.

"Follow me outside." I lead the way like a mother duck with a string of ducklings trailing behind.

Once everyone is on the sidewalk, I speak loudly. "My grandfather took a fall and I'm in town for a short while to make sure he's okay."

A young girl calls out, "Melissa Shakes from the Elk Lake High School *Tribune*. Are you going to be doing any more films for Wonder?"

That's when I take a closer look at my audience and realize most of them are kids and not real reporters at all. *Look at me, thinking I'm all that.* "Yes, I am, Melissa. I've signed on to do another film with them, but I don't have all the details yet."

A slightly older boy steps forward and wants to know, "Is it true you're dating Reba Simms? I mean, she's hot and all, but how in the world did you meet her?"

"I'm not dating Reba Simms," I tell him. "I was with a friend when Miss Simms asked if I would take a selfie with her. I just met her today and only for a few minutes."

"I told you!" a girl in the back shouts. "Reba is a total liar!"

"My sister doesn't lie!" comes a quick retort.

"Who's your friend?" another voice calls out.

"I'm going to keep that to myself for now," I tell them. "I'd appreciate it if you all would give me some space while I'm at the hospital. I know the staff doesn't need any disruptions while they're trying to take care of patients."

Walking back into the building, I have to laugh at myself that I thought there was a mob of serious reporters stalking me. I've only made one big film, and in today's world that's not such a big deal.

The only people who care that I'm in Elk Lake appear to be teenagers and Reba Simms. And maybe Faith, too. I hope.

CHAPTER TWENTY-SEVEN

FAITH

"Teddy is being stalked by the press at the hospital," I tell Anna while putting a wooden wedge under a table leg to balance it.

"What press? You mean, Vonnie Shepard at the *Gazette*?" Elk Lake's gossip columnist has gotten in trouble more than once for some shady reporting. Like the time she suggested Jeanie Coolage from the Permanent Wave was using straight bleach to color people's hair. Jeanie sued for slander and the *Gazette* had to pony up a thousand dollars in damages. Ever since then, Vonnie's column has been rather brief.

"I don't know if Vonnie's part of the problem." I pull a hair tie out of my pocket and make quick work of assembling my hair into a makeshift bun. It's only June and already the mugginess of summer has made the air feel swampy. "Teddy wants me to bring him a disguise so he can get out of the hospital unnoticed."

"What kind of disguise?" Anna sits down on one of the folding chairs. It's on a slant, much like the table, which causes her to tip over onto the ground. I reach out to help her up, but she pulls me down with her.

Growing up hasn't quashed any of my friend's playful impulsiveness. "I need to go," I tell her as I roll on the ground. "I have no idea where I'm going to get a costume though."

"I think my parents have an old Chucky one in the basement from when we were kids."

"And that would help him stay under the radar, how?"

Sitting up, she says, "He doesn't have to wear the wig or carry the knife. He could just wear the striped shirt and overalls and look like a giant toddler." She cocks an eyebrow before adding, "Badum bum."

That's when an idea hits me. "Does your mom still have that old reggae wig she wore that time for Halloween?"

"The one with the crocheted Rasta hat?" She tips her head to the side and thinks for a moment. "I think so. You want him to wear that? He'll look sketchy."

"He will not. He'll just look like a white guy with a seriously misguided sense of fashion."

Anna sticks out her hand for me to help her up. Once she's on her feet, she asks, "Do you want one of my mom's hippy skirts to go with it?"

"Sure," I tell her. I'm not necessarily suggesting Teddy wear drag, but if he's serious about not being recognized, that might not be a bad idea.

Once I'm loaded down with an odd array of clothing—Anna added an old pair of her dad's fishing overalls in case Teddy wanted to go in that direction—I head out to my car.

"Can you believe I'm only going to be single for two more days?" She seems to regret saying that because she follows it up with, "I'm sorry."

"Why?" I demand. "You're getting married. You should be excited. Heck, I'm over the moon for you!" I reach out to give her a one-armed hug.

"I could just shoot Astor," she groans. "What kind of best man pulls a dumbass stunt like this right before their best friend's wedding?"

"In his defense," I say. "he wasn't planning on telling me until after the wedding. It's my fault things went down the way they did."

Anna stops walking and jabs her pointer finger at me. "Don't you dare take responsibility for this."

"I'm not taking responsibility for his cheating," I tell her. "Just for him telling me about it with such craptacular timing."

Opening my car door, I throw the armload of disguise paraphernalia onto the back seat. Then I pop the trunk to get an old shopping bag to put everything into. No sense walking into the hospital advertising that we're trying to pull one over on people. When everything is packed, I turn around and tell my best friend, "We're going to have a great weekend, and we aren't going to let Astor ruin anything."

She walks into my arms and lays her head on my shoulder. "You'll still be next," she says. "Once Chris and I get back from Paris, I'm going to make it my mission to find your perfect guy."

I give her a tight squeeze before releasing her. "As you're kind of responsible for Astor, I'm gonna take a pass."

"But you already told me I could make a list." When I don't respond right away, she reminds me, "The other day when we were talking about how you might be falling for Teddy ..."

"Oh, that. Fine," I tell her. "You can make a list, but I'll pick the names that interest me." *I really do have to stop thinking about Teddy as a possible candidate for my heart.*

On the way to the hospital, I turn on the radio. Dawn's favorite song from her teenage years comes on—Midnight Oil's "Beds are Burning." She used to get Anna and me to dance to it with her when we were in kindergarten. We'd stand out in their backyard with our arms straight out to our sides. When she'd hit play on her portable CD player, we'd all spin around like we were pretending to be flying airplanes. I dream of us doing that with our kids—with Dawn at the helm, of course.

There's no crowd of reporters when I pull up to the hospital, which makes me wonder how Teddy got rid of them already. Grabbing the bag from the backseat, I make my way through the hospital entrance just as Vonnie Shepard runs past me. Her blonde hair is loose around her shoulders. It looks so frizzy, it would be my vote that she cut it off and start over as the brunette nature intended her to be.

She looks right and then left and then turns around and stares at me. "Faith, did you hear? Teddy Helms is here in the hospital! Apparently, his grandfather lives in Elk Lake."

"That's exciting." *What else am I going to say?*

Her gaze narrows slightly. "But you already know he's in town, don't you? I hear he likes to go to Rosemary's in the mornings."

"Really?" Playing dumb seems like the safest bet right now. "I must have been out on those days."

"Faith ..." Her tone is disbelieving.

"Fine," I tell her. "But like any priest worth his salt, I believe in confidentiality. I'm not going to gossip about my customers."

"What are you, the high priestess of pastries?" She cackles at her own lame joke before asking, "What are you doing here anyway?"

"A friend of GG's was brought in earlier today," I lie like a pro. Lifting my shopping bag in the air, I tell her, "I'm bringing her a change of clothes."

Vonnie doesn't seem all that interested in GG's friend's health, so there are no follow-up questions. Instead, she walks three steps away to the nearest chair and plops down. "I'm going to sit here and wait until Teddy Helms comes down. Let me know if you run into him up there." She points at the elevator.

"Will do, Vonnie. You have a nice night."

Once I get into the elevator, I realize that Teddy is going to need this disguise after all. I smile as I imagine the look on his face when he sees what I brought for him to wear. I don't run into anyone on the second floor, so I go right to Theo's room. I tap on the door lightly before turning the handle. I'm not at all prepared for the sight that greets me.

CHAPTER TWENTY-EIGHT

TEDDY

"Hey, stranger." I hear Faith's voice before I see her. I'm lying on the floor with my back half hanging out from under my grandfather's bed. "You okay down there?" she wants to know.

After pushing myself back with my arms until I think my head is clear, I sit up. I misjudged the distance and promptly clock myself on the metal bed frame. Holding onto the top of my head, I tell her, "Just plugging in my phone to charge."

"And you didn't think to use one of the many other more accessible outlets?" She starts to spokesmodel several options while trying to keep from giggling.

Rolling onto all fours, I reach over to the bed to lean on it while I get back on my feet. Once I'm standing, I confess, "Years ago, I saw this movie where an old guy went into the hospital. They put him on life support, but the outlet next to his bed wasn't working."

"And no one noticed?" She's full-on making fun of me now.

"I know it sounds stupid, but it seemed like a small enough thing to check."

She puts a brown shopping bag on the reclining chair in the

corner. "Well, let's hope Theo won't need life support for his hip."
Yeah, I feel like a total idiot right now.

Approaching the chair, I look inside the bag and pull out a pair of dirty bib overalls. Holding them up in front of me, I say, "They smell like fish."

"That would stand to reason as I'm pretty sure the last time they were used was for gutting fish."

The next thing I pull out is a ratty Rastafarian wig. "Where did you get this stuff?"

"Anna's. I was over helping her get ready for the rehearsal dinner BBQ, remember? You're lucky I was there, too. I don't think I have anything costume-oriented at my house." She jerks her head to the side like she just remembered something. "Actually, I have a sexy barmaid costume I wore on Halloween last year. I suppose I could have brought that …"

She sits down on the padded bench against the wall while I put everything back in the bag and move it to the floor. "I don't think I'm going to need a costume, after all," I tell her. "It would seem my big emergency was just a bunch of kids excited that I'm in town."

"And Vonnie Shepard."

Sitting down on the recliner, I say, "I don't know who that is."

"She's the gossip columnist from our local paper. She's waiting for you in the lobby."

I pull the lever on the side of the chair that pops the footstool up. "Elk Lake has a gossip columnist? What in the world could there possibly be to gossip about?"

"Do not underestimate a small town's ability to spill the tea," she says. "Although after the big hair-bleaching scandal last year, she mostly talks about different club news. But now that there's some bonafide dish to be had—*you*—she's on it like the crack reporter she dreams of being."

"There has to be a back way out of here," I say. "Or I could wait her out."

"You can take the back elevator down and go out through the

emergency room exit," she suggests. "Once you get changed that is." She winks while tipping her head toward the bag of tricks she brought.

I push the lever again and my feet land on the floor. "So essentially I'm wearing a wig and dirty overalls?"

"I brought you a skirt if you prefer. It's clean."

"Are you serious right now?" I can't help but laugh with her.

She stands up and crosses the room. "Wait here," she says right before walking out the door. She comes back fewer than five minutes later, holding a pair of scrubs and a lab coat. She hands them to me.

I take the offering while asking, "Why didn't I think of that?"

"Probably because you didn't know who to ask. If the person giving you the disguise tells anyone else, the disguise is no good."

Kicking off my shoes, I say, "Thank God you knew who to ask."

She shakes her head. "I just borrowed them from a utility closet. There's a whole stack in there."

"So, we're stealing them?" That doesn't feel right, but I suppose it's a better option than wearing fish guts.

"We're *borrowing* them. I'll wash them and return them before anyone knows they're missing. Either that or I'll sell them on eBay and make a fortune. You know, Alpha Dog's getaway clothes?" When I shake my head, she adds, "I'll split the proceeds with you."

Once my shoes are off, I take the clothes to the bathroom on the other side of my grandfather's bed. "I'll be right out."

After changing, I realize the disguise isn't that great. I just look like me in scrubs. "Do you have one of those shower cap things and a mask?" I call out.

"Nope. But this should do the trick." I reach my hand out the door as she thrusts the wig through the opening. Once I put it on, I decide I look pretty cool. "Dr. Ganja at your service," I say while walking out of the bathroom.

Faith releases a loud guffaw. "Dawn would seriously love that.

You should wear it to the rehearsal dinner tomorrow. If you can come, that is."

"You want me to wear the skirt, too?" I tease.

She waves her hands in front of her. "No way. You're there to make Astor rethink the terrible way he treated me. I don't want him deciding I'm rebounding with someone who dresses like Anna's mom."

"I can see that." I walk over to the side of my grandfather's bed to say goodnight, but he's still sleeping, so I jot down a note and leave it on his nightstand. Then I ask Faith, "You ready to sneak me out of here?"

"I'll show you the way, but I think it's best if I go out the front door. That way I can keep Vonnie busy while you make your escape."

"I owe you one," I tell her.

"No more than I owe you," she says. She's staring at me like she wants to say something else, but she doesn't.

"You want to have supper tonight?" I ask on impulse. I mean, I'm going to be alone. She's going to be alone. Why not be alone together?

What I figured would be an easy yes is nothing of the sort. Faith stalls a minute and starts to snap her fingers nervously before finally saying, "I don't think so. Not tonight."

"But I thought we were friends."

"We are ..."

"But?" I prompt.

"I'd just rather be on my own tonight. You know, take a bubble bath and go to bed early."

"If that sounds better than having supper with me ..." *I'm clearly pouting.*

"I like you a lot, Teddy, and I love spending time with you. You know that."

"So then have supper with me."

She shakes her head. "I need some time to get in the right headspace for tomorrow night."

"You're still pretty upset about Astor, huh?" The guy only broke up with her a month ago. Yet, I suppose I've been cocky enough to think that spending time with me has been just as good, if not better, than dating that loser.

Instead of answering my question, Faith opens the door and walks out into the hallway. She turns her head from side to side before stepping back into the room. "I'll go first. Take a left down the hallway to the service elevators at the back wall. I'll show you where to go from there."

I don't want to leave her like this, so I reach out and take her hands in mine. "You're a great friend."

Instead of returning the compliment, she squeezes my hand before pulling hers away and hurrying down the hallway. After she's been gone a couple of minutes, I look out and make my break. As I near the elevator, I see her talking to someone. She says, "What are you doing up here, *Vonnie?*" She shoots me a panicked look before telling the woman, "I thought you were going to wait downstairs."

Vonnie doesn't look anything like I expected a newspaper reporter to look. She seems more like a middle-aged soccer mom in nicotine withdrawal. She answers Faith, "I thought he might be trying to make a break for it out the back door. I mean, if I were famous, that's what I'd do."

Faith turns around so her back is toward me while making a frantic gesture with her hands for me to turn around. As much as I want to try to convince her to have dinner with me, I know the best thing to do is steer clear of this reporter.

Maybe I'll stop by her house anyway. What's she going to do, turn me away with the bag of Chinese food I'll have with me?

CHAPTER TWENTY-NINE

FAITH

According to Anna, Astor is coming into town tonight. I don't know what comes over me, but after leaving the hospital, I drive over to the Trout Lodge on the outskirts of town. I can't bear the thought of seeing Tiffany for the first time at the rehearsal dinner in front of so many people. I need to find out what I'm up against before then so I can somehow prepare myself.

Also, I don't trust myself to be alone with Teddy tonight. I'm more than a little afraid that one of these times I'm not going to be able to stop myself from announcing the feelings I'm having for him. And no good can come from that.

Stopping off at the Quickie Mart, I pick up a giant sack of treats to keep me company. I must look like a castaway buying food for the first time in a month. But as no one appears to be watching me, maybe I can keep this indulgence to myself.

Surprisingly enough, the parking lot at the Trout Lodge is packed with cars. Elk Lake attracts a lot of fishermen, but July is when they usually descend upon us en masse. Finding a parking spot between two pickups, I back in so that the front end of my car is slightly in front of theirs. This allows me to see who pulls into the lot without blowing my cover.

Turning off the ignition, I crank up the radio before digging into my bag. I'm going to start out slowly and eat Tic Tacs for a while. If Astor and Tiffany show up soon, I might not even need to dig into the chips and candy bars. Although now that I have a dress that fits, I'm pretty sure I'll do that anyway.

Forty-five minutes, one hundred and eighty Tic Tacs, and two bottles of water later, I have to pee so badly there's no help for it; I have to leave my car. I weigh my options of going into the Trout Lodge vs. jumping over the short brick wall that lies between me and the gas station. Ultimately, I decide the gas station is a safer choice.

After getting the key from Tommy Howard, who was in my graduating class in high school, I hurry around the side of the building to the unisex bathroom. Upon entering, I can't help but wonder if there's some kind of code where you're not allowed to own a gas station if you promise to keep the facilities clean. This room is so gross I can't even. But of course, I do.

Tommy's talking to someone when I go back inside to hand over the key—and perhaps a few tips on the many wonderful uses of Clorox. He's chatting with a gorgeous blonde who cannot possibly be local. Her whole body is probably the width of one of my thighs, and her legs—which are bare from the hem of her short shorts to her feet—are so long I bet a giant could use them for toothpicks.

While I love Elk Lake, I often struggle with the exotic city women who come here during the summer. I mean, most of my shorts used to be jeans. They're so worn I wouldn't be caught dead leaving my house in them. This chick probably spent a hundred bucks on her toddler-size apparel.

"You don't have any Evian in the coolers," the woman complains. She seems to be having a hard time showing facial expression, which leads me to guess the Botox has left her features incapable of movement.

Tommy is leaning on the counter, positively drooling. "We have a whole bunch of other water though."

"I don't like the taste of those," she pouts.

It's all I can do not to shout out, "For the love of God, it's hydrogen and oxygen molecules. Purified water doesn't have a taste!" But I don't. I just stand there and watch one of nature's anomalies bitch about something that would get her laughed out of any third world country on the planet.

"Do you have any sesame water?" *What the heck is that?*

"What in the heck is that?" Tommy asks, proving that all of us locals are bereft of city slicker ways.

"Sesame is very healthy," she tells him condescendingly. "It's full of plant-based protein and it's high in fiber." Tommy looks stumped.

I finally step forward and put the keys on the counter while announcing, "In Elk Lake we eat meat and fish for protein and if we're constipated, prunes usually do the trick. Isn't that right, Tommy?"

He laughs, "You know it, Faith. I had a burger for supper just tonight and if it gets stuck, I'll eat a handful of plums."

"Faith?" the woman gasps like Tommy just called me Adolf Hitler. She looks me up and down like she's inspecting a rare fungus. "Your name is Faith?"

"Um, yes?" I look more closely at her, wondering where our paths have crossed before and how I could have forgotten. "Do we know each other?"

She laughs nastily. "No."

Okay, then. I give Tommy the side-eye before shrugging my shoulders. "See you later, Tommy."

"Bye, Faith."

The woman offers nothing. I'm still looking over my shoulder, unwilling to break the staring contest that seems to have started between us, as I open the door to leave. Arms grip me around the waist when a very familiar voice says, "Hey there, watch where you're going." I turn around and I'm staring right at Astor. "Faith?"

"Astor?" *Crap.* "What are you doing here?" My heart starts to race in triple time and my arm pits feel like someone turned a garden hose on them. I'm hot and cold and every temperature in between.

"Chris's wedding?" His gaze darts to the woman I now know is Tiffany. He adds, "This is uncomfortable."

This is so far beyond uncomfortable I don't have the words. "Yeah ..."

Blondie walks up to us and grabs ahold of Astor's arm like he's the last lifeboat leaving the *Titanic*. "You're *that* Faith?" she asks unpleasantly. I want to slap her senseless.

"The one and only," I tell her. With superhuman power I did not previously know I possessed, I force my soul to reenter my body long enough to stick my hand out. It's a gesture of manners that Emily Post herself would applaud. "You must be Tiffany."

She looks down at my hand like I licked it before offering it to her. *Why didn't I think of that?* "I just had my nails done," she says as though that's the reason she won't shake my hand.

I look down at her nails, and while they do look lovely, I'm one hundred percent sure she uses a gel polish that dries in twenty seconds. "Okay, then." I turn to step around Astor and leave this hellhole.

He reaches out and touches my elbow to stop me. "We should talk, don't you think?"

"Why?" Tiffany and I ask at the same time.

His eyes drift to his new girlfriend. "Will you give us a minute, Tiff?"

She makes no effort to move, so I say, "Seriously, Astor. We're good. You're with Tiffany, and I'm with Teddy. There's no reason this should be uncomfortable."

His expression is vaguely hurt, like it's no fun for him to break up with me if I'm not going to pine for him. What a jerk. "We were together for ten months," he says. "Surely, there's something we need to say."

"Well, nine, actually ..." I let my gaze linger on the interloper.

Tiffany looks like she's ready to lunge at me. *Bring it, bitch.* But I don't say that. Instead, I go with, "I think everything has turned out for the best."

"So, we can be friends?" He sounds astonished at the concept. And rightly so, as I would no sooner be his friend than I'd invite a Sasquatch to supper while lying enticingly on a platter garnished with parsley.

"There's no point in us being friends," I tell him plainly. "But we don't have to be enemies." Look at me taking the higher ground. I'm clearly channeling Mother Theresa here.

Tiffany pulls on Astor's arm. "We should go."

"Where are you staying?" I ask, pretending not to know the horror of their accommodations.

"Some place called the Trout Lodge," he says. "It's supposed to be right around here." He looks outside like he's not at all impressed by the neighborhood. Which stands to reason as it's not that impressive.

I can't seem to stifle the joyous trill of laughter that bursts out of me. "The Trout Lodge? Why in the world would you stay there?"

"Is it horrible?" Tiffany demands nervously.

"That's one word for it," I tell her. I'm enjoying this so much.

"It was the only place with a vacancy." Astor looks positively panicked.

"I'm sure you'll be fine," I tell them. "A lot of fishermen like to stay there because they're allowed to keep their fish in the bathtub."

"What?" Tiffany attempts to contort her face into a look of horror.

"I'm sure they clean between guests," I tell her. I'm actually not sure at all and wish I could be a fly on the wall when she sees her weekend digs. "I have to go," I tell them, finally feeling like I have the upper hand.

"We'll see you tomorrow night then," Astor says. "And Faith, I'm really sorry."

I turn to Tiffany before smiling brightly. "I have a feeling you're going to get everything you deserve, Astor."

He looks nervous. "Thank you?"

"No, thank *you*," I tell him before walking out the door. I was so nervous Tiffany would make me feel horrible about myself, but the truth is, *she's* horrible. If Astor was looking for a stuck-up city gal, he hit the mother lode with her.

While I still feel a little off-center, I realize that my life is a lot better without Astor in it. I want to be with someone who, like Mark Darcy in *Bridget Jones's Diary*, likes me just as I am. I realize now that I'd never have that with Astor. He's so busy trying to show people he's better than they are that he's not living his life for himself.

There's an uncharacteristic bounce in my step as I hop over the brick wall to my car. I know to the depths of my heart that I'm too good for Astor Hill. Now all I have to do is find a nice straight guy who thinks the same thing.

My spirits suddenly plummet.

CHAPTER THIRTY

TEDDY

I'm parked in front of Faith's house for an hour before I start feeling stalkerish. The woman should be allowed not to see me if she wants. How egocentric to assume she'd jump at the chance to have supper with me.

Pulling into my grandfather's driveway, a feeling of melancholy slams into me. I get out of the car and walk up the back steps to let myself in through the kitchen. Opening the refrigerator, I pull out a beer and pop the lid off. Then I saunter into the living room and turn on some lights. I take a long pull of the microbrew before plopping down on the sofa.

It's weird being here without my grandfather. Even though he hasn't been a ball of energy, his presence is huge, and I'm really going to miss it. Pulling my phone out of my pocket I punch in Terri's number. Without any pleasantries, she demands, "How is he?"

"He's in a lot of pain," I tell her. "The doctor scheduled surgery for tomorrow at two."

"Wow, that's fast."

"Apparently they like to do a replacement within twenty-four hours of the injury. The patient has an easier recovery time that way."

"How are you doing?" Terri sounds concerned.

"I wish you were here," I tell her. "It's lonely being at the house by myself."

"Where's Faith?"

"She had other plans tonight." Terri is clearly not going to believe me when I tell her there's nothing going on between us, so I stop trying to convince her.

"And tomorrow is the rehearsal dinner for Faith's friend?"

"Anna, yeah. I'll head over there after Theo gets out of surgery."

"You'd better look great," she warns. "Faith needs this win with her ex."

"You're certainly championing her ..." I take another swig from my bottle.

"Why wouldn't I? If she's important to you, then she's important to me."

"Any chance you and Kay might come out sooner than later?" I know I sound a touch needy, but I could really use my best friend right now.

"As a matter of fact," she says, "we're in the process of clearing our calendars for next week."

"Next week, as in three days from now?"

"Yes," Terri says. "You know we both think of you as family, and when one of us is in need, the rest of us will show up. That's the rule."

"I haven't even told my mom about Theo yet," I tell her. I didn't call her right away because I didn't want to freak her out at work, and then I just forgot. "I'd better give her a ring before she hears the news on television."

"You do that," Terri says. "Suggest that she might want to come out the week after we leave so that you're not left alone."

"You afraid I can't handle it? I live alone in LA," I remind her.

"You can handle anything, Teddy. I just want to make sure you have a constant stream of support."

"Thanks, Ter. Come to think of it, Mom should probably come out while I'm in Canada. That way, Theo will have someone when I'm not here." I kick my feet up onto the coffee table and slump down into the couch.

"That sounds like a good plan," she says. "In the meantime, get your best guest suite ready if you ever want me to visit again." She continues, "I'm thinking beachy, without being kitschy."

"I'm not sure I'll have time to do a full renovation," I tease. "How about we start with clean and go from there?"

"Deal. In fact, Kay and I can decorate our own room while we're there. You know, personalize it so it's not too hokey."

"It sounds like you're planning to move in," I joke.

"I suppose we'll have to if you're going to be there as much as I expect you will."

"I'll talk to you tomorrow, Ter. I love you."

"I love you, Teddy." She clicks off before saying anything else.

I have another beer before calling my mom. When she doesn't answer, I leave a message telling her that grandpa is going to be fine and that if she wants to come out to visit, she might consider doing that while I'm in Canada. I don't bother telling her that I'm buying my grandfather's house and that he's moving into a nursing home. There will be plenty of time for that later.

Rifling through one of the kitchen drawers, I find a stack of takeout menus and decide to order myself a pizza—I didn't end up taking Chinese to Faith's after all. Once my order is placed for my double pepperoni, light cheese, mushroom pie, I head down to the dock while I wait for it to be delivered. One of the first things I'm going to do is buy some kind of boat. Something more than a rowboat, but not necessarily a full-on speed boat. Although maybe a speed boat if I want to water ski again.

I kick my way down the wood chip path to the dock, reminiscing about my childhood. I used to spend hours in areas just like this, collecting little hoppy toads that I'd take home to the terrarium Theo set up for me.

I smile when I remember how the tank was always empty in the morning. Gram said they must have gotten lonely for their families and hopped out. I didn't find out until I was in college that she let them go every night after I went to bed. Memories like this are so special. They make me feel warm and loved, while simultaneously tugging at my heartstrings.

As I reach the dock, I walk right out to the end. I stare out onto the placid lake, watching the occasional ripples made by surfacing fish. I'm tempted to jump in, but I don't want to miss my pizza delivery.

Slipping off my shoes, I sit down at the edge and put my feet into the cool water. I immediately feel the cares of the day leach out of me. I used to love living in Santa Monica where I could hit the beach every day if I wanted to. Now that I'm in Sherman Oaks, I'm lucky to get there every few weeks.

Life is a funny thing. I spent my whole twenties trying to make it as an actor. I dreamed of hitting the big time so all the sacrifice would be worth it. But as I sit here, I realize I lost years not being in the place I've always wanted to be. Elk Lake has always felt like my home, and at the moment I don't ever want to leave.

I look across the water at Faith's dock, and before long I spot her walking down her path. Unlike me, she doesn't seem interested in anything but the water in front of her.

My mouth goes dry as she lifts her arms up and pulls her sundress over her head, exposing the soft curves of her body. She's wearing a blue one-piece but it's every bit as erotic to me as a string bikini might be. I'm hypnotized by the sight of her and while I long to call out to her, I dare not. Instead, I just watch.

Faith flings her dress to the side before running full speed to the end of her dock. Instead of diving in gracefully, she jumps and lifts her legs into a cannon ball. She screams when she hits the water. She's a big kid like me, and I can't stop the grin that overtakes me.

I sit quietly and watch her splash around, occasionally diving deep and popping up in another location. She looks like a playful dolphin. I wonder if this is the reason she didn't want to eat with me. She needed time alone to frolic in the water. I can totally understand that.

As much as I wish I were over there with her, I find that my current view is so delightful I'm hard pressed to be too disappointed. I like Faith so much, and the more I get to know her, the more I can't imagine a life without her.

If everything goes well this weekend, I might just make my move.

CHAPTER THIRTY-ONE

FAITH

I wake up early and refreshed to go into the bakery and work on Anna and Chris's wedding cake. As I'm no longer nervous about confronting Astor and Tiffany, I slept like the dead. Seeing them together made me realize that Astor was never the man for me, and he and Tiffany are disgustingly perfect for each other.

Strolling out of the walk-in with an armload of butter, Esmé announces, "I'll apply the bark to the cakes tomorrow so condensation doesn't form when we take them out of the refrigerator."

"Thanks, Esmé." When the timer rings, I pull four raspberry and cheese coffee cakes out of the oven. I let them cool for a few minutes before giving them a light drizzle of icing. Then I pack them in boxes to take over to the Walkers.

As I go out the backdoor to the parking lot, I'm full of what I can only describe as contentment. There might be a side of hope in there somewhere, too. It's beautiful early summer, and my bestie is going to get married tomorrow. Nothing can make this weekend anything short of perfect.

Driving over to Anna's house, I let my mind drift to memories of our lifelong friendship. Our summers were full of sleepovers, campouts, and BBQs. We spent every day swimming, tubing, or traipsing through our small town on one adventure or another. Elk Lake was the perfect place to grow up, and while I'm now farther away than ever from becoming a mother myself, I can't wait to raise my own children here.

I knock on the Walkers' front door before turning the handle and letting myself in. "It's me, Faith," I call out. "I brought coffee cake!"

Anna's dad, Randal, shouts, "If it's not raspberry, you'd better leave now!"

"Ha, ha," I holler back. "Of course it's raspberry."

He pops around the corner with a huge smile on his face. "It's happening, Faithy!"

I walk into his arms for a hug, and tell him, "My parents are sorry not to be here, but they bought tickets for a cruise before they got their save the date card."

He steps back and takes the bakery boxes from me. "No worries at all. I'm glad they're making the most of their lives in Florida."

"Have you ever been tempted to head south to get away from the freezing winters?" I ask.

He shakes his head. "Never. I find the contrast between the seasons makes me appreciate whichever is currently at hand."

"That's how I feel, too," I tell him while following him into the kitchen. "Where's Dawn?"

"She's upstairs panicking about her mother-of-the-bride dress." He shakes his head while adding, "She thinks it's too boring."

"I suppose it is a bit boring considering her normal style," I say. "Is Anna upstairs, too?"

"Yes, ma'am. You go on. I'm just going to sit down and eat one of the coffee cakes before the ladies know they're here."

"The whole thing?" I laugh.

He winks. "If you tell them you only brought three they won't know the difference."

"Sorry, Randal. They asked for four and if they think I only brought three then I'm the one on the hot seat."

"Fine." He sits down at the table and opens one of the bakery boxes. He cuts off a third of the cake with a table knife and puts the giant piece up to his mouth. "If I'm going to get into trouble, I'd better make it worth it."

I turn around and head back out to the living room where the stairs to the second floor are located. Taking them two at a time, I sing the lyrics of "Going to the Chapel."

"Faith!" Anna meets me at the top of the stairs wearing her "Bride to Be" robe. We got a little carried away when she got engaged and practically bought an entire wardrobe declaring her upcoming marital status. She hands me a t-shirt. "I got this for you."

I open it up to find that it reads "Future Bride to Be." "I bought it when you and Astor were still dating, so if you don't want to wear it, you don't have to."

I follow her into her room while pulling off the T-shirt I have on and replacing it with this one. "There are other fish in the sea, my friend. And I'm gonna find one of my very own."

She smiles slyly. "I sense a story."

"I ran into Astor and Tiffany at the gas station last night." Her eyebrows nearly hit her hairline and she stops dead in her tracks. "Tiffany is everything you'd expect her to be."

"Blonde, skinny, and full of herself?" she guesses.

"I see you you've met her ..." I know she hasn't, or she would have told me.

"That's exactly the kind of woman I visualize Astor being with. Fake as her highlights."

"Are you sure Chris didn't tell you about her?"

She shakes her head. "No way. I was so mad at him for keeping Astor's secret, I told him I was considering canceling our wedding."

"You didn't!"

She takes me by the hand and leads me over to her childhood

bed. As we sit down, she says, "I did. I'm sorry to say I didn't mean it though. But Chris has to know he's not allowed to keep secrets from me. Certainly not secrets that have anything to do with my soul sister." She squeezes my hand before pushing herself up against the stack of pillows at the head of her bed. "Tell me everything."

I shrug nonchalantly. "There's not much to tell. She's exactly like you described her, only she's also a total shrew."

"Did you punch her in the face?" Anna sounds excited by the possibility.

"Nope. I figure the two of them are enough punishment for each other."

"So, you're not pining for Astor anymore?" she asks hopefully.

"Not in the least," I confirm.

"And it's not because you think you're going to turn Teddy straight?"

If only I could. "No. Teddy is a great friend, and if nothing else, he's shown me how I deserve to be treated. I like him a lot, but I'm not going to pin my hopes on him having a miraculous transformation."

"Wow. Good. Great!" she says. "You don't know how happy this all makes me."

"I'm prepared to have the time of my life this weekend," I tell her. "Now, what do you need me to do?"

"My mom has a bunch of friends coming over in an hour to finish getting ready for tonight. I suppose you and I can do anything we want." She adds, "As long as we're at the church by five."

"You want to go roller blading?" We spent our entire high school career on roller blades and only stopped the summer after high school when I broke my ankle.

"I don't want either of us breaking anything before tomorrow," she says. "How about if we go see *Notting Hill* over at the Silver Screen? There's nothing like some vintage Julia and Hugh to get us in the mood for a wedding tomorrow."

"That sounds perfect," I tell her. "And when it's over, we can go out to lunch. Should we invite Chris?"

She shakes her head. "No, he's busy playing host to the guests coming into town from his side. I should probably be doing the same, but today is our last day together with me as a single lady, and I want to enjoy it to the fullest."

"You're hiding from Chris's mom, aren't you?" I guess.

"Most definitely. If I hear one more time how I'm not including Chris's heritage in the wedding, I'm going to scream. Chris made every decision with me, so it's on him to placate his mother."

Within minutes, we've said goodbye to Anna's parents and are in my car driving downtown. I park right in front of our old-fashioned movie theater that plays nothing newer than the turn of the century. Before getting out of the car, I tell Anna, "I just know everything is going to work out beautifully for both of us."

"I do, too, Faithy," she says. "I do, too."

As we enter the theater, I get a glimpse of a woman walking into Rosemary's, which is just across the street. There's something about her that draws my attention, but I can't say what it is. All I know is the hairs on the back of my neck are standing on end, and I don't feel quite so confident anymore.

CHAPTER THIRTY-TWO

TEDDY

I overslept this morning, a fact I attribute to all the tossing and turning I did last night. Thoughts of Faith filled my head to the point I couldn't seem to let unconsciousness take a hold of me.

The first thing I do when I wake up is to call my grandfather. He answers the phone groggily. "What?"

"Good morning to you, too," I say with an excess of enthusiasm. "How did you sleep?"

"I broke my hip, Teddy. I slept like the devil was chasing me."

"Even with all the painkillers?"

Instead of answering, he asks, "Are you on your way over?"

"I will be in about ten minutes," I tell him. "What can I bring you?"

"I'd tell you to bring me some pajamas, so my butt doesn't have to hang out, but I'm guessing they won't let me wear them." He thinks for a minute before asking, "How about an egg sandwich from the diner?"

"You aren't supposed to have anything to eat today, remember?"

"*Yesss*, I remember." *He clearly didn't.* "Bring me some chicken broth then. I'm allowed clear beverages until three hours before surgery."

"Will do," I tell him. Then I add, "Mom left me a message late last night. She'll come out to stay while I'm in Canada shooting. She said to tell you that she loves you and she'll call you later today."

"The vultures are circling, are they?"

"Grandpa, that's a horrible thing to say."

"I know it." He sounds mildly contrite before adding, "I just hate to be the reason for so much fuss, you know?"

"Mom didn't get a chance to fuss over Gram," I tell him. "She went too quickly. Please allow her the privilege of spending as much time with you as she can." I don't want to chastise him, but I think he needs to remember how important he is to our family.

He neatly changes the subject. "Why don't you stop at the bakery and bring me some cookies for after surgery?"

"Being that you won't be allowed to eat them until tomorrow, I'll bring them fresh, then." No sense tempting him.

"I'm hanging up now." And he does just that. I know he must be more than a little nervous about surgery today, so I cut him some slack.

I hurry to get out of bed and then I jump into the shower. I'm out of the house and on my way into town within ten minutes. Maybelle, at the diner, tells me she's going to need to defrost the soup, and that it will take twenty minutes or so. I take the opportunity to sit down and order myself that egg sandwich Theo wanted.

While I wait for my food, I look out the window and watch as Elk Lake starts its day. Moms pushing strollers, young kids running toward the park, and packs of teenagers starting to form. It's everything I remember it being when I was a kid.

My eye briefly catches sight of someone walking into the bakery. Something about her is very familiar, but she moves too quickly for me to identify her. I like the idea of getting to know people in town and becoming part of the landscape. I find it comforting.

So far, I've only had a few incidents of being recognized by a group of people, and they didn't prove to be so bad. I imagine that sooner or later, I'll just be another townsperson to them.

Maybelle brings my sandwich and refills my coffee before announcing, "The broth will be ready to go in five. Do you want anything else with that?"

"No, thanks," I tell her. "Just the check."

When she walks away, I dig into my outrageously delicious breakfast—two fried eggs with bacon, cheese, and hollandaise, all on a toasted square roll. I can't stop the groans of appreciation that flow out of me.

Once I'm done eating and Maybelle drops my to-go order, I put cash on the table and head out the door. I'm tempted to cross over to the bakery to see why that woman seemed so familiar to me, but I'm sure I'll see her again some other time. Right now, I want to get the soup to Theo while he can still drink it.

Once I'm in the car, I connect my Bluetooth and call Faith. Her phone rings four times before going into voicemail. I leave the following message: "Hey, Faith. Theo's surgery is at two. He should be done and in post-op at four. I figure that should give me plenty of time with him so that I can meet you over at the Walkers' house at six thirty. Give me a call when you get this."

Once I get to the hospital, I park quickly. There are no reporters or teenagers to greet me as I walk in, which is nice. When I get to Theo's room, I knock gently before opening the door. "Hey, Grandpa, it's me," I say as I enter. He looks old and tired, and I immediately worry that he might not be up to this surgery.

"Did you bring soup?" He pushes the button on the side of his bed to lift his head.

"I did." I approach his bed and start to unpack the little brown bag from the diner. "Maybelle assured me it's straight broth with no noodles or chicken."

"Yuck." He picks up the paper cup and takes the lid off. "Teddy," he says after blowing on his soup for a minute.

"Yes, Grandpa?"

"If I die ..."

"You're not going to die," I interrupt him.

He rolls his eyes before saying, "Even if I don't go today, we both know I'm the next one on the chopping block." He's got me there. He continues, "If I die, I want you to mix my ashes with Gram's and put us in the travel chest in the dining room."

"The dining room of your house? Wouldn't you prefer to be interred somewhere or sprinkled someplace meaningful to you both?"

"It's your house now," he says. "And that's where we want to be." He takes a sip of his broth before saying, "I'm not sure how this whole afterlife thing goes, so I want to make sure part of me will always be with my Abigail."

My eyes start to get watery. That's totally sweet, if not highly unorthodox. I try to imagine telling my dinner guests someday that my grandparents are joining us, via the old steamer trunk under the window. Yeah, I think I'll forget to mention that. "Don't you want Mom to have your ashes?" I ask.

"Abigail and I always wanted to be in Elk Lake, so I would prefer if you would just do as I ask and let us stay in the trunk."

"You've got it," I tell him. It seems like a small enough thing if it will bring him some peace. "Anything else?"

"I think it's time for you to get back in the swing of things and find yourself a nice girl." Before I can comment, he adds, "I like Faith." His head bobs up and down sharply to emphasize his declaration.

"I like her, too."

"A blind man could see that, Teddy. It's time you quit running from your life just because you're afraid of being hurt. It's time to take a chance, son."

"Okay," I tell him. And I mean it. I've spent enough time with

Faith to know that I see something in her. I don't know if we'll be forever, but I sure would like the opportunity to find out.

"You mean it? You're not just saying that to get me off your back?"

"I mean it, Grandpa. I would like nothing more than to start dating Faith."

He puts his broth down and announces, "In that case, I think I'm going to live."

"Just like that, huh?" I ask with a laugh.

"Yes, sir, just like that. I'd like to see Abigail's and my great-grandbabies. And now that I'll have a whole bunch of people to take care of me down at Vista Pines, I figure I might as well sign up for a few more years."

Pulling the reclining chair closer to his bed, I sit down and tell him, "Things better go well with Faith if you're expecting to meet those great-grandchildren that quickly."

"I have a feeling ..." he says with a twinkle in his eye.

I hope he's right. I'm ready to enter the next phase of my life, even if it means turning down movie roles so I can spend more time here. I want what my parents and grandparents had. I want to raise a family with the woman I love more than I want a life in Hollywood. But hopefully I can have both, at least for a while anyway.

After Theo finishes his soup, he leans his head back and closes his eyes. I do the same, letting my brain be free to explore all the wonderful possibilities of my future.

CHAPTER THIRTY-THREE

FAITH

During *Notting Hill*, it occurs to me that Teddy and I are kind of like the characters Anna Scott and William Thacker from the movie. Anna Scott's famous/Teddy's famous; Anna's hunted by the press/Teddy's stalked by the high school newspaper; Anna begs him to love her/I want to beg Teddy to love me ... Ugh. It's the first time I've watched Julia and Hugh in these iconic roles and felt depressed.

After lunch, my Anna and I walk over to the elementary school playground and sit on the swings. We don't quite fit like we used to, but that doesn't stop us from kicking off the dirt and setting ourselves into motion. "When we were eight," Anna says, "I used to think I was going to grow up and become an astronaut."

"I remember that! You begged your parents to send you to camp at NASA, but they sent you to church camp instead."

"Yup. Instead of learning about the planets, I got a nasty case of scabies with a poison ivy chaser. Good times."

"Remember when we were ten and the circus came to town? I think that was the best summer of my life."

She leans back so that her body sails through the air in a straight line. "That's because you won three hundred bucks at the traveling bingo stand outside the gates, and you didn't tell your parents. We had a killer time spending that money."

"I think Sam at the Purple Cow thought we'd knocked over a bank. I was worried he was going to ask my parents why I seemed to have a never-ending supply of twenties." I stop pumping my legs to let my swing slow. "We should head back to your parents' house and get you ready, Mrs. Tanaka ..." I tease Anna by using her soon-to-be surname.

She drops her feet to the ground and drags them until her swing stops. "Every time I hear Mrs. Tanaka, I think of Chris's mom." She bodily shudders. "Do you think that woman is ever going to like me?"

"Grandbabies are miracle workers," I tell her. "I predict that once she's holding a little Anna or Chris, she's going to melt."

"Either that, or she's going to start telling me how to parent my child." She mimics, "Vegetables with every meal, and no sugar except on Sundays ..."

"Ew, is that how Chris was raised?"

"He says yes, but he's so normal it's hard to imagine."

As we walk through town to get my car, I ask, "You want to see the wedding cake?"

"No way! I want to be surprised."

Once we get to her house, I tell her, "Go on in and get ready. I'm going to go home and change. I'll meet you at the church."

"What are you wearing tonight?" she asks.

"That will have to be another surprise," I tell her. "I'm pretty sure the dress I was going to wear will be tight in the waist, so I'm going to have to dig around for something that was purchased before Astor and I even started dating."

As soon as I pull into my driveway, I check my phone for messages. The only one is from Teddy, asking me to call him back. "How's Theo?" I ask.

"So far so good. I'm just waiting for the surgeon to update me. What did you do last night?"

"I went across town to see if I could get a glimpse of Astor and Tiffany checking into their motel. And I did."

"You sound pretty happy about that," he says. "Did she have bucked teeth and a giant wart on her nose?"

That image causes a chuckle. "Wouldn't that be great? But, no. She's pretty perfect."

"Then why are you so happy?"

Walking through my back door, I tell him, "I've decided I don't want a picture-perfect life. It seems like too much work to keep up that kind of image."

"Good for you. A lot of people never come to that realization and spend way too much time trying to paint an ideal vision of their lives. Personally, I blame Instagram."

"Yes, well, I'm enlightened now," I tell him. "In fact, I'm pretty sure that I need to go clothes shopping because I don't feel any pressure to stay thin."

"Did Astor pressure you?" He sounds appalled.

I think for a moment before answering. "Not in so many words. It was more how he always turned down dessert for both of us when we ate out, or how he'd order glasses of wine instead of a bottle, so I wouldn't be tempted to have more. He'd even tell the waiter not to bring us any bread before dinner."

"What an ass!" Teddy declares, which causes me to giggle. "Remind me to take you out for a dinner of bread, butter, wine, and crème brûlée. We'll go next week."

"If you do that, Alpha Dog is going to look like Thor in *Avengers: Endgame*," I tease.

"Don't worry, my trainer will beat it out of me. Hang on, will you?" I hear him talking to someone in the background, and when he gets back on the phone he says, "Theo just got out of surgery and the doc said he did great. It looks like I'll be right on schedule."

"Give him my love," I tell him. "I've got to get to the church, so I'll see you later."

After hanging up, I dig through my closet and pull out a crisp white cotton blouse and a baby pink skirt with an elastic waistband. I add a stretchy belt and a pair of white sandals before declaring myself ready for the wedding rehearsal.

I'm the first attendant to arrive at the church, as is the maid of honor's duty. Anna is a little nervous because her two cousins who are also standing up for her are in the middle of a major fight. Tanya's boyfriend recently told her sister Tracy that she was a nasty shrew, and now Tracy is going out of her way to prove him right. Their mother promised them separate vacations to Hawaii if they could get through the weekend without making a scene.

I see Chris before I see Anna. He walks up to me and gives me a quick hug. The first thing he says is, "I'm a total rat for not warning you about Astor. I just didn't know how."

"Don't worry about it, Chris," I tell him. "I'm okay. I'm also probably better off without him."

"I hear you met Tiffany." He raises one eyebrow in question.

"She's lovely," I lie.

"Like a piranha after a three-day cleanse."

"You don't like her?" I'm delighted.

"She's no you," he says kindly.

Anna scurries down the aisle toward us. She squeals, "Faaaaaaaith!!!" Then she launches herself into my arms. "You ready?"

"As I'll ever be ..." I tell her. "How about you?"

She leans toward me like she's going to tell me a secret, but instead she yells in my ear, "I might be a little drunk."

"How are you drunk already? I just left you forty-five minutes ago."

"My mom's been working on her ever since she got back from your girls' day," Chris says. "She thought Anna's place was at her mother's side helping to get ready for the BBQ."

I take up for my friend. "Dawn would have never let her help."

"That's what I said." Anna releases a loud hiccup. Then she looks at Chris and says, "That's what *she* said." And she convulses in laughter at her joke.

Astor chooses that moment to join us. "Hello."

"Hey, man," Chris says. "You're with me." He grabs ahold of Astor's shirt to pull him away.

"Hey, Faith," Astor says as he's being dragged up the altar.

I offer a small wave, but nothing more. While I'm no longer raw over the breakup, I don't have any interest in going out of my way to be nice.

Anna's cousins are standing by the door leading into the sanctuary, so we hurry to take our place in line behind them. As soon as the minister cues the organist, we're off.

CHAPTER THIRTY-FOUR

TEDDY

I spend an hour with Theo after his surgery. He stays asleep, which the doctor said to expect. In fact, he'll be out of it the rest of the evening.

I hurry home to change clothes before going over to the Walkers'. Faith said it was fine if I wore shorts, but I put in a little extra effort and change into freshly pressed khakis and a white linen button-down shirt. I want her to be proud to be seen with me. Plus, there's still evidence of the waxing, so there's that...

When I get to Anna's house, I walk around the back path as instructed. The party seems to be in full swing with a group of men standing around the grill and an equally large number of ladies carrying platters to a picnic table.

I spot Faith before she sees me, and I simply stand back and stare at her. She's gorgeous. Her hair is up in a tidier bun than usual, and her lips look deliciously kissable. It's all I can do not to go over and find out for myself.

When she turns around and scans the crowd, her eyes land on me. The smile that takes over her face is radiant. She waves before hurrying to my side. Conscious that we're putting on a show, I open my arms for her to run into. Which she does. She wraps her arms around me and declares, "You look gorgeous!"

"I wanted to make sure Astor knew what great hands you're currently in," I tell her.

"Don't be obvious, but he's the guy with sandy blond hair standing next to Chris. Chris is the guy with his arms around Anna."

She takes my hand and leads me toward a keg located under a large maple tree. Taking a red cup off the stack, she says, "I'll pour your beer so you can take a peek."

I do as instructed. "He's short." It's the only thing I can think to say.

"He's almost five ten. That's not short."

"I'm six two," I tell her. "He's short."

"What do you think of Tiffany?" she asks. "She's the blonde who looks like she's been surgically attached to Astor."

I'm quiet for a minute while I try to formulate my answer. She's certainly pretty enough, but there's something missing, I decide. "She looks like she's trying too hard. You know, too much makeup, too much jewelry." I look at Faith's fresh face with no more adornment than a pair of small earrings, and tell her, "You're way hotter."

"You're the best gay boyfriend ever!" She hands me my beer.

"About that ..." I start to say.

She looks at me with wide eyes. "Yes?"

"No more calling me gay this weekend. I'm your boyfriend and that's how I'm going to act."

She smiles coyly. "So, you're going to hold my hand and kiss my cheek and call me pretty?"

"And then some ..."

The air between us starts to crackle with electricity. "Teddy ..."

Instead of letting her finish her sentence, I lean toward her and give her the gentlest of kisses. Her lips are soft, and full, and so sweet, I immediately want more. But I'm not about to have our first real kiss be in front of a crowd. That's something for just us.

As I reluctantly pull away from Faith, I hear Anna say, "Hello, Teddy!"

I turn to her and offer her a kiss on the cheek. "The beautiful bride-to-be."

"This is my fiancé, Chris." She indicates the man at her side.

"Congratulations, Chris. You're one lucky guy."

Chris smiles infectiously. "Thank you." He nods his head toward Faith. "So are you."

"Yes, I am," I agree. But before we can small talk anymore, the band starts to make sounds like they're getting ready to play.

Anna says, "My parents hired our favorite local band, Wild Boar on the Shore."

"That's some name," I say.

"They're some band," Chris offers. "Lots of old-timey Americana music that really gets your feet tapping."

When the opening strains of "Istanbul (Not Constantinople)" fill the air, I ask Faith, "You ready to cut a rug?"

She takes my hand in hers and leads me toward the makeshift dance floor. "I don't know if we can waltz to this one."

In an effort to show her how flexible the waltz can be, I pull her into my arms. We dance and twirl and have the best time I can remember having. After the song ends, Astor approaches us with his new girlfriend, and Tiffany does not look very happy.

"Faith," he says. "This must be Teddy." When his eyes lock on mine, he demands, "Teddy Helms? You're dating Teddy Helms?"

It's suddenly very nice to be recognized. I put my hand out to shake his. "Hello. Who are you?"

"I'm Faith's boyfriend." *Oh yeah, he's mad.*

"*Ex*-boyfriend," Tiffany announces before pushing Astor out of the way to get closer to me. He staggers slightly before reclaiming his balance.

"Ah yes, I think Faith might have mentioned you." I say that in such a way as to suggest that she did so while comparing him to rotten fish.

Astor stares at Faith and demands, "How did you meet Teddy Helms?"

I answer for her. "My grandfather lives in Elk Lake. I just bought a house near Faith's."

"You're going to live *here*? I thought you lived in Hollywood or something."

I offer a slight shrug. "I'll live wherever Faith is." Then I look at her and pucker my lips in an air kiss.

"But you don't even know her yet." *This guy really is an ass.*

"What's to know?" I ask him. "Faith is beautiful and kind, and she makes the best cookies in the whole world." Astor looks like he's about to blow a gasket, which compels me to add, "Only an idiot would let her go."

He sputters and gasps, "Are you calling me an idiot?"

Instead of answering, I entwine my fingers through Faith's. "How about if we go and get supper?" Then I lead her away.

Faith is positively vibrating next to me. As we near the buffet, she squeezes my hand and says, "If this was a movie, you'd be nominated for an Academy Award!"

"How so?"

"You were so convincing, you had me believing that you were in love with me!"

Instead of continuing on our current trajectory, I change direction and lead us toward a copse of trees, tripping twice as I go. I stop behind a large oak and turn around so that I'm facing Faith. "I'm not gay," I tell her.

You'd think I'd just told her I was a draconian lizard from a far-off galaxy the way she's looking at me. "What do you mean you're not gay?"

"I mean just that. I'm not gay." I hurry to explain, "When we first met, you asked me if my boyfriend had ever cheated on me. I replied that I *had* been cheated on. I did not specify the sex of the person who did so."

"Lindsey's a girl?" she demands disbelievingly.

"Yes."

"You're straight?" She's really having a hard time accepting this.

"Yes."

"And you never thought to tell me?"

"I'm sorry," I say. "You thinking I was gay sort of went along with my trying not to be recognized."

"But I've known who you really are for days now. Why didn't you tell me everything then?"

I inhale deeply. On the exhale, I confess, "Because I like you, Faith. A lot. And because you recently broke up with your boyfriend, and I didn't want to be the guy who jumped in and preyed on your vulnerability. You also mentioned that you were glad I was gay and I didn't want to let you down."

She stares at me without blinking. "You like me, like a straight guy likes a straight woman?"

"Very much," I tell her. "So much that I get distracted and keep stumbling over my own two feet when I'm near you. You make me nervous."

"You're blaming your giant circus feet on me?" I love how she teases me.

I take a step toward her. "I'm normally very suave around women. Yet, I've got no game with you at all. That must mean something."

She looks like a feather could knock her over. "And you're not gay?"

"I am so not gay."

"Do you want to ... you know ... kiss me? Right now?" She's so adorable I can barely keep my hands to myself.

"I would like nothing more." Yet I don't move for fear that I'll break the spell that seems to have formed around us.

Faith doesn't wait for me to make the first move. Instead, she launches herself into my arms and presses her mouth to mine. It's our first kiss and it's insanely wonderful. We stay connected for what feels like an hour—the best hour of my life. When she finally disconnects, she says, "I've been wanting to do that since the first day we met."

"Really?"

"Really," she says. "But I thought you were gay, and I was losing my mind." Then she tells me, "You're not the first gay guy I've been attracted to." She doesn't say more, so I don't ask.

Instead, I tell her, "Well, being that I'm straight and you're straight, and I'm going to be spending a good deal of time in Elk Lake, do you think you might consider dating me for real?"

She shakes her head like she's about to say no, but instead says, "I would be an idiot not to!" Then she lunges at me in another soul-searing embrace.

"Faith," I tell her, "I never thought I'd feel like this about a woman again. I was so torn up after Lindsey, but you … you feel like my other half. You feel like a part of me, and I never want to let you go."

"Then don't ever let me go. Teddy, you are everything I've ever wanted in a man. You're perfect."

After several more kisses, we're finally ready to go back to the party. We no longer have to pretend we're a couple, because we definitely are a couple. It's the best I've felt in years.

As we approach the buffet, I imagine how excited Theo and Terri are going to be when they hear our news, and suddenly, I can't wait to tell them.

CHAPTER THIRTY-FIVE

FAITH

Teddy. Isn't. Gay. Teddy isn't gay. Teddyisntgay. Those words run in a loop through my brain. *And he likes me!* How is that even possible? I mean I cried all over him on several occasions, I've eaten in front of him like I was angling to win placement in the *Guinness Book of World Records, and* I let the man wax my mustache!

Not only did I never expect to meet a movie star, but I sure as heck didn't think I'd date one. I mean, I live in Elk Lake, Wisconsin, of all places. But here I am, being wooed by Alpha Dog himself. It's an astonishingly bizarre thing.

It turns out, the best part of the night is not getting my revenge on Astor, which had once been my sole motivation. The best part is being able to kiss Teddy and have it be for real, not just an act we are putting on.

We dance to probably ten more songs, both lively and slow, and each time I'm in Teddy's arms I feel like I've come home. When we're not dancing, we hold hands wherever we go, which is often only to find a tree to kiss behind. I don't want to PDA all over Anna's party.

On one such occasion, I lean my forehead against his, and say, "This seems too good to be true."

"Why?" he wants to know. "Why can't it simply be our time?"

"Because you're Teddy Helms and I'm a small-town bakery owner. To quote *Sesame Street*, one of these things is not like the other."

He stares deeply into my eyes. "Are you saying that you only started to have feelings for me once you knew I was famous?"

"Heck, no! I liked you the first day I met you and I thought you were gay then. If anything, your being famous is a hindrance."

"How so?"

"I have so much more to worry about now. I mean, what are the chances you're going to want to keep dating a nobody from a small town?" I hurry to add, "I'm not saying that you're shallow, I'm merely pointing out the disparity of our lives."

"I spent my summers here from the time I was seven years old, Faith," he says. "Elk Lake feels as much like home to me as any place I've ever lived. More so, in that I've always dreamed of coming back and settling here someday."

"So if one of the Kardashians sets her sights on you, I'd have nothing to worry about."

He looks appalled. "Not at all." He winks before adding, "Although if Alexis Bledel suddenly became single ..."

"Rory, from *Gilmore Girls*?" I can't help but laugh. "She *is* pretty hot."

"She was my childhood crush." He confesses, "I even tried to see if my agent could find a way for me to meet her after Lindsey and I broke up."

"And?" *Do I really have something to worry about here?*

"Terri told me that she's not my matchmaker. Also, I met Alexis *and her husband* at a movie premiere, and while she was lovely, there were no sparks."

"*And* she's married." I want to make sure Teddy respects the institution.

"Which obviously would have killed the deal had there been any sparks." *Nice.*

"I used to be in love with Henry Cavill." I tease, "In fact, I still might be."

He brushes a wisp of hair off the side of my face. "Thanks for the heads up. I'll make sure to do everything in my power to keep you two apart." Then he wraps an arm around my waist to pull me close. "How late should we stay?"

"Are you ready to leave?" I rapidly bat my eyelashes to let him know I'm not opposed to the idea.

He grins broadly. "Only if you are ..."

"I don't go all the way on the first date," I tell him primly. Although that might be a rule I may need to rethink in the next hour. Even though I didn't know Teddy was straight, I feel like we've pretty much already dated for a month.

"I don't either." He leans down so that his nose is next to my ear. He runs the tip of it down my neck like he's trying to inhale me. "But there are still all kinds of fun things we can do without doing *that.*" He lets the possibilities linger in the air.

"Follow me," I tell him before practically sprinting toward Anna. When I get to her side, I fake a giant yawn, and loudly announce, "Boy, am I worn out. I think I need to go home and get some sleep, so I look my best for your wedding tomorrow."

When Teddy shows up at my side, my bestie looks at him and then back at me. I told her the truth about Teddy when she followed me to the bathroom earlier in the night. She's beyond excited for me. "Go," she says. "But just so you know, I know you're not going to sleep." Then she winks.

Before we can make our escape, Astor walks over and stops next to me. "Faith, would you do me the honor of a dance?" I look behind him for Tiffany, but she's nowhere to be seen.

"Faith and I were just leaving," Teddy answers for me.

"So soon?" Astor wants to know. "Don't you think her place is here with her friend?"

"Her friend is just fine," Anna inserts her two cents. "Where is *your* friend?" Her tone has a definite edge.

"Tiffany wasn't feeling well, so she went back to the inn." He looks at me again in a manner that appears to be something like longing. Mere weeks ago, this would have thrilled me, but right now I could not care less.

"No more dancing for me," I tell Astor. As an afterthought, I add, "I hope Tiffany is feeling better tomorrow." If he could read my mind, he'd know this was code for, "I hope you both come down with the worst case of food poisoning possible."

As we turn to leave, I hear Astor beg, "Faith, please ..."

He must think he has some bionic power over me, but he doesn't. Not anymore. And that's not just because Teddy has declared his interest in me, either. There was something about seeing Astor with Tiffany that made it crystal clear we are not meant to be together. While I have no idea what's going to happen between me and Teddy, I do know that Teddy has never made me feel like I wasn't good enough.

I don't turn around to say anything else to Astor. Instead, I simply pick up my pace up the path. When Teddy and I get to the front yard, I find that my car has been blocked in. "Do you mind driving?" I ask him.

"Not at all. Where are we going?" He leads the way to his SUV.

"I thought I'd take you out to my pier. That is, if you're up for a little late-night swim."

"I don't have my suit with me." He's trying to sound innocent but it's not working.

"I don't think you'll need one," I tell him. I sound all coquettish, like some Victorian-Era miss, suggesting she might hold hands with a man without her gloves on.

"Well, then ... I suppose I don't mind getting my pants wet ..." He opens the passenger side door for me before running around to let himself in. Once he pushes the button to engage the ignition, the air fills with the sweet strains of "Just the Way You Are" by Bruno Mars. I've always loved this song.

Instead of putting the car into gear, Teddy turns to look at me. He reaches out to caress the side of my face, and then like some 90s rom-com moment amped up to eleven, he starts to sing the lyrics of the song. He knows every word.

I'm so lost in the moment, I can't tell if it's really happening or I'm having a particularly vivid hallucination. While I didn't detect any pot in the brownies, that may be because Dawn went straight for LSD. When the song is over, Teddy says, "This is how I feel about you, Faith. You are perfect for me, and I hope to God I'm perfect for you."

How is it possible that this amazing man is already saying such lovely things to me? So I ask, "How can you feel like that already?"

"We became friends first," he says. "People always put their best foot forward when they start dating, and sometimes months go by without ever knowing who the real person is."

I snort. "And the first time you met me, I spilled boiling hot water on you and cried about another man. I can totally see how that must have been a huge turn on."

"You were vulnerable, and sweet, and open. You weren't trying to impress me. You were just being you, and I was hooked."

"Teddy Helms," I tell him, "I don't even care if you're lying right now."

He leans over the console and every so gently kisses me. When he pulls back, he says, "I will never lie to you, Faith." His face turns red as he adds, "No more lies by omission either, I promise."

"I believe you," I tell him. And I really do. Teddy does not strike me as the kind of man to make up feelings just to get a woman in the sack. Heck, according to him, he's hardly dated at all since his breakup with Lindsey. I cannot imagine a woman being so stupid as to cheat on someone like him.

When we get to my house, I lead the way up to the front door. "I'm just going to go upstairs and get some beach towels."

He reaches out and catches my hand. "Are you sure we need them?"

"Unless you want to freeze when we get out of the water," I say.

He shakes his head. "What if we skipped the swim?"

And that's all the encouragement I need to call off any lake activities.

CHAPTER THIRTY-SIX

TEDDY

After talking all night, with some phenomenal kissing and snuggling thrown in, I fall asleep with Faith in my arms. I know it sounds trite, but I don't know where I end, and she begins. It is an experience like none other.

I've been awake for thirty minutes and all I can do is stare at her. Faith is an amazing woman—so loving, passionate, and beautiful ... I did not expect to stay with her tonight, but once she fell asleep, I couldn't bring myself to leave.

I doze off again and dream about the summer I had my first kiss at that beach party down at the lake. I've never really had a clear memory of the girl's face, but in my recollection, I superimpose Faith's image onto hers.

Our kiss is no tentative, unsure thing either. It's a connection of two souls destined to be together. It's a promise that we'll find each other again someday.

Even in my sleep, I start to think that maybe my mom made me watch one too many rom-coms. I mean, what grown man thinks stuff like this? But then I console myself that if Colin Firth could say the things he did as Mr. Darcy, then at least I'm in good company.

I hear Faith stirring before I open my eyes—the squeak of the bed springs, her stepping on a creaky floorboard. I don't want her to have time to second guess anything, so I don't pretend to stay asleep. Instead, I accuse, "Trying to sneak away from the scene of the crime, are you?" Then I open my eyes and I'm greeted by the sweetest smile.

"I don't have to sneak around in my own house," she says as she walks over to my side of the bed and sits down. "How did you sleep?"

"Like the dead," I tell her. "I did have a dream though ..."

"Oh, yeah? What did you dream?" She bites her lower lip in such a tantalizing way, I almost lose track of my thoughts.

"Before I tell you, I want you to tell me about your first kiss."

She sits up straighter. "Why?"

"Humor me," I tell her.

She tips her head from side-to-side while furrowing her brow like it's taking some effort to remember. "He was a summer visitor. I didn't even know his name."

That sort of catches me off guard. I never told the girl I kissed my name either. I was leaving the next day to go back to Scottsdale, and I figured it was romantic to just go up to her and kiss her. In retrospect, it sounds more pervy than anything, but she went for it, so who was I to complain?

"How could you kiss someone without knowing his name?" I ask. I'm clearly not judging, just curious.

She shrugs. "I'd seen him around the beach, and we used to smile at each other, but we never talked. Then that night, he walked up to me and said, 'I'm leaving tomorrow ...'"

I cut her off, "And I didn't want to go without making sure you remembered me."

Her mouth opens wide, and she looks like she just saw a ghost. "It was you?"

"I dreamed about it," I tell her.

"*You* were my first kiss?" She sounds as astonished as I am.

"You were my first kiss, too," I tell her, suddenly wanting to pull her into my arms and never let go.

"But you must have been fifteen or sixteen."

"What's your point?" I tease.

"Only that you were so cute, I imagined you'd had plenty of experience before that night." Her face flushes an adorable pink.

"I guess I just picked the right girl to kiss," I tell her.

"I never saw you after that ..." she says. "I looked for you the entire next summer."

I explain, "That was the year before I grew six inches and gained thirty pounds. I'm pretty sure that even if you did see me, you wouldn't have recognized me."

"Did you look for me?" she wants to know.

"Don't be mad," I tell her. "But I started dating my first girl-friend when I went back to Arizona, and I kind of forgot about you."

"How in the world could I be mad about that?" She confesses, "I went back to school and fell madly in love with Adam Sanchez."

"Oh, yeah? What happened with Adam?" I find I'm oddly jealous of this boy from her past.

"Lots," she says. "He dated Belinda Flock, Maria Gomez, Taylor Heinz, and Bethany Lark, and that was just freshman year."

"But not you?" I ask.

She shakes her head. "Never me."

I tease, "When we tell this story to our grandchildren someday, let's say that I ruined you for other men."

Her eyes appear to glow with delight at the very thought of a future life together. If we don't get out of this bed, I may just make a move in that direction. As I don't want her to feel pressured, I ask, "Do you have any breakfast food in your refrigerator, or should we go out to eat?"

"We don't have time to go out," she says. "I have to be over to Anna's at two for hair and makeup. It's already eleven."

"Eleven!" I never sleep this late. "That's still enough time to go out for a bite."

"No, sir. I'm having my nails done at noon, so that only leaves time to take a shower and grab a piece of toast or something."

Sitting up, I throw my legs over the side of the bed. "You go. I'll figure out breakfast for us." She stares at my bare chest so intently, I add, "Unless you want to skip your nail appointment."

That causes her to hop off the bed with a flirtatious smile. "Pretty nails are a must. Call me when breakfast is ready." She closes the bathroom door behind her.

As I get out of bed, I think about calling Terri and updating her on my developing relationship with Faith. But then I realize how much fun it will be to introduce them and let her figure that out for herself.

I go downstairs and rifle through Faith's refrigerator. I pull out eggs, bacon, and grapefruit. Then I start a pot of coffee. While waiting for my skillet to heat, I call Theo at the hospital. He answers the phone by saying, "Where are you? I'm starving, and I'm in no mood for hospital food."

"I overslept," I tell him, not yet ready to say anything more. I think I'll kiss Faith in front of him and let him figure out our new status for himself. "I can be over in an hour. Do you want that egg sandwich?"

"I want a french dip and an extra side of french fries. And don't forget you were going to stop at the bakery and get those cookies."

"Are you allowed to eat that much so soon?" I ask. "I don't want you to get sick."

"I need to eat so I can heal. Now get moving." He hangs up the phone.

I wonder if Faith will be available to visit Theo tomorrow, so we don't have to wait too long to tell him about us. The news is going to make him so happy.

I enjoy the sizzle and popping sound of the eggs as I crack them into melted butter. Then I put some bread in the toaster and cut the grapefruit in half. Moments later, everything is ready to go. I call up the stairs to Faith, "Breakfast is ready!"

She practically skips down the stairs before kissing me. "Good morning, again."

"Something's made you happy," I say. "Care to share?"

She walks past me toward the kitchen. "I just have a great feeling about today, that's all."

"A great feeling about today or about us?" I ask.

She stops walking and turns around. "How about this? I just feel great, and a lot of that has to do with you."

Putting my hands on her waist, I pull her close. "I feel pretty wonderful, too." Then I lean down and press my lips to hers, all the while thinking how incredibly my life is turning out. I have the career of my dreams, I'm buying a great house, and I'm falling in love with my first kiss.

Life cannot get any better than this.

CHAPTER THIRTY-SEVEN

FAITH

I have never been this happy, and that includes the time my parents gave me a puppy for Christmas. I don't think the euphoria is all due to Teddy, either. Had I still thought he was gay, I might still be a little depressed about Astor's cheating. But even so, when I saw Astor with Tiffany, the truth hit me like a punch to the face.

I was the one always trying to please him. I went to Chicago to see him, instead of him coming to me. He always chose the restaurants we ate at and the activities we participated in. He even told me how to dress, going so far as to take me shopping to pick out clothes I would have never chosen for myself. Clothes I spent a fortune on. No man is going to have control of my self-esteem again.

I believe with all my heart that Teddy likes me for me. He's right when he said that being friends first made a huge difference in how quickly we connected emotionally. I've never been friends with a man before dating him, but it's something I'm now totally sold on.

Once I get to the nail salon, I decide to go with a classic french tip. Working with my hands as I do, I never bother getting my nails done. But Anna's wedding is certainly reason to celebrate with a gorgeous manicure.

Megan, the nail technician, says, "You're going to look great today!"

"I feel great," I tell her.

"You look like a woman in love." She puts my hands under the UV light while asking, "Are you?"

"I'm definitely in *like*," I tell her. I'm not about to confess anything more to a total stranger.

"Well, good for you. Not everyone is so lucky." She tightens the lids on the nail polish, while adding, "I had a woman in here yesterday who was big and pregnant, and her baby daddy left town on her. She's here trying to find him and make him take responsibility."

"Ouch," I say. "That has to be really hard."

"She seems to think that once he knows she's pregnant he'll do the right thing."

"Oh," I say. "I thought he left town because she was pregnant."

She shrugs. "I wasn't too clear on that myself, but I didn't want to ask too many questions. I find that people share a lot more if I just let them talk." The look of surprise on my face has her adding, "It's a boring job. There's only so much speculating a person can do about what all that gunk is under everyone's fingernails."

"I guess I can see that." Note to self: If I ever get another manicure, bring an audio book to keep from spilling my life secrets to the manicurist.

Once I get to Anna's house, Dawn opens the door before I even knock. "Faithy, you're here!" She pulls me close and does a little dance around me.

"Today's the big day, Dawn!"

She puts a hand to her chest and exhales like she's trying to blow up an air mattress with one breath. "Yes, it is. My little girl is all grown up and getting married." She lets out an ear-shattering squeal of delight before saying, "And I understand that you have a new man."

"Maybe," I tell her. "I mean, I like a guy. Teddy. You met him last night."

She smiles mischievously. "Anna tells me he's in the movies."

"He was Alpha Dog," I say proudly.

"Honey, I have no idea who that is, but I'm happy for you. Just make sure this one knows your worth." I briefly wonder if *anyone* thought Astor and I were good together.

"Will do." Then I ask, "What's the deal with the brownies for the party favors? Did you decide to keep them legal?"

"I had to." She sounds disappointed. "The trial batch Rosemary made for us to sample kept me high for a week."

"Gram made you pot brownies?" I ask with a good deal of shock. She never said anything to me.

Dawn nods her head. "Don't worry, she made them over here, so she didn't bring the fuzz down on your bakery."

"The fuzz?" I love Dawn, but her vocabulary sometimes catches me off guard.

"Yeah, you know, the coppers, the po po."

"I appreciate your not jeopardizing my livelihood," I tell her sincerely. "Also, I'm relieved you've decided against dealing drugs."

"It's not dealing if you give them away." She waves her hand in front of her face. "I'd move to Colorado or Oregon in a heartbeat, but Randal won't hear of it."

"I'm glad you're staying," I tell her truthfully. Then I give her another quick hug and run up the stairs.

Anna is in her bedroom, sitting at her vanity, getting the final touches put on her updo. "You look like a queen!" I exclaim. And she does. Her box braids have been wound around her head along with additional fake braids. The overall effect is that of an actual crown of hair.

When she sees me in the reflection of her mirror, she spins

around and declares, "That's because I am a queen." Then she jumps up and comes over to hug me. "How did last night go?"

"It was a great BBQ," I say evasively.

"That's not what I was asking, and you know it! How was your night *after* the rehearsal dinner?"

I had a good night's sleep."

"Faith Audrey Reynolds ... spill it!"

That's all the encouragement I need. I mean, if a gal can't confess the details of her love life to her best friend, who can she talk to? I tell her everything.

"And he stayed over?"

"He sure did, but I kept to my rule."

"Even so, you're one fast worker." There's a degree of awe in her voice. Probably because I have never been a fast worker in the past. In *that* way, anyway.

"Only because Teddy's not into dudes. If he actually were gay, I'd still be pretty pitiful."

"You were never pitiful." She takes my hand and pulls me over to the chair at her vanity and then pushes me to sit down. "I overheard a fight Tiffany and Astor had last night."

"A fight?" I try not to sound too excited but I'm not sure I'm successful. "What did they fight about?"

"You." Her hands are on her hips in the fiercest of Anna poses. She looks like a warrior from *Black Panther* getting ready to go into battle. *Except she has way more hair.* "Tiffany told Astor it was clear he still had feelings for you and that she was nobody's second choice."

"Astor does not have any feelings for me," I assure her.

Shaking her head rapidly, she says, "Of course not. He's just jealous that you've moved on with a movie star. That's really chapping his ass."

"He can't stand to think I'm with anyone better than him. What a turd."

Anna pulls over a chair and sits next to me while the hairdresser starts to brush out my hair. "Tiffany said if he didn't get his act together, she wasn't going to the wedding with him today. That's when she left."

"You know what's weird?" I ask. "I don't care if she comes or not."

"That's because you're in love with Teddy. You moved on like it was some kind of Olympic event." She giggles.

"I'm not sure I'm in love with him, yet," I tell her.

"You're both single and free, and only seeing each other. It's only a matter of time," she predicts.

"I think you're right." I've never felt about a man the way I feel about Teddy. "He's raised the bar pretty high," I tell her.

"And he's buying Theo's house, so I'm not going to lose you to a glamorous Hollywood life."

"I'm not going anywhere," I assure her. Then I say, "Just wait until you see the dance we've been working on. It's spectacular."

"I can't wait," Anna says. She stands up and walks across the room toward her dress, which is hanging on the back of her closet door. "Today is the first day of the rest of both of our lives. And as long as Mrs. Tanaka stays ten feet away from me at all times, I predict it will be a doozy."

"It would be a doozy if she got *within* ten feet of you, too," I joke.

Anna shakes her head. "*That* would be a potential lawsuit. And before you say my future mother-in-law would never sue me, let me inform you that she's threatened to leave the ceremony if I don't promise to honor Chris in our vows."

"Are you serious? No one does that anymore."

"No one from this century, anyway," she says.

"What are you going to do?"

She shrugs. "I have no idea. Chris told me he'd take care of it. So, either he will, or his mother is going to do her darndest to ruin my day."

"Oh, Anna, this is the last thing you need. I'm so sorry."

"I can't say I'm surprised," she says. "Chris's mom always wanted him to marry a Japanese girl. She hated me at first sight."

"She just doesn't know how great you are. Give it a little time."

"It's been two years, Faith. At this point, I just want her to stay the heck out of my way."

"Maybe your mom should sneak her a pot brownie." Her eyes pop open in interest, so I explain, "GG made a batch that kept your mom loopy for a week."

"Is that what the package in the freezer is all about?" She starts to laugh before explaining. "They're wrapped in a plastic baggie and sealed with duct tape. She's written a *Little Einsteins* quote on the front."

I think for a second before guessing, "We're going on a trip on our favorite rocket ship?"

"That would be the one."

"I don't really think you should drug her," I say. "I was just kidding."

Anna scrunches up her face. "I wouldn't. But that's not to say I'm not going to imagine what it would be like." Then she declares, "I'm off to grab some cookies from the kitchen. Do you want milk with yours?"

"Are adult polar bears white?" I ask, referring to the most boring documentary we had to watch our junior year of high school.

"They may have white fur, but they all have black skin," she reminds me with a wink.

When she walks out of the room, I smile at the girl doing my hair. "Anna is the best person in the whole world. I hope nothing goes wrong to screw up her big day."

And then like a prophet of doom, the stylist releases the mother of all curses. "What could possibly go wrong?"

CHAPTER THIRTY-EIGHT

TEDDY

The church is packed by the time I get there. Theo made me go back to the diner twice. Once for more au jus for his sandwich, and a second time for an order of pancakes that he only took two bites of. I'm more relieved than ever he's going to be moving into a facility that will take care of all his needs. I no longer think I'm up for the task.

As I step into a pew, I introduce myself to the man I'm sitting next to. His name is Sam and he's the boyfriend of one of Anna's cousins. "Do you know a lot of people here?" I ask.

"No, you?" he wants to know.

"I'm dating the maid of honor," I tell him proudly. "I pretty much just know Faith, Anna, and Anna's parents."

"I'm in the same boat," he concurs. "They're all good people except for Tanya's sister Tracy. That girl could make a hyena cry."

When the procession starts, all eyes turn to the back of the church. Sam points to the first woman walking up the aisle. He whispers, "That vision of loveliness is my Tanya." The next woman looks exactly like her, yet his face turns to disgust. "The ugly one is the devil's handmaiden, Tracy." It must be odd to be in love with a woman who's an identical twin to the one you hate, but I don't feel like it's my place to comment.

Faith is the next one through the doors, and she takes my breath away. Her dark hair is swept up in some kind of intricate bun, with curled tendrils framing her face. Her dress shows off all her charms from the waist up, while the skirt flutters around her like an angel's gown. I can't wait to see what happens to it once we hit the dance floor.

Anna is last, and she's a beautiful bride. She walks with the bearing of a queen marching to her coronation. Sam whispers, "Tanya's going to look like that soon."

"Are you engaged?" I ask as Anna passes our pew.

He pats his jacket pocket. "Tonight, if all goes according to plan."

As we sit down the minister welcomes us by saying, "Fifty percent of marriages end in divorce." *What the heck kind of way is that to start a wedding?*

He quickly adds, "Which means marriage is fallible and fragile, and it requires attention and love to keep things on track." I guess that's a little better.

He goes on to tell us about Anna and Chris and the importance of their commitment to each other.

Chris steps froward and takes Anna's hands in his. "My parents always wanted me to marry a nice Japanese girl who would let me be the king of my castle." There are a few snickers from the congregation at that. He quickly adds, "Anna, you have been the most unexpected and delightful surprise. I don't know what I've done to deserve you."

Smiling at her, he adds, "You are not submissive. Instead, you are a force of nature that will clearly always rule at my side. I couldn't be luckier." He puts a ring on Anna's finger. "This ring is a symbol of eternity, which is how long I will love you." There are a few sniffles at this point.

Chris gets down on one knee and continues, "I will cherish you always. I will help you and support you in times of joy, sadness, and turmoil. You are my person, Anna." This time, the bride wipes a tear from her eye.

The whole congregation laughs at his final declaration. "I will honor you on Mondays, Wednesdays, and Fridays, but I suggest we take Sundays off."

Anna helps Chris to his feet and then keeps ahold of his hands. "Christopher Tanaka, you are the only gift I need. You're correct that I won't stand back and let you take charge. We're going to do that together." She glances out into the congregation and appears to make eye contact with someone. "*Our* life, *our* rules."

Then she turns back to Chris. "I will try to honor you on Tuesdays, Thursdays, and Saturdays, but I make no promises. What I do promise is to put us first before anything or anyone." *Again, I sense she's making a point to someone else.*

"I will always love you, I will help you, and I will support you in all ways. You are my person, forever." She puts the ring on Chris's finger, and when the minister pronounces them husband and wife, the congregation applauds enthusiastically. After a couple additional prayers, songs, and communion, the ceremony is over.

Faith walks down the aisle next to Astor, but she only has eyes for me, and I couldn't be prouder.

As soon as everyone leaves the sanctuary, I hurry to find her. When I do, I tell her, "The bride was beautiful, but she has nothing on the maid of honor."

"Hey, you." She leans in and softly kisses my lips. Astor is standing uncomfortably close and he's glaring at us.

Pulling Faith to the side, I ask, "What's up with your ex?"

"Oh, my God, wait until I tell you." And then she does. It looks like our plan to make his royal highness jealous has worked beyond all expectations.

"So is Tiffany here?" I start to look around.

"I don't know yet," Faith answers. "But I don't care. We're going to have a great time either way."

I lead her toward the exit where the bride and groom are

greeting their guests. "What's the plan now? Do you come with me to the country club, or do I meet you there?"

"I can go with you," she says, "but I need to stay here long enough to see Anna and Chris off. It's the maid of honor's duty to be at the bride's beck and call."

"Can I help you do anything while we wait?" I ask.

She takes my hand and starts to walk toward the staircase at the side of the narthex. "We can clean up the bride's changing area and make sure everything is packed." We also take some time to enjoy several kisses that make me more certain than ever that one day I'll be declaring my own vow, to Faith.

When we get back upstairs, she pulls me out front where everyone is lining the steps to send the bride and groom off. Faith hands me a small bottle of bubbles. "Blow these as they walk by."

"I thought throwing rice was the thing."

"We blow bubbles now," she says.

"Do you want bubbles blown at your wedding?" I ask her flirtatiously.

She gives me the side-eye. "Maybe. How about you?"

"I want ham sandwiches."

Faith snorts so loudly that people turn to stare. "Ham sandwiches? Why?"

"I like them, and you know, I might be hungry."

Anna and Chris glide past us in a veritable cloud of floating spheres. It's such an enchanting sight, I tell Faith, "I've changed my mind. I want bubbles."

Once the bride and groom are in their limo and pulling away, everyone else does the same. After we get into my car, I tell Faith, "I've never been to the Elk Lake Country Club."

"It's beautiful." She sounds wistful. "My parents never belonged, but I love going to weddings there."

"Does Anna's family belong?"

As we turn down Country Club Lane, she says, "They're way too free-spirited to be country club types, but Anna and Chris joined. They thought it would be a good way to build their client list, being that they're both just starting out fresh in Elk Lake."

"That makes sense," I say. "How about you? Have you ever wanted to be a country club queen?"

She shrugs her shoulders. "Maybe someday if I win the lottery and become a lady who lunches."

As we pull through the double wrought iron gates, I let out a low whistle. "Call me crazy, but I kind of want to join. I'd feel like royalty pulling up to my castle."

After we park, Faith leads the way to the rose garden. "Cocktails and hors d'oeuvres are being served here for the next hour. Unfortunately, I can't stay for that. I need to go take wedding pictures."

"You go," I tell her. "Just meet me back here before supper."

Faith tips her head up and kisses me tenderly. I gently nibble on her upper lip before saying, "I can't wait for this wedding to be over."

She winks playfully. "Me either. But first, we dance!" Then she hurries into the rose garden, leaving me to wonder at my good fortune.

CHAPTER THIRTY-NINE

FAITH

I drink a whole glass of champagne while waiting for the photographer to decide which lens to use. At this rate, we're going to be here all night.

I'm doing my best to keep my distance from Astor, but he seems hell bent on talking to me. He's currently maneuvering around Anna's cousins to get to me. When he reaches my side, he says, "You look very beautiful today, Faith."

"Thank you." I don't feel like there's anything more to add, so I don't.

"You know," he says, stepping even closer, "I always thought you and I would be the next to get married."

I choke on my drink. "Seriously?"

The expression on his face indicates that I've hurt his feelings. *Good.* "Didn't you think we were slated for marriage?" he wants to know.

"Maybe at one time," I tell him. "But that ended when I found out about Tiffany." I look around, scanning the crowd behind him. "Is she here?"

"She was still feeling poorly from last night. I told her not to worry about coming."

"What a waste to travel all the way to Wisconsin and miss the fun." *Also, I hope her room smells like grouper.*

"Faith." He clears his throat like he's either going to tell me his deepest darkest secret or recite the Gettysburg Address. "I made a big mistake."

"Did you order the fish instead of the beef?" I ask sarcastically. I do not want to hear his confession, but it doesn't look like that's going to stop him.

"I started to get nervous by how close we were getting, and I think that caused me to sabotage our relationship."

I shrug my shoulders casually. I have nothing to say.

"What I'm saying," he persists, "is that I don't want to be with Tiffany, I want to be with you."

"I'm seeing someone," I tell him. "Teddy Helms, remember?"

"You've only just started seeing him," Astor says. "Surely, you can't be that serious yet."

"We were friends before we started dating," I say. "It feels like we've been together a long time. I have very strong feelings for Teddy."

Astor shoves his hands in his tuxedo pockets in an aw-shucks kind of way that does not look natural on him. "We were together for ten months, Faith."

"Nine," I remind him. "Then you started cheating."

"I told you that was a mistake. Isn't there some way you can find it in your heart to forgive me?" Not too long ago, I dreamed of him saying something like this to me. Now, I find myself revolted by his spineless display.

"Oh, I forgive, you, Astor. In fact, I think you did me a big favor." I drive the last nail into his coffin by adding, "I'm glad to have found out what you're really made of before getting in any deeper. So, thank you."

"That's not fair," he pouts. "I was scared. That's all."

"If that's the kind of man you become when you're afraid, I

want nothing to do with you." Taking a page from Tiffany's book, I tell him, "I'm nobody's second choice."

He seems to take the hint because he moves back next to Chris without saying anything else. Thankfully, the photographer finally gets going, and we bang out the wedding photos quickly.

After a half hour, the photographer announces that he only has a few more pictures to take of the bride and groom. Anna reaches to take my hand. "Tell my mom it's time to move everyone into the dinner tent. Oh, and alert the band to be ready to announce us."

"I'm on it." I tell her, "Anna, this was the best wedding ever. You and Chris are perfect for each other."

She shimmies with delight. "We really are."

Astor tries to walk with me as I stroll across the lawn toward the rose garden where the cocktail hour is being held. "Faith, wait up."

I stop moving all together and turn around to glare at him. "I've been as nice about this as anyone could be," I tell him. "But you are not taking the hint. Leave me alone, Astor. I don't want anything else to do with you. Not now. Not ever."

"Faith ..." His whine makes me wonder how I ever found him attractive.

In lieu of responding, I pick up my pace and leave him in my dust. It's a good feeling.

Teddy spots me as soon as I near the floribunda bushes and he saunters toward me. "Hey, beautiful."

I can't stop the smile that overtakes me. "Hey, handsome."

"I hope you're ready to dance." He shrugs his eyebrows up and down.

"Oh, I'm ready. But first I have to find Dawn and tell her it's time to move everyone into the tent."

I take his hand and lead the way to Anna's mom, who's talking to the sheriff. We hear her tell him, "Magic mushrooms have been used for centuries to increase spiritual growth and enlightenment."

Sheriff Miller nods his head stiffly. He looks like he wishes he was anywhere else. "I understand you can fly to South America and take them legally there."

"It's expensive to fly to South America," Dawn says. "I'm thinking of starting a petition and working toward getting a law passed. If there's one thing there's a shortage of in this country, it's spiritual awareness."

"I wish you luck," Sheriff Miller says before bowing his head and excusing himself.

As he leaves, I hurry over. "Hey, Dawn. It's go time. Anna and Chris are almost done."

Dawn immediately puts two fingers into her mouth and lets out an eardrum-busting whistle. Once she has everyone's attention, she calls out, "Let's eat!" As she leads the way to the tent, the guests follow behind with various expressions of amusement on their faces. Dawn is certainly one of a kind.

I hurry up to the bandstand and tell the lead singer that the bride and groom will be here soon. Then I turn around and tell Teddy, "We're sitting over there." I point to table one.

"Don't you have to sit at a head table or something?"

"Nope. Anna and Chris are sitting alone so people have an easier time coming up to them to talk. That means you and I get to eat together."

"Wonderful." He pulls me close to his side. "I can't imagine spending a nicer evening with you," he says.

"You're a romantic, aren't you?" I ask.

He sounds serious as he says, "I'm only going to love one woman, Faith, and that woman is going to be my everything. My partner, my lover, and the mother of my children. I guess I'm just old-fashioned like that."

"I don't want a big, complicated love affair either. I just want a nice life with a nice man, and no drama."

He takes two champagne glasses off the tray of a passing waiter and hands one to me. Lifting his in the air, he says, "To no drama." I toast to that enthusiastically.

After the band introduces Anna and Chris, we all sit down and enjoy a delicious meal. Anna's cousins and their dates are at our table, which is an odd experience. Tanya and Tracy go out of their way not to talk to each other, so Teddy and I stay in our own little bubble. By the time our dishes are cleared away, I'm slightly buzzed and feeling no pain.

Anna and Chris are called up for the first dance, which is followed by the parents' dance. Before starting the third song, the lead singer announces, "We have a special number for you next. Some of you older folks might remember The Hooters doing it in the eighties, but we've put our own spin on it." Then he says, "Will Faith and Teddy please take the dance floor?" I'm glad they didn't use Teddy's last name. So far, his presence hasn't caused a big stir, and I'm guessing that's because most people here don't know who he is.

"This is it!" Teddy grabs my hand and leads the way.

Once we're situated, the band starts to play their upbeat and slightly sped up version of "And They Danced."

Much like the lyrics suggest, I feel like we're riding high on a wave of romance. We turn, and spin, and two-step like we were born to be together. Like we're two halves of the same whole. It's a transcendent experience. By the second refrain, Teddy lifts me high and flips me over the top of his head with ease. My skirt moves so fast that gravity doesn't have a chance.

When the song ends, we're the center of a standing ovation. I briefly catch sight of Astor's back as he leaves the tent. *Hurray, he finally got the message!*

And then I see someone else. It's the woman who was going into the bakery yesterday. And just like that, I know who she is.

CHAPTER FORTY

TEDDY

"Teddy!" I turn to see Lindsey waddling toward me from across the dance floor. *She* was the woman I saw going into the bakery yesterday. It's no wonder I didn't recognize her right away, as she wasn't pregnant the last time I saw her.

My brain immediately scrambles trying to remember how long ago that was. Seven months? Eight, now? *Oh, hell no.* She cannot be here to tell me that baby is mine. There's no way.

I pull Faith off to the side so that Lindsey can't make as big of a scene as I'm guessing she's intent on making.

Faith whispers, "That's Lindsey Flint who used to be on *Finding Dr. Hawks.* She's the Lindsey you dated, isn't she?"

I nod my head. "Yes. But I have no idea what she's doing here."

"It looks like she's about to give birth." Faith doesn't sound nervous, which is probably because she doesn't know that Lindsey and I slept together in November. My stomach feels like it's trying to exit my body via my esophagus. I'm both nauseated and choking with fear at the same time.

"Teddy!" Lindsey finally gets to my side. She looks at my arm around Faith's waist and demands, "Who's your friend?"

"This is Faith," I tell her before demanding, "What are you doing here?"

"Didn't Terri tell you I've been looking for you? My God, I've called a thousand times."

"She did," I tell her. "But you should know by now that I don't want to be found by you. How *did* you find me, anyway?"

"You were all over the internet with your arms wrapped around your *other* friend. Reba Simms, was it?"

"Faith is the only woman I'm dating," I tell her. I feel Faith tense at my side. She's clearly getting an idea of the kind of woman my ex has turned out to be.

Lindsey turns to glare at Faith while loudly declaring, "I hope you don't mind that your boyfriend is having a baby with me."

"What?!" This from both me and Faith.

"That is not my baby," I tell Lindsey plainly.

"Oh, but it is, Teddy. You remember that night I stopped by our house, don't you?"

Faith slips out of my arms and takes a step away from me. I try to pull her back, but she shifts her body, making it clear she wants no part of me right now. *Damn it!*

Looking around, I discover we've become the center of everyone's attention. There are several phones pointed in our direction, making it obvious this scene will be replayed all over the internet by tonight.

I turn to Faith and quietly tell her, "I need to talk to Lindsey privately. I'll find you as soon as we're done. Okay?"

Her face is so pale, she looks like she's going to pass out. "Faith, are you okay?" She nods her head, so I add, "I'll be right back. Don't go anywhere." Another nod.

I tell Lindsey, "Let's find someplace more private to talk." I stalk off toward the club house without bothering to see if she's behind me.

I hear her tell Faith, "Don't expect him back. We have a lot of plans to make."

Regardless of how many people are now filming us, I shout back to Faith. "I'll be back!" *Who do I think I am, Arnold Schwarzenegger in* The Terminator?

Instead of responding, Faith turns and walks in the other direction.

I don't stop moving until I reach the expansive patio outside the country club. Then I open the first door I come to and walk inside. As soon as it closes behind me, I watch as Lindsey slowly nears the patio. She doesn't appear to be in any hurry.

When she finally gets inside, she demands, "Why didn't you wait for me?"

"Are you kidding me right now?" I fire back. "You followed me to Elk Creek, you've crashed a wedding, and you're pregnant. I don't think you have any right to be angry with me."

"Really?" Her hands are on her hips which pushes her belly farther forward. "I've been trying to get a hold of you for months! I had to follow you here so I could talk to you."

I point at her bulge and say, "That's not mine."

"Oh, but it is. Seven and a half months ago we were busy making this little guy."

"How?" I demand. I'm not really asking how he was made, more like how it was possible that she got pregnant. "We used protection," I remind her.

She scoffs nastily. "Yeah, Teddy, 'cause that always works."

"How do I know the baby isn't Tom's? Or any other man's for that matter," I demand. "I know you said you two were broken up at the time, but *we* were broken up and still … you know …" I point at her stomach again.

"Tommy already took a paternity test," she says. "And you were the only other guy I'd been with around that time."

How can this be happening now, when I've finally found an amazing woman like Faith? I want to scream! "I want a paternity test, too," I tell her.

She shrugs her shoulders. "Fine. But I've never lied to you before, Teddy, so why would I lie about this?"

"You cheated on me," I remind her. "Forgive me if I'm having a hard time trusting you."

She takes a step toward me. "We were good for a lot of years, Teddy."

"Until I wasn't enough for you," I remind her.

"I made a mistake that I've regretted ever since."

"You mean you've regretted it since I became Alpha Dog," I tell her.

"That's not true, Teddy. I always believed in your career. I always knew you were going to hit it big ..."

I interrupt, "Which is why, when you left, you told me that you were going to hitch your wagon to a star and that wasn't me."

She lowers her eyes. "That was awful of me. I should have never said that."

"But you did, Lindsey. And I've moved on."

"How could you have possibly moved on?" she demands. "I know for a fact that you haven't been in Elk Lake for that long."

"That has nothing to do with anything. I like Faith a lot."

"I'm having *your* baby," she reminds me. Her demeanor seems to soften as she asks, "How did you meet Faith, anyway?"

"We met at her bakery," I say. "The first day I got here."

"Ah, she couldn't resist Alpha Dog, huh?"

"That's not how it was at all." In an attempt to defend Faith's intentions, I tell her, "She didn't even know who I was. She'd just broken up with her boyfriend."

Lindsey laughs. "Yeah, I'm *sure* she didn't know who you were. Don't be naive, Teddy."

"She didn't. She was upset because she had to be in this wedding with her ex. She couldn't have cared less who I was."

"And out of the goodness of your heart, you offered to be her date?"

"Yes," I say plainly.

Lindsey tips her head back and laughs. "So this is nothing more than a pity date! God, Teddy, you had me worried there for a minute."

"This is not a pity date," I tell her. "Faith and I have been friends since the day we met, and we've recently become more than that."

Lindsey moves toward a love seat by the window bay and sits down. "You're telling me that you're going to walk away from the mother of your son because of a woman you recently started to date? Seriously, Teddy? I know you. I know how much you've always wanted a family."

She rests her hands on her stomach. "Here we are. Your family. In five weeks, this little bundle is going to meet his daddy, and I'm willing to bet that if he could talk, he'd tell you he wants his mom and dad to raise him together."

"You can't just storm into my life like this, Lindsey. If the baby is mine, I'll take care of him financially, but I'm done with you."

"You need to think about this carefully, Teddy. I made a horrible mistake that I thought ruined any chance we could have at happiness, but now that little Theo is on the way, that could change. We can finally be the family we always dreamed of."

I stand there staring at Lindsey like she's speaking Swahili. Yet even though I'm totally disbelieving this is really happening, there she sits, offering me the one thing I always saw myself having: a family with Lindsey.

CHAPTER FORTY-ONE

FAITH

I'm pacing around the country club bathroom like a caged tiger. *Teddy is having a baby with Lindsey Flint.* My heart is beating so fast I feel like I've just run a two-minute mile. My hopes of us becoming closer are now over. *How can this be happening to me?*

Anna rushes through the door and immediately locks the deadbolt behind her. "Are you okay?"

I catch my reflection in the mirror. I look positively wild-eyed. "I'm not great."

"Did you have any idea?"

"That Teddy had impregnated Lindsey Flint? You know I didn't. There's no way last night would have happened had I known that."

"But they broke up," Anna reminds me.

"So? They're still having a baby together."

"Yeah, but that doesn't mean they're going to get back together," she maintains.

I lean back onto the counter, right into a puddle of water. "We've only been on one real date, Anna," I say. "Based on that, he'd be stupid not to give it another try with Lindsey. They were together for years and Teddy has been mourning her ever since they went their separate ways." I tell her, "I was his first real date since her."

"Seriously?" She sounds completely horrified.

"That's how much he loved her. Now tell me he's going to want to stay with me."

Anna looks very unsure, so I add, "Also, I'm not sold on the idea of dating a guy with a newborn. Not only do I not want to jump right into diapers, but what if we don't work out? I can't let myself fall in love with a child that I will have no rights to."

Someone knocks on the bathroom door, and Anna yells at them, "This bathroom is out of order! Go someplace else!" Then she shakes her head. "That's a good point."

"It is," I tell her. "Not to mention that Teddy is a movie star and I'm nothing close to that. This has got to be the universe's way of telling me to save myself."

"Oh, Faithy." Anna wraps her arms around me. "I can't believe this is happening."

I hiccup against her neck as tears start to pour down my face. "I can. I've never had great luck with men. I think it might be time for me to consider the convent life."

"Don't be ridiculous." She holds me closer. "You're a wonderful woman who has a lot of love to give. You'll find some-body someday."

"Astor wants me back," I tell her.

She looks appalled. "What did you tell him?"

"I told him to take a hike, that I was seeing someone else."

Anna steps back so that she can look me in the eye. "You would never consider getting back together with him, would you?"

"Yuck, no! I'm not an idiot."

"Good." She wets a hand towel before blotting my face with it. "Do you want to go home?" she asks. "I can have my dad take you."

"I want to leave more than anything in this world," I tell her.

"But I'm not going to. I've given men enough power over me to last a lifetime. No, I'm going to go back out there and enjoy your wedding reception."

"You're going to get drunk, aren't you?" *She knows me well.*

"Could be," I tell her.

"What are you going to do about Teddy?"

I push myself off the counter and blot at my skirt with a dry hand towel. "I'm going to cut him loose."

"And if he doesn't want to go?"

I shrug my shoulders. "I don't really care what he wants. I'm looking out for number one from this point on."

"Good girl." Anna pinches my cheeks for color and then takes my hand and leads me out of the bathroom.

Her mother is standing there waiting for us. "You doing okay, honey?" she asks me.

I fake a smile. "You bet I am, Dawn. That whole scene just caught me a little off guard."

She nods her head, but she still looks concerned. "It's time to cut the cake if you two want to come back to the tent."

I didn't even take time to inspect the final product. In fact, I was having so much fun I didn't see Esmé set it up. "How does it look?" I ask.

"Like something you'd find in a medieval forest," she says excitedly.

I smile at Anna and say, "I put extra cherry brandy in the smallest cake. I think I might eat that all by myself."

"You can have whatever you want, Faithy. You certainly deserve it." Then we walk hand in hand back to the tent.

Once we reach our destination, everyone stops talking. They simply stare at me. *Such good times.* Chris runs over to join us and leans in to whisper in my ear, "You've got this, Faith, because we've got you."

"Thanks, Chris."

He points to a table where my grandmother is sitting. "Rosemary doesn't seem to know what's going on. I think she missed the whole thing."

"Good," I tell him. "I'll go sit with her and pretend my life is great." I head in the direction of GG, feeling a renewed sense of resolve that I can get through the rest of the reception.

When I get to her side, she says, "Hi, honey. You having fun?"

"Tons." She doesn't seem to register the sarcasm.

"I'm getting kind of tired," she says. "You don't suppose you might be able to drive me back to Vista Pines, do you?"

"Do you want to stay for cake?" I ask her.

"After the cake," she says. "You know Black Forest is my favorite." GG looks so old to me right now, which is not how I'm used to seeing her. I know she's slowing down, but she's normally so full of life.

GG and I watch while Anna and Chris cut the cake. When they're done, I ask a waiter to wrap up a couple pieces from the top tier for us. I haven't seen Teddy yet, and I want to make our escape before he comes back. *If* he comes back.

Anna and Chris are sitting at their little table for two feeding each other when I arrive. "This cake is amazing, Faith!" Anna says.

"I'm having seconds for sure," Chris adds.

I smile at their compliments. "I know I said I was going to stay, but GG is wiped out. I think I'll take her home and maybe stay with her for a while."

Anna stands up. "I love you." Then she tells Chris, "Give Anna your car keys. She came with Teddy."

Chris hands me his keys with a smile. "We'll pick it up tomorrow."

Pushing past the emotion clogging my throat, I tell them, "I love you. I'm sorry for ruining your wedding."

"You didn't ruin anything," Anna says.

Chris adds, "Not everyone's wedding reception goes viral. This will certainly be something to tell the kids someday."

"Is it already online?" I feel renewed panic start to build.

"I have no idea," he says. "But while you were gone, people were pretty busy on their phones. I'm guessing it's only a matter of time."

"Have you seen Teddy?" I ask him.

"He told me to tell you that he'd catch up with you tomorrow. He didn't want to turn the reception into any more of a circus."

"That was nice of him." *What else can I say?*

"Maybe you can go to his house and see him after you get Rosemary home," Anna suggests.

"I don't think so. Not tonight anyway." I hug them both. "Have a great rest of your night and call me before you leave for Paris tomorrow."

"I could stay," Anna offers.

"We could go to Paris in the spring," Chris adds.

"No way! You two need to celebrate your marriage. I'll still be here when you get back."

As I walk toward GG, my heart feels like it's sinking into a pit of doom. Anna and Chris are happily married, Teddy and Lindsey are having a baby, and then there's me. All alone and on my own, once again.

I think I'm going to stay that way for a long while, too.

CHAPTER FORTY-TWO

TEDDY

The last thing I wanted to do was leave Faith at the reception without saying goodbye. But I had no choice. When Lindsey left to go back to her bed and breakfast, I went back to the tent to find Faith. I was like a fresh bucket of chum thrown into a pod of hungry sharks. Suddenly everyone knew who I was, and they all wanted to know about Lindsey.

I asked Chris to tell Faith that I'd be in touch tomorrow. Even though my intentions were pure, I don't imagine she's taking my abandonment well. Add that to the fact that my ex is pregnant and chose her best friend's wedding reception to announce the news to the world. I'm most definitely in a load of trouble.

As I pull out of the parking lot, I'm tempted to go straight to the hospital to see Theo, but then I'd have to tell him what I'm doing there. So instead, I drive back to my house where I promptly open two beers and take them out on the back porch with me. I drink them like a double fisted drunk.

I take the next two out to the dock, where I set up a weird kind of stakeout. Instead of looking at the water, I turn around and stare at Faith's house. Then I pull out my phone and call Terri.

"Hey," she answers. "I thought tonight was the big night."

"It is. Or was, rather," I tell her.

"Oh, no. What happened?"

"Lindsey showed up."

"To the wedding?" She sounds as shocked as I was.

"To the reception." I take a swig from bottle one before saying, "Faith and I had just finished our big dance number, and there she came waddling across the dance floor."

"Waddling?" Terri laughs. "Did she get fat after leaving the show?"

"Yup," I tell her. "But not because she's eating too much. She's pregnant."

"WHAT?" Terri yells so loudly I pull the phone away from my ear. "What do you mean she's pregnant?"

I'm not sure how to make that any clearer, so I tell her, "She said it happened when she came by our house."

"She says it's yours?"

"Why else would she have shown up in Elk Lake?" I ask.

"Maybe to pawn off someone else's baby on you?"

"I thought that too, but she said Tom and I were the only men she'd been with and that he already took a paternity test."

"So? That doesn't mean anything."

"Terri," I tell her. "When Lindsey and I were together, I was the one pushing to get married and have a family. She could not have cared less."

"What's your point?"

"My point is that if this weren't my baby, I'm betting she would have had an abortion." I continue, "She knows I'm not stupid enough not to get a paternity test, and if that test came back negative, I'd walk for sure."

"And according to her, she's been trying to get a hold of you for months. Oh, my God, Teddy. It might really be yours."

"She refers to the baby as little Theo," I tell her.

"It's a boy?" I hear her groan on the other end of the line.

"And my grandfather just told me that seeing my children is

giving him a new lease on life. Of course, he was talking about me and Faith having kids someday ..."

"How is Faith taking this?"

"I can't imagine well," I tell her. "I left before I had a chance to talk to her. The whole episode was being filmed, by the way. I'm surprised you haven't seen it online yet."

"I was taking an internet break day. Kay's been complaining that I spend so much time on my computer that she never gets to see me on the weekends." I hear her tell Kay, "Babe, it's Teddy. All hell has broken loose."

Kay says, "Fine, go online, but when we leave for Wisconsin on Monday, no more."

Terri whispers into the phone, "I'm on my way into the other room. Hang on." I hear her clicking away at her keyboard before she says, "Holy shit, it's everywhere!" Click, click, click. Then I hear the whole thing second hand. When it's over, she says, "You're going to have to make some kind of statement."

"Why?"

"Because people are going to want to know," she says. "And because if you say your piece upfront, they will be more likely to let you be."

"How about if I say I'll comment once the paternity test comes in?"

"That makes you sound cold," she says. "It's better to say that Lindsey just told you about the baby and that you need a few days to absorb everything. You know, ask for the privacy they won't give you, but tell them you'll make a statement soon."

"And then what? Tell everyone how excited we are that we're going to be parents? I'm not excited, Terri. I don't want kids with Lindsey."

"That ship may have already sailed, my friend," she says. "If Lindsey isn't lying about you being the dad, then for your image alone, you're going to need to publicly be happy about this baby."

"I don't give a crap about my image," I tell her. "What I care about is hurting Faith."

"Well, if this baby is yours," she says, "you're going to have to care about your image. Because you're going to have a child to support."

My brain feels like it's about to explode. "I need to go, Terr. I've got some thinking to do."

"I'm so sorry this is happening, Teddy. Kay and I will be there the day after tomorrow to help."

"What are you going to do?" I ask ungratefully. "Invent a time machine and kidnap me on the night of conception so I can't make such an idiotic mistake?"

"I would if I could," she says. "But being that that isn't likely, we'll just wrap you up in our love, so you don't feel so alone."

"You're the best, Terr." Then I say, "I'm only half-way drunk. I'm going to go so I can get busy finishing the job." Then I hang up.

I continue to stare at Faith's house for another hour or so. Her lights never come on, so I can only assume she stayed at the reception. I hope she's somehow able to have a good time, although I highly doubt that's going to be the case.

When I finally go back into the house, I look for something more potent than beer—like grain alcohol. The only thing my grandfather has is vermouth, and I can't quite imagine getting drunk on that. So, I grab the last beer and go and sit in his chair in the living room.

Staring around the sparsely decorated room, I can't help but wonder what I'm going to do if Lindsey's baby really is mine. If he is, then I'm not going to want to live on the other side of the country from him. And I'm positive Lindsey is not going to want to relocate to Wisconsin. Even if she's cool with it, I'm not sure Faith would be.

I suppose I'll just have to go back to Sherman Oaks and finish renovating my house, so I'll be able to keep little Theo when it's my turn with him. Little Theo ... the name pulls at my heart strings. I always told Lindsey I wanted to name our first son Theo, after my grandfather. She's either honoring that, or she's playing one hell of a vicious mind game with me. I guess I won't know the answer to that until we get the results from the paternity test.

I immediately pull out my phone and google where we can get that done. It looks like the first step is to find a doctor who will order one and then go to a lab for Lindsey to have a blood draw. All they need from me is a cheek swab.

If I'm being honest with myself, I don't know what to hope for. I don't want to have a baby with Lindsey, but if he already exists, I never want him to feel like he was a mistake. And the best way to make sure that doesn't happen would be to marry his mother.

CHAPTER FORTY-THREE

FAITH

"I'm thinking about marrying God," I tell GG as soon as we get into Chris's car.

I'm not sure what I think her response should be, but I don't expect her to say, "Word on the street is He isn't that great in the sack."

"GG!" Even though I didn't grow up going to church often, that still sounds sacrilegious to me.

"Don't have a cow." She buckles her seatbelt. "I think God has a better sense of humor than anyone gives Him credit for."

"In what way?" I back out of the parking space.

"Have you ever seen naked people? Now that's funny."

She may have a point. "Well, at this juncture, I'm not looking for anyone who's good in bed. I'm sick of men and all their crap."

"That pregnant gal was carrying your new beau's baby, huh?"

"You caught that?" So much for Chris thinking GG was oblivious.

"Honey, I could have caught that with my eyes closed and my hands tied behind my back."

"I'm so embarrassed," I tell her. "I can't believe that scene had to play out at Anna's wedding."

"You have nothing to be embarrassed about," she tells me. "As far as I saw, you and your date are the victims here."

I turn left off Country Club Lane. "How do you figure Teddy was a victim?"

"You don't think he invited that girl to Anna's reception in hopes she'd make a scene, do you?"

"I suppose not."

"And he seemed quite shocked by the state of things." She puts her hands out in front of her like she's acting act out the word pregnant in a game of charades.

"I think he was," I agree.

"So then why are you talking about hitching yourself to the Big Guy?"

"Because I don't want to date a man who's having a baby with another woman. I would have never gotten involved with him had I known that."

GG lets her head drop back against the head rest. "You know what they say, Faith." Before I can venture a guess, she tells me, "Man plans, and God laughs."

"What does that even mean?" I demand hotly. I'm not mad at GG, but darn if she doesn't say the craziest things at times. I reference, *God isn't that great in the sack …*

"It means that for all the planning we do, there will always be outside forces that get in the way of our being able to forecast the future. Do you think those poor suckers on the *Titanic* had any clue what they were in for? It didn't matter that they had all their outfits planned for every meal or that they were expected at one gala or another upon arrival in New York. No sir, they planned, and God laughed."

"I highly doubt God laughed at that tragedy, GG."

"He wasn't laughing at the tragedy, Faithy. He was laughing at man's arrogance to think they had any control over the future just because they'd made plans."

I drive quietly the rest of the way to Vista Pines, thinking about that. How can we not make plans? Making plans is the only thing that brings order to our chaotic human experience.

After parking at Vista Pines, I get out and open the door for GG. When she steps out, she says, "I think we'd all be better off living like those Zen folks."

"What Zen folks?" I wonder if the nursing home has a new club.

She takes my arm and walks slowly next to me. "You know, those Buddhists. They live in the here and now. They don't get bogged down with all that future nonsense."

"My here and now isn't that spectacular," I tell her grumpily.

"Mine is." She squeezes my arm. "I'm walking with my best girl on a beautiful summer night, and I have cake to eat as soon as I get inside."

Leave it to my grandmother to pull me out of my pity party. "I love you, GG."

"I love you too, honey. I know tonight has taken you by surprise, but I don't think you need to make any decisions for a while."

After getting to GG's room, I help her get into her pajamas. Then I take her hair out of her bun and brush it for her. Once she's sitting in bed, I open the containers of cake and hand her one. "Shoot," I remember. "It's got cherry brandy and you're not supposed to mix alcohol with some of your meds."

She waves her hand in front of her face before opening her bedside drawer and pulling out a bottle of vodka. Holding it up, she says, "I like to think those warnings are nothing but gentle suggestions."

I don't know whether to laugh or scold her. "GG ..."

"What's the worst thing that can happen to me? I'll die? Please. I've already got one foot in the grave and another on an oil slick."

"Don't say that."

"Honey, you gotta live while you're alive. You can't let fear rule your choices." She unscrews the vodka bottle and takes a swig out of it. She offers me one, but I just shake my head, so she screws the lid back on and puts it back in her drawer.

After taking my first bite of cake, I ask, "What would you do if you were me?"

She thinks for a moment before asking, "What would I have done fifty years ago when I was young, or what would I do now with all of my vast experience with life?"

"Both."

She puts her fork down. "If I were in your situation when I was twenty-nine, I would have probably thought my whole life was over."

"And now?" I prod.

"Now, I'd stand still for a minute and let the dust settle. Then I'd take each situation as it came. I wouldn't make any rash decisions like running off to a nunnery."

"So just wait and see, huh? That doesn't sound like it will be too easy," I tell her.

"Life isn't easy, Faith. There are moments for sure, but they're always followed by challenges. What you have to remember is that the challenges don't define you."

"How do you feel about me spending the night here?" I ask.

She scoots over in her little twin bed and pats the mattress next to her. "I always have room for you, baby."

My eyes start to water. "I'll sleep on your reclining chair, GG. But thank you."

GG picks up the telephone next to her bed. "Jocelyn, it's Rosemary in room one twelve. Do you have a rollaway bed I can use for the night? Uh, huh. Yup. Okay. Thanks."

"I didn't think you were allowed to have overnight guests," I say when she hangs up.

"Why would you think that?"

"I don't know, maybe because your room isn't that big?"

"I can have someone spend the night up to three times a month," she tells me.

"Why didn't I ever know that?" I ask.

"Because you have your own life, and you spend enough time with me as it is. I never wanted you to feel like you had to sleep over on top of everything else you do."

"It wouldn't exactly be a chore, GG." I'm hurt that I never knew this was an option.

"I come and stay with you once in a while," she says. "That's enough." Then she points across the room at a chest of drawers. "There are some nightgowns in the top drawer. One of those should fit you okay for the night."

I open the drawer and immediately feel like I'm five years old. Touching the variety of silky nylon gowns transports me. I pick up a pink one and take it into the bathroom. It's ridiculously short and a little tight in the chest, but it will work.

When I get out of the bathroom, I find that GG has already gone to sleep. Someone also brought in a folding bed and left it right next to her. I open it up and push it so that it's an extension of her mattress. Then I get in and take her bony hand in mine.

I don't go to sleep right away. Instead, I lie there and try my hardest to stay in the moment. I feel the breath fill my lungs and can almost visualize it as it leaves my body. After several minutes, I'm left with one clear thought. *Life is not easy, but that doesn't mean I should go out of my way to make it any harder.*

CHAPTER FORTY-FOUR

TEDDY

My first conscious thought is that my head feels like I've fallen out of a two-story window and landed on it. I put my hands on top of my hair and squeeze hard to stop all the throbbing. It doesn't work.

I sit up slowly, hoping the room will stop spinning so fast. *How in the world am I drunk on two glasses of champagne?* Then I remember the five beers and tumbler full of vermouth—which was just as gross as it sounds. It's all I can do not to throw up at the memory.

Staggering into the bathroom, I take three aspirin out of the cabinet and swallow them with a handful of water from the sink. Then I brush my teeth with vigor to scrub off all the little fur coats that grew on them during the night.

Once I get to the kitchen, I put on a pot of extra strong coffee and force myself to drink a glass of orange juice. After my first cup of caffeine, I realize how hungry I am.

I decide to head over to Rosemary's for something sweet, and hopefully a chance to talk to Faith. I'm not sure what I'm going to say to her, but I can't let any more time go by without addressing last night.

Nick greets me with, "Teddy Helms is in the house!" This, of course, causes every person there to turn around and stare at me.

"Is there some reason you had to do that?" I hiss as I approach the counter.

His face turns bright red. "I'm sorry, I always greet people I know by their full name. I wasn't thinking."

I believe him, so I decide not to hold a grudge. "Is Faith in?" I ask.

"After last night?" He sounds shocked at the very idea.

"You know about last night?"

"*Everyone* knows about last night, Teddy."

I look over my shoulder to see that my back seems to be the main focal point in the room. "Can I get a triple espresso and a couple of donuts to go?"

Nick gets my order together. As he puts it on the counter, he looks over my shoulder and says, "Trouble, man. Lindsey just got here." I'm about to ask him how he knows her, but then think better of it. *Everyone knows* according to him.

Lindsey steps up behind me and greets, "Teddy."

"Lindsey. What are you doing here?"

"You neglected to give me your phone number last night before leaving the country club." She points to Nick. "This lovely man told me the other day that you stop by here most mornings, so I thought this would be my best chance to continue our discussion."

I turn to Nick. "I thought you'd gotten that out of your system …"

He shrugs half-heartedly. "I did too, sorry."

Lindsey takes my arms and says, "We need to talk."

"Not here," I tell her. I lead the way out the front door and start to walk down the street toward the park. Luckily, no one seems to be following us. As soon as we get to a park bench, I sit down and gesture for her to join me.

She sits next to me and then takes my bag and pulls out a donut for herself. "You don't eat donuts," I say in shock. Lindsey usually doesn't eat any simple carbs.

"Your son does," she tells me before taking a bite.

"Is he really mine, Linds?" I ask.

"Yes, Teddy, he is. Listen …" She stops to take another bite. After swallowing it, she continues, "I'm sorry about the way this went down. I hadn't intended to blindside you at a public event, but I couldn't get ahold of you any other way. Believe me, I've tried."

"You could have told Terri what was going on and she would have called me," I suggest.

"I didn't know that you'd want Terri to have this information," she says.

"Terri is my best friend. Why wouldn't I want her to know?"

She shrugs. "It just seemed like the right thing to do was to tell you first and then let you share the news with whomever you wanted to."

I guess that makes sense. "I'm surprised you decided to have the baby," I tell her.

"I am too," she says bluntly. "It's not that I never wanted to have kids, Teddy. It's just that I didn't want them as much as you did."

"Then why are you having this one?" I'm not trying to be unkind; I just really want to know.

"Because I'm thirty-two and not currently employed. I figure now is as good a time as any."

"That doesn't sound like you." I take a giant bite of the remaining donut.

Lindsey reaches over and touches my hand. "I wouldn't be having this baby if the father was anyone but you, Teddy. You will be a great dad, and even though you clearly think I'm the most selfish woman in the world, I want the best thing for my child."

"God, Lindsey …" Her words are touching but there's so much negative history between us, it's hard to take them at face value. "What did Tom say when he found out the baby wasn't his?"

"He was disappointed. He was hoping that having a baby together would be enough reason for me to go back to him."

"Why did you break up?" I ask, not sure I really want to know.

"Tom knew that I still loved you, and he gave me an ultimatum. I had to either quit pining for you and dedicate myself to him, or I had to go. I left that afternoon."

"So, you were still with him when we …" I point to her stomach. "I thought you said that you'd already broken up."

"I knew you would have never been with me if you thought that Tom and I were still together." She lowers her head in what appears to be shame. But I know Lindsey and she's shameless.

"So, you tricked me?"

"It might look like that, but that's not what I was trying to do. I just wanted to remind you how good we were together. I wanted you to think about giving me a second chance."

I take the lid off my espresso and take a long sip. It's so hot it chars some taste buds on its way down my throat. "What do you expect me to do?" I finally ask.

"What do I want you to do, or what do I expect you to do?" she asks. She doesn't wait for me to answer. "I want you to give me another chance. I want that for me and our son, and for you too, Teddy. I *want* us to be a happy family. In lieu of that happening, I want you to enjoy being a dad. We could share custody, and both be active parts of little Theo's life."

"I'm buying my grandfather's house," I tell her.

"In Elk Lake? How are you going to make that work?"

"Terri has already booked me for the next Alpha Dog movie. I'll just go to LA when I need to and then fly out of here for whatever location I'm shooting at."

"You seriously want to live in Wisconsin?" It's like I just told her I wanted to retire to the outer ring of Saturn.

I did, but now I have no idea if that will still work. If Faith decides she wants nothing more to do with me, I won't want to run into her all the time. "That's my plan," I tell her.

"What about me?"

"As I haven't been thinking about you," I tell her, "I don't know. I guess I could stay in LA for part of the year, and you could come here for part of the year. That way Theo would have us both."

"I don't want to live in Wisconsin, Teddy."

"I guess that's something we'll have to work out then," I tell her. I'm in no position to do that right now as I haven't even talked to Faith. And then like Heathcliff staring off into the moors in *Wuthering Heights*, I see her like a phantom drifting closer.

I stand up and tell Lindsey my phone number. Then I say, "Let's get together again before you leave town."

"You're just walking away from me? Why can't we talk now?"

"Because we aren't the only ones this affects," I tell her.

She turns around and sees Faith. "You can talk to her any time," she says angrily. "Right now, you and I have a lot to figure out."

I look down at Lindsey and stare at her hard, before saying, "Faith is important to me."

"And I'm not?"

"You have been nothing to me for months," I tell her honestly. "You can wait." Then I turn off and run down the sidewalk toward the woman I know I've started to fall in love with. Heck, I'm probably already there.

CHAPTER FORTY-FIVE

FAITH

I wasn't originally scheduled to work today, but there doesn't seem to be any reason for me not to go in. Maybe Esmé can enjoy an unexpected afternoon off.

As I walk past the park, I start to feel the endorphins kick in. I expect I'll be doing a lot of walking in the next weeks for that very reason. I'm about to cross the street when I see Teddy coming toward me. He waves, which means there's no point in trying to hide. Although, I do glance wistfully toward a large trash can. *Yes, that's what my life has come to—I yearn to jump into the garbage to hide.*

"Faith!" he calls out as he jogs toward me.

"Teddy. How are you?"

His posture straightens as we both stop walking. "Not great. How are you?"

"We must have both caught the same bug," I say, trying for some levity.

"I told Lindsey that I need a paternity test."

I nod my head. "That makes sense."

"I can't really make any decisions before then."

I continue nodding stupidly.

When neither of us speaks, I start to walk again. Teddy stays at my side. While I once felt perfectly natural and comfortable next to him, I now feel awkward and uneasy. I finally say, "I wish you and Lindsey the best."

"What? Why?"

"Because you're having a baby together." I want to crawl into a hole.

"We don't know the baby is mine, yet," he says.

"Why would Lindsey fly all the way out here if it weren't?"

Teddy lifts one shoulder in a half-shrug. "I don't know. But I don't think I should be making decisions for the rest of my life based on her word. Do you?"

"Look, Teddy"—I stop walking and face him—"I don't have any hold on you. In fact, we barely know each other, so if the baby is yours, I think you should go be with Lindsey."

He's quiet for a long stretch of time, which makes me think he agrees with me. When he finally speaks, he says, "I'm going to work on getting that paternity test right away. Before Lindsey leaves Elk Lake."

"You do what you have to do," I tell him. Standing next to him is wreaking havoc with my senses. I want to reach out and touch him; I want to kiss him. But neither of those things is in my best interest. "Call me when you know the results."

"Can't we spend some time together today?" he asks.

"To what end? If the baby is yours, we should not be getting any closer."

"You wouldn't want to keep seeing me if I'm the father?" I'm not sure what *he* wants, but I get the sense he's trying to get as much information as he can so he can make his own decision.

"No," I tell him plainly. "I don't."

He shifts from side-to-side nervously. "I guess I don't blame you."

"I just broke up with someone I thought I'd be with for the rest of my life, Teddy," I tell him. "And I don't want to jump into something that could affect the life of a child."

I'm not sure how I think he'll respond, but I'm surprised when he says, "You'll be a great mother someday." I can feel the angst radiating from him.

"I hope so," I tell him. "But for the record, I'm not going to go out of my way to fall in love with a man who already has kids. Children need to be a parent's first priority, and I'd like to have that spot in someone's heart before being replaced."

"So you don't want to see me anymore? Even as a friend?"

"Not if you're Lindsey's baby daddy." When we reach the front door of the bakery, I tell him, "I hope you understand. But even if you don't, I need to do what's right for me."

"Of course you do." He leans in like he's going to kiss my cheek before catching himself. Taking a tiny step back, he says, "I'm sorry, Faith. I like you so much."

"I like you too, Teddy, but let's not fool ourselves into thinking we're closer than we are. Neither one of us needs that kind of complication right now." It's a cold thing to say, but I can't help myself. Because it's the right thing to say.

"My friend Terri and her wife are coming tomorrow. I know she wanted to meet you."

The last thing I want to do is to get to know any more people from Teddy's life. It's already going to be hard to keep my distance from Theo. I was hoping to introduce him to GG. She loves playing cruise director and helping new residents acclimate to Vista Pines.

I tell him, "I don't think I should be getting more involved in your life right now."

He looks like he's in physical pain as his features contort in what I'm assuming is an attempt to smile. "I'll let you know as soon as I learn anything. I'm not sure when that will be."

Instead of dragging this conversation out any further, I simply tell him, "Sounds good." Then I turn and walk into the bakery alone. I'm greeted by several flashes from people's phones. That scene from *Notting Hill*, when Spike opens his front door and is greeted by the press, flashes through my brain.

While I'm not sure I have the guts to brazen this moment out with the same confidence he had, I force a smile to my face. "Good morning!" I call out cheerfully. Nick jolts like he just stuck his finger into a live outlet.

"Faith!" he declares. Then he rushes around the counter to greet me before quietly whispering, "What are you doing here?"

"Why wouldn't I be here?" I ask. "It's my bakery."

He moves so that his back is facing our audience. "Yes, but last night at the wedding ..."

I don't have a chance to reply because the door opens, and a news camera crew walks in. An overly styled woman in a hot pink suit shoves a microphone in my face. She says, "Talia Harper from the Associated Press. Faith, can you tell us how you're feeling today?"

I have two options right now. I can run into the back and refuse to come out, or I can face the music and pretend I'm fine. I choose the latter. "I'm feeling pretty good, Talia. Why do you ask?" *I didn't say I was going to make this easy for her.*

"According to every gossip site online, you're in the middle of a complicated love triangle with Teddy Helms and Lindsey Flint. How do you feel about Teddy being the father of Lindsey's baby?"

I don't bother to dispute the possible paternity. Instead, I say, "I think babies are a great thing. I wish Teddy and Lindsey all the best."

"So, you're taking yourself out of the picture, are you?"

I briefly consider taking her microphone and hitting her over the head with it. Instead, I opt for a classier approach. "Teddy and I are friends. I'm not sure where you heard that we were anything more."

Instead of answering, she takes her phone out of her pocket and holds it up to me. She must have twenty pictures of me and Teddy kissing at Anna and Chris's rehearsal dinner. *Crap.*

I don't have a chance to comment before the door opens again. It's Astor. "Faith!" He sounds overly excited to see me, being that the last time we spoke I told him to hit the bricks.

"Astor, what are you doing here?" I ask him while he insinuates himself between me and the photographer and kisses me on the cheek.

"Where else would I be?" He turns and smiles into the camera before adding, "I'm always around for my girl."

Talia jumps on that like a horse fly on a fresh cow patty. "Are you saying that you and Faith are dating?"

"We've been together for ten months," he tells her.

"Really? I heard that Faith and Teddy Helms were an item." She clearly senses a lie when she hears one.

"We took a little break," he tells her. "But we're back together now. Isn't that right, Faith?"

This is my chance to set the record straight and dump Astor publicly and forever. But I don't say anything right away because this is also my chance not to be cast in such a negative light in front of the whole world.

I do not want to be remembered as the woman Alpha Dog dumped for his ex.

CHAPTER FORTY-SIX

TEDDY

After leaving downtown, I spend the rest of my Sunday with my grandfather at the hospital. I don't say anything about how Faith and I had started to see one another. No sense in getting Theo's hopes up only to dash them. I do, however, need to tell him about Lindsey.

Once he finishes his pudding cup, I jump in. "It looks like you might be a great-grandfather before you'd thought."

His brow furrows into a frown. "How's that?" He does not sound pleased.

"Lindsey showed up yesterday in Elk Lake nearly eight months pregnant."

"You two broke up two years ago."

"We did," I confirm. "But we spent one night together almost eight months ago."

He doesn't say anything for the longest time, and I start to wonder if he heard me. "Grandpa?"

"Dammit, Teddy!" He does not sound happy. "Why would you have done something so stupid? The woman cheated on you."

"She did. And I don't have any decent excuse for my behavior other than to say when she showed up at my house, I was feeling particularly vulnerable."

"She was only there because you'd become more successful than Tom," he says harshly.

It hurts like hell to hear that, even though it's probably true. "I know."

"Once a cheater, always a cheater," he says.

"I'm sure there are people who make mistakes and learn from them." I'm not trying to defend Lindsey as much as I'm trying to figure out if I believe what I just said.

"Are you seriously saying that you'd be willing to stake your happiness on Lindsey's word that she's learned her lesson?"

"What other choice do I have if it turns out I'm her baby's father?"

Theo presses the button on his remote that raises his legs. He shifts to a more comfortable position before saying, "Don't let that child grow up thinking it's secure in a loving home, only to make it a product of divorce. Better to let them always think of their parents as separate entities."

"It's a boy," I tell him. "Lindsey wants to name him Theo."

"Of course she does. If acting doesn't work out for her, she could investigate becoming a professional manipulator."

"Are you saying you wouldn't be happy if the baby is mine?" I hate having this conversation with him at all, let alone while he's in the hospital recovering from such a harrowing surgery.

"I'm saying let's wait and see before we throw a parade."

Before I can respond, a nurse comes rushing in. "Mr. Helms," she says. "You're wanted in the emergency room."

My first thought is that something happened to Faith. I jump to my feet and demand, "Why?"

"Your wife is in labor," she says. "They're working to admit her now."

"He's not married!" Theo shouts.

She sounds flustered by that news. "Oh, well then, your girlfriend."

I don't bother to correct her assumption. "Is she okay? She's not due for six more weeks."

"That's something you'll have to ask the OB on duty. I was just told to come get you."

I turn to my grandfather. "I'll be back as soon as I can."

"I wouldn't be upset if the baby is yours, Teddy," he says quietly.

"Thanks, Grandpa," I tell him. Then I turn and follow the nurse out of the room. I don't know much about babies, but I don't think six weeks early would be life threatening. At least I hope not.

By the time I get down to the ER, they've already moved Lindsey to the maternity wing. The nurse at the desk sees me coming and says, "She's in labor room six, Mr. Helms."

I run down the hall in the direction she's pointing. As I pass labor room three, I hear Lindsey yell out in pain before declaring, "I changed my mind, I don't want this baby!"

I walk through her door and rush to her side. "What happened?"

"Your son decided to come early," she hisses through a contraction.

The nurse next to her bed adjusts what I'm assuming is a saline drip. She says, "Ms. Flint was brought here by ambulance when she fainted on Main Street. Her blood pressure is dangerously high."

"You fainted?" I'm more than a little concerned at that news.

"Luckily a nice stranger was nearby." Oh yeah, she's mad that I left her to go with Faith.

I ask the nurse, "Is there some way you can stop the labor, so the baby isn't born so early?"

"At this point," she says, "we usually rush the mother in for an emergency C-section so no other problems arise. Like pre-eclampsia. But the doctor will be in shortly to talk to you."

Once she leaves, I sit down next to Lindsey and take her hand. "I'm sorry," I tell her. "I should have stayed with you."

Her body seems to relax like the contraction has passed. "I'm sorry, too. I have no right to be mad at you, Teddy. I made my bed."

We sit quietly, both absorbed in our thoughts, until the doctor comes in. He's older, probably in his sixties, and he has an upbeat, energetic presence. "Looks like we're going to meet a baby today!" he says excitedly.

"Are you doing a C-Section?" Lindsey asks nervously.

He picks up the chart at the end of her bed and flips through it. "The baby's heart rate is high. Coupled with your blood pressure, I think that would be the safest option for both mother and son."

"Are they in any danger?" I ask, suddenly feeling a connection to Lindsey's unborn child for the first time.

"There are always risks," he says. "But we're going to do everything in our power to make sure they both stay healthy." He looks at his watch. "We have an operating room booked in thirty minutes. That'll give you both time to get ready."

I look over at Lindsey and her face is unnaturally pale. "You okay?" I ask her.

She shakes her head. "I'm not sure I'm ready for this."

The doctor tells me, "The nurse will come in and give you a pair of scrubs. Then she'll show you where to get cleaned up." This is the first I'm even thinking about being there for the delivery.

He tells Lindsey, "You just sit back and try to stay calm. You're in good hands, young lady. I've delivered more than four hundred babies by C-Section in my career."

As he leaves the room, Lindsey squeezes my hand. "What am I doing?"

"I think you're having a baby," I tell her.

"No, I mean, why am I having a baby? I've never really wanted a baby." She sounds panicked.

"You're going to do great, Linds. You've got this."

"Please tell me that you're going to love him," she says. "One of us has to."

Instead of bringing up the paternity test, I tell her, "Of course I'm going to love him. And so are you."

"Oh, my God … a baby! I mean, I've felt him kicking around like a blackbelt but now he's coming out. He's real!"

I feel a hurricane of emotions right now. I haven't even had a chance to get used to the idea that I might be a father, and now I'm minutes away from meeting my son. It's a lot to take in. I decide the best thing for both me and Lindsey right now is to be a united front. If this baby is mine, I want to remember his birth as a time of joy, not suspicion.

"Lindsey Ann Flint," I tell her, "we've talked about this moment a lot during our years together. I say we enjoy it."

Her eyes fill with tears. "Thank you, Teddy. Thank you for being you. You truly are going to be an amazing dad."

I give Lindsey a kiss on the forehead as the nurse comes in. "Mr. Helms, if you'll follow me, I'll show you where to get ready for the delivery." I smile at Lindsey. "Okay, Mom, I'll see you on center stage."

She smiles weakly. "Okay, Dad, see you there."

As I walk out of her hospital room, I can't even begin to imagine the day ahead of me.

CHAPTER FORTY-SEVEN

FAITH

Work is a revolving door of persistent members of the press. As sad as I am, I'm starting to feel a sense of relief that Teddy and I aren't a couple. I do not want to spend my life feeling like everything I do is so interesting to countless strangers.

When my phone rings at five, I pick it up grumpily. "What?"

"Is that anyway to talk to your best friend?" Anna asks.

"Sorry. It's been a day," I tell her.

"I'm sure," she says. "I just wanted to let you know that we picked up the car and we're almost to the airport. Oh, and we got the house!" *Insert excited squeal here.*

"I'm so happy for you, Anna! That's the best news ever."

"Just think of all the fun we're going to have picking out paint colors and carpet and new counter tops ..."

"Isn't that something Chris will want a say in?" I ask.

"He'll be happy with whatever we choose," she says. "I just wanted to let you know before we left for Paris."

"Thank you." I turn off the lights in the bakery and let myself out the front door. "I can't wait."

"I know you're not too excited now, but I predict you will be," she says mysteriously.

"Why is that?"

"Because you can't be sad forever, and the contractor I hired is gorgeous!"

I groan loudly. "No, thank you. Not interested."

"Give yourself some time to come down from this week." I hear mumbling in the background. "Chris says that if he were into guys, he'd jump at a chance with Chip."

"Chip? Uh, no."

"What's wrong with Chip?"

"He sounds like he's either a country club snob or chipmunk," I say unkindly.

"We'll talk about it when I get home." She changes the subject. "What do you want me to bring you for a souvenir?"

"An Eiffel Tower snow globe," I tell her. I don't share anything about today with Teddy or the reporters. No sense in sending her off on a bad note.

"You're on," she says. "Love you, Faithy! Talk to you soon!"

"Love you," I tell her before signing off.

I'm nearly to the park when I'm approached by yet another reporter, full-on with camera crew behind him. Before he has a chance to say anything to me, I demand, "What's wrong with you people? Why can't you just leave me alone?"

"Faith Reynolds?" he asks.

"Like you didn't already know that."

He signals the camera before asking me, "How do you feel about Lindsey Hart giving birth to her son right here in Elk Lake?"

What kind of dumb question is that? "I'm pretty sure she's going to have him in California."

He shakes his head, "We've just received a tip that Theodore James Helms was born thirty minutes ago at Elk Lake Community hospital."

My knees suddenly go weak, and I worry that I'm about to

crumple in a heap at this man's feet. For all of my bravado, I'm really a total mess. I force myself to inhale deeply before answering, "I wish them all well."

"Are you and Mr. Helms still dating?" As much as I toyed with the idea of letting the press think that Astor and I had gotten back together, I ultimately chose to tell them the truth. I don't want any links to my ex. Not after what he did.

I stop walking and tell the reporter," I'm not sure why it's your business, but I'm not with Teddy or Astor. I'm just a girl who runs a bakery in Elk Lake, Wisconsin. Surely, that can't be of any interest to you."

He starts to look uncertain, like I might be on to something. "But the pictures of you and Teddy tell another story."

"Did I kiss Teddy Helms?" I ask. "Yes, I did. Does that mean I'm in love with him? No, it does not. Now please, please leave me alone and find someone else to torment." I walk down the sidewalk on my own.

I feel oddly detached from my body, like the news of Lindsey having her baby has severed a cord to reality. So much for having to wait to find out if the baby is Teddy's. He's sure to discover the truth of paternity relatively quickly now. The whole thing makes me feel nauseated.

I don't know what to do with myself when I get home. Anna is on her way to Paris and Teddy is at the hospital. I dare not go out for fear that I'll continue to be targeted by every media person currently in town.

I decide to pour myself a bowl of cereal and go out back. Instead of sitting at the table, I plop down on the deck, crisscross applesauce—just like I did when I was a kid. I find the warmth from the sun-heated boards oddly comforting.

In the last month, my life has gone from the ridiculous to the sublime and right back to the ridiculous. Maybe I should take a page out of Anna's book and get out of town for a while. Although I can't really miss work this time of year without hiring someone else.

Before I can come up with any firm plans, I hear someone call my name. It's Missy Corner and she's standing at the bottom of the steps that lead up to the patio.

"Hey, Missy, what are you doing here?"

She starts to climb slowly. "I thought you might need someone to talk to."

Missy and I have always been friendly, but we've never been friends. "Are you working for one of the tabloids?" I try to make my question sound like a joke.

She looks hurt. "No. I just heard what happened last night at Anna's wedding. And I know she's on her honeymoon."

"So, you're here to check on me?" That's really nice, and I hate myself for questioning her.

She sits down on a chair nearby. "I know what it's like when things don't turn out how you expect them to."

"Really?" I hate to admit it, but I don't think in all the preparation for Anna's wedding either Anna or I ever asked Missy about her life. Talk about self-centered.

"It's a long and drawn-out story that I won't bore you with now, but suffice it to say, on two occasions I thought I'd met 'the one.' I was wrong both times."

"Were you engaged?" I'd never heard anything about it and that's the kind of thing that spreads like wildfire in Elk Lake.

She shakes her head. "No, but I thought it was coming both times."

"Cheaters?" I ask, feeling a sense of sisterhood with Missy I've never felt before.

"One of them was. The last one died before he could ask me to marry him. His mother gave me the ring at his funeral."

"He died?" I'm beyond shocked. How have I not heard anything about this?

"He lived in Madison," she said. "We spent most of our time there."

I slowly stand up and walk over to take the chair next to

Missy. I sit down and tell her, "That must have been horrible. I'm so sorry."

She nods her head slowly. "Dillion died last year. I'm still not over it."

"How could you be?" I reach out and put my hand on her arm in a what I'm hoping is a comforting gesture.

"My mom seems to think I need to put myself out there again, but I just haven't been able to do that."

A horrible thought hits me that I should probably keep to myself, but I don't. "And you own a bridal boutique! It must be torture watching brides come and go, all getting ready for their big day."

"It hasn't exactly been easy," she says. "But to be honest, I really do love being a part of their special events. I still dream about getting married myself someday."

"I'm sure you will," I tell her, not at all convinced. My own recent disappointments have good and truly dampened my normally optimistic nature.

Missy sighs dramatically. "My mom says I need to stop having a pity party and move on already."

"That seems kind of harsh," I say.

"Mom never understood what I saw in either Matt or Dillion. She didn't think either of them were good enough for me."

"How so?" Again, this is not my business, but I feel oddly better knowing that I'm not the only one to have had her heart broken on multiple occasions. *Disappointment has made me a monster.*

"Matt was a cop, and Mom always thought I should marry a man with a college degree. Dillion was an actuary. She thought that made him boring."

"What kind of man does she see you marrying?" It's not like Elk Lake is full of successful, eligible bachelors. We're mostly a blue-color summer vacation town. So if you're not looking for a fisherman, a minimum wage employee, or a person in lawn maintenance, your pickings are pretty slim.

Missy looks so sad right now, I wish there were something I could do to cheer her up. But maybe I'm helping just by listening to her. I sure hope so.

Missy says, "I think she wants me to marry a doctor or a dentist, or even a schoolteacher. She has some definite ideas about how she expects my life to turn out."

"I think moms just want their kids to be happy," I say. "And I'm willing to bet they'd do anything in their power to make that happen."

Missy sits up straighter. "Enough about me. How are you doing? Can I help you in any way?"

"I wish you could," I tell her. "But as it stands, I'm just sitting around waiting to find out if Teddy is the father of Lindsey's baby. She already had him, by the way. Right here in Elk Lake."

"You're kidding!"

I rest my elbows on the table in front of me in a defeated pose. "I heard it from one of the many reporters stalking me."

"Then he should know pretty quickly if the baby is his."

I nod my head. The thing is that with all the media attention, I'm no longer sure that I want to be with Teddy, even if he isn't the father.

It's possible this whole nightmare might have been a blessing in disguise.

CHAPTER FORTY-EIGHT

TEDDY

I've been staring at little Theo for an hour, and I still can't tell if he's mine. He's adorable and surprisingly big for a preemie, but the doctor said that babies with gestational diabetic mothers are often bigger. That was the first time I'd heard that part of the story.

Lindsey is breast feeding Theo and staring at him like he holds the secrets to the universe. "He's beautiful," I tell her.

She meets my gaze. "He really is. He's just perfect."

"Do you want me to call anybody? Your parents? Your friends?"

"I'd appreciate if you'd call my folks. I'm not sure I'm ready to share the news with anyone else."

"I'm not sure you're going to have a say-so there. I'm guessing word of your delivering here will soon be the talk of the town, and then the press is sure to descend."

"Only because of you. Not me." She sounds annoyed.

"I'm sure you'll get another part in no time and people will start to hound you again." I've always thought that Lindsey was in this line of work for the attention, and she's doing nothing to change my mind. It also makes me wonder if she didn't have this baby just to get her own name back into the press. That thought makes me sick to my stomach.

Later in the evening, Lindsey says, "You don't have to stay. I'm sure you're exhausted, and I could use a break."

"Are you sure?" I really would like some space to think.

"Yeah, go on," she says. "Maybe you can come back in the morning."

"Of course," I tell her. Then I stand up and say, "You did a great job today, Linds. Get some rest."

I touch the baby's cheek while he nurses before turning around and walking out the door. I stop to see my grandfather but he's sleeping, so I leave him a message that little Theo is doing great and that I'll be back in the morning. Then I go home, praying the right thing happens.

Just yesterday, I might have prayed that Theo wasn't mine, but after being there for his birth, and holding him, I'm just not sure what to hope for anymore. Babies are magical little beings and if anything could heal the hurt that's taken place between me and Lindsey, a baby might do the trick.

The last thing I want to do when I get home is tie one on like I did last night. So, I take a hot shower and try to go to bed early. I need clarity, so sleep seems like the best idea.

By nine o'clock, I'm under the covers and ready to turn off the light when my phone rings. It's my mom. *Shoot, I called Lindsey's mom but not my own.* "Hey, Mom, what's up?"

"What's up?" she demands. "We have televisions in Arizona, you know."

Hearing the news on TV must have really blown her mind. "It's been a busy day," I tell her. "I'm sorry I didn't call."

"I'm not sure how I feel about all this. I mean, I've always gotten on well with Lindsey, but I thought you two were good and over. Now I find out there's a baby."

"I don't know if he's mine yet," I tell her. "I'm getting a paternity test."

"Good. Then I'll reserve excitement until you do know. When will that be, anyway?"

"Soon," I tell her, as I pull one of the pillows out from under my head. "I didn't think it was in good taste to ask for it on the day of his birth."

"I guess I can see that. But you call me the minute you know, Teddy. The very second."

"I will, Mom. I promise."

We talk for a few more minutes before saying goodnight. Once I hang up, I turn my phone off so I'm not bothered again. Sooner or later someone from the press is going to get my number and then it will be nonstop ringing.

I sleep surprisingly very well. In fact, I don't wake up until my doorbell starts to buzz incessantly. It must go off ten times before I realize it's not part of my dream. I hurry to pull some pajama pants on and then run down the stairs. Opening the door, I expect to find Terri and Kay—they said they wanted to rent a car to have at their disposal. And while they are there, they've also brought company.

"Tom," I say, full of shock at seeing Lindsey's most recent ex.

"Teddy." Tom looks like he hasn't slept in a week.

"What are you doing here?" I ask him, before shooting Terri a look of total disbelief.

She steps forward and announces, "Tom is here to take a paternity test."

"What?" My gaze shifts to him. "I thought he already did that?"

"No," he says. "In fact, I didn't even know Lindsey was pregnant until Terri called me yesterday."

Terri inserts herself back into the conversation. "I got to thinking that we only had Lindsey's word on whether or not Tom had taken the test, so I decided to call him and find out."

I step back into my house and indicate that my guests should join me. I give Terri a kiss, and then I kiss Kay. I'm sure as hell not going to kiss Tom, but even so, I'm suddenly very happy to see him.

"I can make you some breakfast and then we can go to the hospital," I tell them.

Kay, who is the most petite woman I've ever met, also happens to eat more than a professional linebacker. "I'll get cooking," she says. "You go on up and take a shower and get ready."

I nod my head absently before saying, "Nice work, Terr. For some reason I believed Lindsey. You'd think I would have known better." Anger floods my nervous system at the thought of her flagrant lie that Tom had already taken the test.

"If I had to guess," Tom says, "I'd say Lindsey wants the baby to be yours which is why she never told me."

"But why?" I ask this even though I can guess at the answer.

Tom shrugs. "You're more famous than I am." He says this like it's obvious. I suddenly have the urge to start throwing things.

"I forgot what great pancakes you make," I tell Kay as we all walk into the hospital. We called ahead to find out what kind of scene to expect and were told to come through Emergency. They'd have an orderly there meet us there and take us up to Lindsey's room via the service elevator. I don't know why Lindsey wants a life like this. It's a pain in the backside.

"I'm pretty sure my pancakes are the main reason Terri married me," Kay says.

Terri, who's holding her hand, asks, "How many people do you know who make pancakes from scratch these days?"

Tom, who's been surprisingly quiet, asks, "Do you mind if I go in and talk to Lindsey first?"

I share a look with Terri and Kay before answering, "I guess that's okay."

Once we're on the maternity floor, Tom tells me, "I'll come get you soon." I watch as he walks into Lindsey's room. Boy, do I wish I was a fly on the wall to see her reaction to him.

Tom is in Lindsey's room for forty-five minutes before he comes out. I'm nearly pulling my hair out in anticipation. Terry and Kay took off to the cafeteria a half hour ago, so I've just been sitting here, trying not to lose my mind. It hasn't been easy.

When Tom comes out, he approaches me, and says, "Why don't you go in alone?"

I jump to my feet. No sense asking him questions when I can ask Lindsey herself. I step around him and walk into the room. Lindsey is once again nursing the baby. I don't trust myself to say anything lest it be truly unkind.

When she looks up it's obvious that she's been crying. "Hey."

"I didn't know about Tom until this morning," I tell her.

She nods her head. "I'm not surprised Terri called him. She's always had your back."

I sit down on a chair next to her bedside. "So I guess we're both here to take a paternity test."

Lindsey shakes her head. "No need."

Wait, what? "Why?"

"The baby is Tom's," she says.

The news nearly knocks me off my chair. "Are you serious?"

"Yeah, I am. And I'm sorry."

"You knew the baby was Tom's and you came here to trick me? What in the hell is wrong with you, Lindsey?" I know I've put her on the defensive, but this is insane.

"Between you, me, and Tom, only one of us was born to be a parent. You," she says.

"So you thought you'd pawn another man's child off on me? That's sick." I cannot believe I ever thought I loved this woman.

"It's not nice, but it's not sick. Look," she says, "when I found out I was pregnant, I made sure to hook up with you. I thought you'd take me back then and we could be happy like we used to be."

"So Theo—please tell me you're not going to name him Theo now ..." She shakes her head. "So the baby isn't early, is he?"

"Only six days."

"And you weren't gestational diabetic?"

"That part was actually true." She seems the slightest bit sheepish now.

"So Tom knows the baby is his and I'm free to go?"

A tear slides down her cheek as she says, "I'm sorry, Teddy. I know you don't believe me, and I know you must hate me, but I really thought we'd be good parents together."

"I have no words, Lindsey." I turn to leave, but I stop long enough to say, "Please don't ever try to see me again." Then I walk out, hoping to get back the life I thought I was going to have before Lindsey came to town.

CHAPTER FORTY-NINE

FAITH

I almost don't come into work this morning, but I ultimately decide to keep facing the music head on. By eleven, there's a lull in business and I'm about to go in back and eat the cottage cheese and peaches I brought for lunch. No more cookies and cakes for me until I've safely passed the emotional eating phase of grief.

The bell over the door rings and I look up to see a woman I've never seen before. "Good morning," I say cheerfully. "We're out of sticky buns, but we have plenty of cookies."

She steps toward the counter. "I'll take a dozen gingersnaps, please. My friend says they're the best he's ever had."

I start to pack her a bag. "It's hard to stop at just one."

"You aren't Faith Reynolds, by any chance, are you?" she asks.

I stop packing cookies. "Who wants to know?"

She smiles genially. "Terri Ramirez."

"Teddy's friend?" I start to take the cookies out of the bag and put them back into the glass case.

"Hey, wait! I may be Teddy's friend, but I still want those cookies."

"I told him I didn't want to meet anyone else in his life.

There's no reason to." I do not put any cookies back into the bag. "Why did he send you in here?" I demand angrily.

"He wanted me to tell you that he's in the alley waiting for you." She points out the door. "There are lots of paparazzi down the sidewalk out front."

"Why didn't he just call me?" I demand. My stomach feels like it's bottoming out.

"He felt that he should talk to you in person."

My eyes begin to fill with tears. He's here to tell me that he's Lindsey's baby daddy. I just know it. "I don't want to see him," I say.

"Faith." She sounds so calm and kind. "You liked Teddy once, didn't you?"

Against all good sense, I tell her, "Yes."

"Then as a gesture of good will, please. Please go and hear him out."

"You've been a very good friend to him, haven't you?" I ask, not really expecting an answer.

"He's like a brother to me." She takes a moment to seemingly gather her thoughts before adding, "Straight guys are often threatened by women who don't appear to need men for anything. Teddy has never cared that I was gay, and he's always treated me with respect. He's the most honest and loving person I've ever known."

"Yeah, he's a good one." *What else can I say?*

"He said that if you didn't want to see him that I should tell you it's his prize for letting you wax his legs. I really don't want to know what that's all about, but won't you please give him a chance to talk to you?" She looks so sincere, I can't seem to muster any anger. Instead, I hand her one gingersnap before walking into the kitchen.

I stop to look in the mirror and re-pin a couple of coils of hair that have released themselves from my bun. I don't bother with any makeup.

I open the back door and step out, expecting to see Teddy

standing there, but he's not. In fact, no one is. I'm about to go back inside when I hear the first strains of The Righteous Brothers' "Unchained Melody" start to play. It was the song I was singing when Teddy was watching me through my window.

I look right and left and then right again, before I hear him. "May I have this dance?"

He looks gorgeous in his linen shirt and shorts. Like a city guy ready to spend the day on his yacht.

Why is he tormenting me like this? "No, you may not have this dance," I tell him, all the while pushing his hands away from me. "I told you to call me with the news, not to show up here."

"I had to see you again, Faith."

"No, Teddy, you didn't. You've caused enough confusion in my life; I need you to just leave me alone." I cross my arms like I'm physically trying to protect my heart.

He puts his hands on my elbows to pull me in, but I resist with equal force. "The baby isn't mine," he says.

Wait, what? I stop pulling. "Are you serious?"

"As a heart attack," he says. "Lindsey knew all along he was Tom's. She knew she was pregnant when we slept together. She planned on tricking me into thinking it was mine."

"But wouldn't you have always asked for a paternity test?" I'm so confused right now. Absolutely delighted, but confused at the same time.

"She knew she broke my heart when she left me. And it's possible that had I found out sooner, I might have just gone along with it and accepted the baby as mine."

My arms loosen and fall to my sides. Teddy puts his hands on my waist and pulls me closer, asking again, "Can I have this dance?"

Just as the lead singer croons about how he trembles for his love's touch, my body begins to quake. "I don't know if I want to be in the public eye all the time," I tell him.

"I know I don't want to be ..." He touches the tip of his nose to my temple. I feel his hot breath on my ear, and my whole body erupts with goosebumps.

"As long as you're famous, the press will follow you," I remind him.

"I think they might not be that interested once they know I've moved to Elk Lake. They'll probably only show up when you and I are walking the red carpet together for one of my movie premieres."

At that, I step into his arms with purpose and happily follow along as he starts to waltz. "Are you saying that you're going to live here full time when you're not working?" I can't believe he'd do that for me.

"That's what I'm saying," he whispers in my ear. Then he adds, "Terri and Kay are going to buy my house and tear it down and build their dream home. Being that I barely started unpacking, I don't even have to go back. The movers can just load everything from the garage and I'm good to go."

A wall of fear slams into me that forces my feet to stop moving. "But what if we don't work out?"

"What if we do?" he counters. My heart melts when he says, "I'm just a boy standing in front of a girl ..."

I don't let him finish. "The scary part is that I really want to say yes."

"Then take the leap with me, Faith. Let's give ourselves a chance to be each other's person. You might think I'm a little crazy, but when I had my first kiss, I knew it was something special. I knew the girl was something special."

Happy tears start trickling down my cheeks. "You were *my* first kiss."

"Think of how much our grandkids are going to love this story."

"I'm not marrying you ..." I look into his eyes and add, "yet."

"I'm in no rush," he tells me. "As long as we're together, I'm good."

We continue to dance, wrapped in each other's arms like

there's no place on earth we'd rather be. When the song ends, I ask, "What do we do now?"

"You feel like holding your first press conference?" he asks.

"You want us to tell the press?" A wave of disbelief hits me. "Why would we ever go out of our way to talk to them?"

"Because once they hear what we have to say, they won't be nearly as interested in us."

Suddenly excited by that prospect, I ask, "When should we do it?"

He picks up his phone and makes a call. Putting it on speaker, he says, "We're good for the conference, Terri. Set it up."

"Excellent! How's tomorrow morning at nine right here at the bakery?" Before either of us can answer, she adds, "You'll need to bake extra for tomorrow, Faith. I guarantee a big profit day."

And just like that, Teddy and I get ready to tell the world our news. That we're just a girl and a boy, ready to give love a chance.

CHAPTER FIFTY

TEDDY

Faith and I went to her house last night. We ordered a pizza and stayed up talking long into the night. In a way, I'm kind of glad that Lindsey showed up and threw a wrench into things. It showed both me and Faith that we have a solid enough connection to get through hard times.

I wake up before she does, so I go downstairs and make a pot of coffee. Then I bring her a cup. "Wake up, sleepy head."

She groans as she rolls over. "Can't be morning. Too soon."

"Once you get some caffeine in you, you'll realize how exciting it will be to have this morning over with."

That seems to be enough to catapult her into consciousness because she sits up and reaches for her coffee. "The press conference! What do I wear to something like that?"

"Celebrities tend to go out of their way to look extra shiny and perfect on such occasions. As such, I suggest we look as boring as we can and make them wonder why they even care about us."

She nods her head slowly. "I can look boring."

"I don't believe that for a minute," I tell her. "You're a thousand times more beautiful than any Hollywood starlet I've ever met."

Her cheeks flush prettily as she responds, "You can tell me lies like that forever."

"Not a lie." I sit down on the bed next to her. "You are not only beautiful, but you're kind and loving and delightfully quirky."

"People who make their own coats from the squirrels they hunt are quirky."

"Does that happen a lot around here?" I ask.

"Mr. Fields did that once when I was a kid. It was disgusting."

"I venture to say that kind of behavior is more questionable than quirky," I tell her.

"Fine," she agrees readily enough. "Tell me more nice things. You know, like you've never had a girlfriend so fit and fabulous."

I reach out to her and say, "Curvy and kind …"

"Talented and always camera ready …" She giggles.

Pulling her closer, I counter with, "Good and solid."

She pushes me away. "You make me sound like a table."

"Hey," I tease, "Theo used to make some expensive tables. Do not underestimate the appeal of a custom piece of furniture."

"Fine." She laughs. "If I'm a table, what are you?"

"Breakfast, lunch, and dinner …" I take her coffee from her and put it on the nightstand. Then I kiss her with all the longing in my heart. Faith feels like coming home, and I can never imagine a life without her.

Terri and Kay are already at the bakery when we get there. Terri is roping off an area around the front door to keep the press back. I walk up to Kay and kiss her cheek before asking, "Does she always travel with rope?"

Kay nods her head seriously. "And duct tape, and a shovel…"

Faith says good morning to Kay before announcing, "I'd better get inside and help Esmé and Nick get ready. I'm willing to bet Nick is beside himself with excitement today."

After she walks into the bakery, Terri joins us. "I have an interesting idea that I think might make today go easier for you."

"What's that?" I ask, already knowing that if Terri thinks it's a good idea, it is.

"I think we should have Tom join us." I bristle, so she hurries up to add, "You and Faith can go first, and once you're done, we can sick the vultures onto him. He's cool with it. He knows he has to face the music sooner or later, and he thinks sooner would be better."

I consider it for a moment. "It would make us seem congenial. The press will hate that."

"They'd much rather see the two of you going at it in a fist fight," Terri agrees.

"Let's do it," I say as the first TV van pulls up.

The press start arriving to set up, so we all go into the bakery for some coffee cake to wait.

Nick's hair is purple today and it's spikier than ever. "Teddy Helms!" he calls out loudly. Which is fine because we're the only ones here.

"How are you doing today, Nick?" I ask. "You ready to meet the press?"

"Am I!" he says excitedly. "I've prepared a short monologue in case they want to see what I've got."

"I didn't know you were an actor," I tell him.

He shakes his head. "I don't have any classical training, but I think I could really tear it up on the soaps. You know, a little *Young and the Restless* action?"

"I could actually see that." I make a mental note to introduce him to Terri when she gets off the phone.

Faith walks over to me and says, "I'm terrified."

She's wearing the white shirt and pink skirt that she wore the night of Anna and Chris's rehearsal dinner—the night we became a couple. "You look gorgeous," I tell her. "You have nothing to worry about."

"Is it crazy that I kind of feel bad for Lindsey?"

"It's not crazy because you're such a nice person," I tell her. "Having said that, let's not become friends with her."

"Ew, no. I'm not that nice." Faith laughs. Then she takes my hand and leads me into the kitchen where no one can see us. We kiss between bites of her sour cream coffee cake and pass the time together.

At five minutes until nine, Terri comes back clapping her hands loudly. "It's go time!"

We stand up and follow her out into the bakery and then through the front door. I lean down to Faith and whisper, "We've got this. Just let me do all the talking."

"That's fine by me," she mumbles nervously.

I don't know where Terri found a podium in the last hour, but she did, and it's set up right outside the door. She walks over to it and taps the microphone to make sure it's on. Then she says, "Good morning, I'm Teddy's agent, Terri Ramirez. Thank you all for coming out today."

Random voices call out things like, "Teddy, is the baby yours? Faith, what do you think about your boyfriend being a dad with someone else? Are you two broken up? Are you going back to LA soon, Teddy? What's going to happen with Alpha Dog?"

Terri interrupts them. "Teddy, why don't you come on up and say your piece."

As I approach the microphone, a new slew of queries is released. "I'll take questions when I'm all done," I tell them. Then I launch into my rehearsed script. "As you all know, Lindsey Flint had her baby last night right here in Elk Lake. I know you're all interested in knowing if I'm the dad." The air starts to buzz with loud murmuring.

I ignore it and continue, "I'm not the father of Lindsey's baby."

"But according to the video from the wedding reception you were at, she said you are!" a reporter in the front row says.

"Did you take a paternity test?" someone else wants to know.

"Are you pregnant, Faith?"

I cut them all off. "I've told you the part of the story that affects me. I think it's time to bring out the baby's real dad and let him talk to you."

And just like that, no one is interested in me anymore. Tom walks up behind the crowd saying, "I think you're looking for me." They part for him like he's Moses at the Red Sea.

Meanwhile, Terri pushes me off to the side, and then tells me and Faith, "Go on in, and leave through the back door. I predict you are free to enjoy the rest of your summer."

We follow her instructions, and within minutes, we are on the other side of the building where nobody seems to care who we are anymore. My life in Elk Creek starts for real now, and I can't wait.

"What do you want to do?" I ask Faith.

"Let's go to the hospital and visit with Theo. I miss him. Then let's go to Vista Pines and tell GG our news."

"Will she be happy?" I ask.

Faith smiles brightly. "She'll be ecstatic."

"We still need to introduce her to Theo," I say.

"I predict they'll be great friends," Faith says.

Then she takes my hand and starts to walk. "Come on, let's be normal people for a change."

EPILOGUE

FAITH

One of my favorite parts of classic rom-com movies are the montage scenes where you find out what happens to the couple after the movie ends. Those scenes are often full of kissing, weddings, babies, and so much more. They fulfill the audience's need to know that everything turns out the way they desire it to.

Well, I'm no screen writer, but I am an avid rom-com lover. As such, I think it's safe to say that Teddy's and my montage will include all the necessary ingredients for a blockbuster movie. Don't take my word for it, though. Terri just sent us the script in the mail.

EXTERIOR. THE DOCK ON ELK LAKE WHERE FAITH AND TEDDY (as teenagers) HAVE THEIR FIRST KISS – NIGHT

Two teenagers kiss tentatively.

FAITH (Voice Over)

Never in my wildest dreams did I think
I would fall in love with a movie star.
But that's exactly what happened.

EXT. THE SAME DOCK IN PRESENT DAY—FAITH AND TEDDY HOLDING HANDS

Teddy gets down on one knee with a robin's egg blue ring box. They kiss before Teddy picks Faith up and spins her around.

FAITH (V.O.)

Teddy proposed on the same dock where we
first kissed when we were kids.
Of course, I said yes.

EXTERIOR/INTERIOR VISTA PINES NURSING HOME
Card game being playing in the game room—switch to dance lessons.

FAITH (V.O)

Theo and GG became fast friends.
In addition to being canasta partners,
they're learning how to do the rumba.

EXT./INT BRIDAL BOUTIQUE
Faith and Anna walk into the boutique—Anna hands Missy a piece of paper.

FAITH (V.O)

Once Anna found out Teddy wasn't Lindsey's
baby daddy, she got busy putting together a
list of eligible men for Missy.

EXT./ CHURCH
Faith and Teddy come out of the church together and are met in a cloud of bubbles and one ham sandwich.

FAITH (V.O.)

Teddy decided bubbles made more sense than
ham sandwiches for our wedding. But I never
wanted him to regret that choice so I made sure
one sandwich hit its mark.

EXT. RED CARPET MOVIE PREMIERE

Faith and Teddy getting out of a limousine.

FAITH (V.O.)

The strangest part of being Teddy's wife is
going to his movie premieres. No one in Elk Lake
even looks twice at him anymore, but the minute
we show up in LA, it's constant flashbulbs in our face.

EXT. DOCK ON ELK LAKE

Faith hands Teddy a small, wrapped present. Teddy opens the gift and it's a pregnancy test.

FAITH (V.O.)

But I don't mind showing up for that side of things.
Because when Teddy isn't filming,
he's right here at my side.

EXT./INT. ELK CREEK HOSPITAL

A harried TEDDY pulls Faith into the hospital.

FAITH (V.O.)

Where we're going to stay and
raise our babies together.
Little Theo and Rosemary.

EXT. ELK CREEK PARK

Hooters song "And They Danced" starts to play as Faith and
Teddy spin in a circle with their children.

CREDITS ROLL

COMING SOON: PITY PARTY

What do you do when you own a bridal salon and can't seem to seal the deal on a romance of your own? You have what your mother refers to as a pity party. Then you enlist the help of your friends and get busy changing your destiny.

Pre-order Pity Party today!

ABOUT THE AUTHOR

USA Today Bestseller Whitney Dineen is a rock star in her own head. While delusional about her singing abilities, there's been a plethora of validation that she's a fairly decent author (AMAZING!!!).

After winning many writing awards and selling nearly a kabillion books (math may not be her forte, either), she's decided to let the voices in her head say whatever they want (sorry, Mom). She also won a fourth-place ribbon in a fifth-grade swim meet in backstroke. So, there's that.

Whitney loves to play with her kids (a.k.a. dazzle them with her amazing flossing abilities), bake stuff, eat stuff, and write books for people who "get" her. She thinks french fries are the perfect food and Mrs. Roper is her spirit animal.

Join her newsletter for news of her latest releases, sales, and recommendations. If you consider yourself a superfan, join her private reader group, where you will be offered the chance to read her books before they're released.

Made in United States
North Haven, CT
25 April 2023